THERE'S ONE SIN THAT HITCHCOCK CAN'T STAND

Alfred Hitchcock is the most tolerant of men. He doesn't mind such peccadillos as murder, arson, lying, greed, envy, treachery, torture. But Hitchcock absolutely abhors any form of selfishness—and therefore he's arranged to share his choicest pleasures in inhuman perversity and screaming shock-horror with you, the reader. Now you can join in the master's most fiendish fun and gruesome games—in a collection that includes the greatest terror talents ever and makes you shriek for more.

SCREAM
ALONG WITH ME

ALFRED HITCHCOCK

A DELL BOOK

Published by
DELL PUBLISHING CO., INC.
1 Dag Hammarskjold Plaza
New York, N.Y. 10017

ISBN: 0-440-13633-4

Reprinted by arrangement with
Random House, Inc.

Printed in Canada

Previous Dell Edition #3633
New Dell Edition
First printing—September 1977

ACKNOWLEDGMENTS

FISHHEAD, by Irvin S. Cobb. From *The Escape of Mr. Trimm* by Irvin S. Cobb. Used by permission of Nelson Buhler, Trustee of Trust created by Laura Baker Cobb, widow of Irvin S. Cobb, 274 Madison Avenue, New York, New York.

CAMERA OBSCURA, by Basil Copper. Reprinted by permission of the author. © Copyright 1965, by Basil Copper.

A DEATH IN THE FAMILY, by Miriam Allen deFord. Reprinted by permission of the author. Originally appeared in *The Dude,* November 1961. © Copyright 1961, by Miriam Allen deFord.

THE KNIFE, by Robert Arthur. Reprinted by permission of the author. Copyright 1951, by Grace Publishing Co., Inc.

CASABLANCA, by Thomas M. Disch. Printed by permission of the author and the author's agent, Robert P. Mills. © Copyright 1967, by Thomas M. Disch.

THE ROAD TO MICTLANTECUTLI, by Adobe James. Reprinted by permission of the author and London Authors. Originally appeared in *Adam Reader,* #20. © Copyright 1965, by the Knight Pub. Corp., Los Angeles, California.

GUIDE TO DOOM, by Ellis Peters. Reprinted by permission of Joyce Weiner Associates, London. Reprinted from *This Week Magazine.* © Copyright 1963, by the United Newspapers Magazine Corporation.

THE ESTUARY, by Margaret St. Clair. Reprinted by permission of McIntosh and Otis, Inc. Originally appeared in *Weird Tales.* Copyright 1950, by *Weird Tales.*

TOUGH TOWN, by William Sambrot. Reprinted by permission of Curtis Brown, Ltd. Originally appeared as "Stranger in Town." © Copyright 1957, by Official Magazine Corporation.

THE TROLL, by T. H. White. Reprinted by permission of David Higham Associates, Ltd., London. Copyright by the Estate of T. H. White. All rights reserved.

EVENING AT THE BLACK HOUSE, by Robert Somerlott. Reprinted by permission of McIntosh and Otis, Inc. Originally appeared

CONTENTS

AHEM!

If I May Have a Moment—

I hope no one will construe the title of this tome as a challenge. It is—in case you were so eager to get to the stories that you didn't notice—*Scream Along With Me: Stories That Scared Even Me*. This is meant as a simple statement of fact, not as a summons for you to cry in ringing tones that some of the stories didn't scare *you*. Why the word *Even* is in there I don't know. I proposed to call the book, in a simple and dignified manner, *Scream Along With Me: Stories That Scared Me*. I was overruled. It seems that *Scream Along With Me: Stories That Scared Even Me* has more swing to it. And this is, obviously, the day of the swinger.

For myself, I do no more than affirm that the stories in this book all gave me one or more of the pleasurable sensations associated with fear. Some quite terrified me. Some profoundly disturbed me and left me with a sense of deep uneasiness. Others prickled my nerve ends pleasurably, touched my spine with chills, or made me swallow hard as I registered their impact. Some did several of these things at once.

On that basis I offer them to you, trusting you will share with me these emotions, so enjoyable when they can be experienced in the snug embrace of an easy chair in the comfort of one's home.

And now I relinquish the screen to the main feature.

ALFRED J. HITCHCOCK

FISHHEAD

by Irvin S. Cobb

It goes past the powers of my pen to try to describe Reelfoot Lake for you so that you, reading this, will get the picture of it in your mind as I have it in mine. For Reelfoot Lake is like no other lake that I know anything about. It is an afterthought of Creation.

The rest of this continent was made and had dried in the sun for thousands of years—for millions of years for all I know—before Reelfoot came to be. It's the newest big thing in nature on this hemisphere probably, for it was formed by the great earthquake of 1811, just a little more than a hundred years ago. That earthquake of 1811 surely altered the face of the earth on the then far frontier of this country. It changed the course of rivers, it converted hills into what are now the sunk lands of three states, and it turned the solid ground to jelly and made it roll in waves like the sea. And in the midst of the retching of the land and the vomiting of the waters it depressed to varying depths a section of the earth crust sixty miles long, taking it down—trees, hills, hollows and all; and a crack broke through the Mississippi River so that for three days the river ran up stream, filling the hole.

The result was the largest lake south of the Ohio, lying mostly in Tennessee, but extending up across what is now the Kentucky line, and taking its name from a fancied resemblance in its outline to the splay, reeled foot of a cornfield Negro. Niggerwool Swamp, not so far away, may have got its name from the same man who christened Reelfoot; at least so it sounds.

Reelfoot is, and has always been, a lake of mystery. In places it is bottomless. Other places the skeletons of the cypress trees that went down when the earth sank still stand upright, so that if the sun shines from the right quarter and the water is less muddy than common, a man peering face downward into its depths sees, or thinks he sees, down below him the bare top-limbs upstretching like drowned men's fingers, all coated with the mud of years and bandaged with pennons of the green lake slime. In still other places the lake is shallow for long stretches, no deeper than breast-deep to a man, but dangerous because of the weed growths and the sunken drifts which entangle a swimmer's limbs. Its banks are mainly mud, its waters are muddied too, being a rich coffee color in the spring and a copperish yellow in the summer, and the trees along its shore are mud-colored clear up to their lower limbs after the spring floods, when the dried sediment covers their trunks with a thick, scrofulous-looking coat.

There are stretches of unbroken woodland around it and slashes where the cypress trees rise countlessly like head-stones and footstones for the dead snags that rot in the soft ooze. There are deadenings with the lowland corn growing high and rank below and the bleached, fire-blackened girdled trees rising above, barren of leaf and limb. There are long, dismal flats where in the spring the clotted frog-spawn clings like patches of white mucus among the weed stalks and at night the turtles crawl out to lay clutches of perfectly round, white eggs with tough, rubbery shells in the sand. There are bayous leading off to nowhere and sloughs that wind aimlessly, like great, blind worms, to finally join the big river that rolls its semi-liquid torrents a few miles to the westward.

So Reelfoot lies there, flat in the bottoms, freezing lightly in the winter, steaming torridly in the summer, swollen in the spring when the woods have turned a vivid green and the buffalo gnats by the million and the billion fill the flooded hollows with their pestilential buzzing, and in the fall ringed about gloriously with all the colors which the first frost brings—gold of hickory, yellow-russet of syca-more, red of dogwood and ash and purple-black of sweet-gum.

But the Reelfoot country has its uses. It is the best game and fish country, natural or artificial, that is left in the South to-day. In their appointed seasons the duck and the geese flock in, and even semitropical birds, like the brown pelican and the Florida snake-bird, having been known to come there to nest. Pigs, gone back to wildness, range the ridges, each razor-backed drove captained by a gaunt, savage, slab-sided old boar. By night the bull frogs, inconceivably big and tremendously vocal, bellow under the banks.

It is a wonderful place for fish—bass and crappie and perch and the snouted buffalo fish. How these edible sorts

live to spawn and how their spawn in turn live to spawn
again is a marvel, seeing how many of the big fish-eating
cannibal fish there are in Reelfoot. Here, bigger than anywhere else, you find the garfish, all bones and appetite
and horny plates, with a snout like an alligator, the nearest
link, naturalists say, between the animal life of to-day and
the animal life of the Reptilian Period. The shovel-nose
cat, really a deformed kind of freshwater sturgeon, with
a great fan-shaped membranous plate jutting out from
his nose like a bowsprit, jumps all day in the quiet places
with mighty splashing sounds, as though a horse had fallen
into the water. On every stranded log the huge snapping
turtles lie on sunny days in groups of four and six, baking
their shells black in the sun, with their little snaky heads
raised watchfully, ready to slip noiselessly off at the first
sound of oars grating in the row-locks.

But the biggest of them all are the catfish. These are
monstrous creatures, these catfish of Reelfoot—scaleless,
slick things, with corpsy dead eyes and poisonous fins like
javelins and long whiskers dangling from the sides of
their cavernous heads. Six and seven feet long they grow
to be and to weigh two hundred pounds or more, and
they have mouths wide enough to take a man's foot or a
man's fist and strong enough to break any hook save the
strongest and greedy enough to eat anything, living or
dead or putrid, that the horny jaws can master. Oh, but
they are wicked things, and they tell wicked tales of them
down there. They call them man-eaters and compare them,
in certain of their habits, to sharks.

Fishhead was of a piece with this setting. He fitted
into it as an acorn fits its cup. All his life he had lived
on Reelfoot, always in the one place, at the mouth of a
certain slough. He had been born there, of a Negro father
and a half-breed Indian mother, both of them now dead,
and the story was that before his birth his mother was
frightened by one of the big fish, so that the child came
into the world most hideously marked. Anyhow, Fishhead
was a human monstrosity, the veritable embodiment of
nightmare. He had the body of a man—a short, stocky,
sinewy body—but his face was as near to being the face
of a great fish as any face could be and yet retain some
trace of human aspect. His skull sloped back so abruptly
that he could hardly be said to have a forehead at all;
his chin slanted off right into nothing. His eyes were small

and round with shallow, glazed, pale-yellow pupils, and they were set wide apart in his head and they were un-winking and staring, like a fish's eyes. His nose was no more than a pair of tiny slits in the middle of the yellow mask. His mouth was the worst of all. It was the awful mouth of a catfish, lipless and almost inconceivably wide, stretching from side to side. Also when Fishhead became a grown man his likeness to a fish increased, for the hair upon his face grew out into two tightly kinked, slender pendants that drooped down either side of the mouth like the beards of a fish.

If he had any other name than Fishhead, none excepting he knew it. As Fishhead he was known and as Fishhead he answered. Because he knew the waters and the woods of Reelfoot better than any other man there, he was valued as a guide by the city men who came every year to hunt or fish; but there were few such jobs that Fishhead would take. Mainly he kept to himself, tending his corn patch, netting the lake, trapping a little and in season pot hunting for the city markets. His neighbors, ague-bitten whites and malaria-proof Negroes alike, left him to himself. In-deed, for the most part they had a superstitious fear of him. So he lived alone, with no kith nor kin, nor even a friend, shunning his kind and shunned by them.

His cabin stood just below the state line, where Mud Slough runs into the lake. It was a shack of logs, the only human habitation for four miles up or down. Behind it the thick timber came shouldering right up to the edge of Fishhead's small truck patch, enclosing it in thick shade except when the sun stood just overhead. He cooked his food in a primitive fashion, outdoors, over a hole in the soggy earth or upon the rusted red ruin of an old cook stove, and he drank the saffron water of the lake out of a dipper made of a gourd, faring and fending for himself, a master hand at skiff and net, competent with duck gun and fish spear, yet a creature of affliction and loneliness, part savage, almost amphibious, set apart from his fellows, silent and suspicious.

In front of his cabin jutted out a long fallen cotton-wood trunk, lying half in and half out of the water, its top side burnt by the sun and worn by the friction of Fish-head's bare feet until it showed countless patterns of tiny scrolled lines, its under side black and rotted and lapped at unceasingly by little waves like tiny licking tongues. Its f rther end reached deep water. And it was a part of Fish e d, for no matter how far his fishing and trapping might take him in the daytime, sunset would find him back there, his boat drawn up on the bank and he on the outer end of this log. From a distance men had seen him there many times, sometimes squatted, motionless as the big turtles that would crawl upon its dipping tip in his absence, sometimes erect and vigilant like a creek crane, his misshapen yellow form outlined against the yellow sun, the yellow water, the yellow banks—all of them yellow together.

If the Reelfooters shunned Fishhead by day they feared him by night and avoided him as a plague, dreading even the chance of a casual meeting. For there were ugly stories about Fishhead—stories which all the Negroes and some of the whites believed. They said that a cry which had been heard just before dusk and just after, skittering across the darkened waters, was his calling cry to the big cats, and at his bidding they came trooping in, and that in their company he swam in the lake on moonlight nights, sporting with them, diving with them, even feeding with them on what manner of unclean things they fed. The cry had been heard many times, that much was certain, and it was certain also that the big fish were noticeably thick at the mouth of Fishhead's slough. No native Reelfooter, white or black, would willingly wet a leg or an arm there.

Here Fishhead had lived and here he was going to die. The Baxters were going to kill him, and this day in midsummer was to be the time of the killing. The two Baxters—Jake and Joel—were coming in their dugout to do it. This murder had been a long time in the making. The Baxters had to brew their hate over a slow fire for months before it reached the pitch of action. They were poor whites, poor in everything—repute and worldly goods and standing—a pair of fever-ridden squatters who lived on whisky and tobacco when they could get it, and on fish and cornbread when they couldn't.

The feud itself was of months' standing. Meeting Fishhead one day in the spring on the spindly scaffolding of the skiff landing at Walnut Log, and being themselves far overtaken in liquor and vainglorious with a bogus alcoholic substitute for courage, the brothers had accused him, wantonly and without proof, of running their trot-line and stripping it of the hooked catch—an unforgivable sin among the water dwellers and the shanty boaters of the South. Seeing that he bore this accusation in silence, only eyeing them steadfastly, they had been emboldened then to slap his face, whereupon he turned and gave them both the beating of their lives—bloodying their noses and bruising their lips with hard blows against their front teeth, and finally leaving them, mauled and prone, in the dirt. Moreover, in the onlookers a sense of the everlasting fitness of things had triumphed over race prejudice and allowed them—two freeborn, sovereign whites—to be licked by a nigger.

Therefore, they were going to get the nigger. The whole thing had been planned out amply. They were going to kill him on his log at sundown. There would be no witnesses to see it, no retribution to follow after it. The very ease of the undertaking made them forget even their inborn fear of the place of Fishhead's habitation.

For more than an hour now they had been coming from their shack across a deeply indented arm of the lake. Their dugout, fashioned by fire and adz and draw-knife from the bole of a gum tree, moved through the water as noiselessly as a swimming mallard, leaving behind it a long, wavy trail on the still waters. Jake, the better oarsman, sat flat in the stern of the round-bottomed craft, paddling with quick, splashless strokes. Joel, the better shot, was squatted forward. There was a heavy, rusted duck gun between his knees.

Though their spying upon the victim had made them certain sure he would not be about the shore for hours, a doubled sense of caution led them to hug closely the weedy banks. They slid along the shore like shadows, moving so swiftly and in such silence that the watchful mud turtles barely turned their snaky heads as they passed. So, a full hour before the time, they came slipping around the mouth of the slough and made for a natural ambuscade which the mixed breed had left within a stone's jerk of his cabin to his own undoing.

Where the slough's flow joined deeper water a partly uprooted tree was stretched, prone from shore, at the top still thick and green with leaves that drew nourishment from the earth in which the half-uncovered roots yet held, and twined about with an exuberance of trumpet vines and wild fox-grapes. All about was a huddle of drift— last year's cornstalks, sheddy strips of bark, chunks of rotted weed, all the riffle and dunnage of a quiet eddy. Straight into this green clump glided the dugout and swung, broadside on, against the protecting trunk of the tree, hidden from the inner side by the intervening curtains of rank growth, just as the Baxters had intended it should be hidden, when days before in their scouting they marked this masked place of waiting and included it, then and there, in the scope of their plans.

There had been no hitch or mishap. No one had been abroad in the late afternoon to mark their movements—and in a little while Fishhead ought to be due. Jake's woodman's eye followed the downward swing of the sun speculatively. The shadows, thrown shoreward, lengthened and slithered on the small ripples. The small noises of the day died out; the small noises of the coming night began to multiply. The green-bodied flies went away and big mosquitoes, with speckled gray legs, came to take the places of the flies. The sleepy lake sucked at the mud banks with small mouthing sounds as though it found the taste of the raw mud agreeable. A monster crawfish, big as a chicken lobster, crawled out on the top of his dried mud chimney and perched himself there, an armored sentinel on the watchtower. Bull bats began to flitter back and forth above the tops of the trees. A pudgy muskrat, swimming with head up, was moved to sidle off briskly as he met a cottonmouth moccasin snake, so fat and swollen with summer poison that it looked almost like a legless lizard as it moved along the surface of the water in a series of slow torpid s's. Directly above the head of either of the waiting assassins a compact little swarm of midges hung, holding to a sort of kite-shaped formation.

A little more time passed and Fishhead came out of the woods at the back, walking swiftly, with a sack over his shoulder. For a few seconds his deformities showed in the clearing, then the black inside of the cabin swallowed him up. By now the sun was almost down. Only the red nub of it showed above the timber line across the lake, and the shadows lay inland a long way. Out beyond, the big cats were stirring, and the great smacking sounds as their twisting bodies leaped clear and fell back in the water came shoreward in a chorus.

But the two brothers in their green covert gave heed to nothing except the one thing upon which their hearts were set and their nerves tensed. Joel gently shoved his gun-barrels across the log, cuddling the stock to his shoulder and slipping two fingers caressingly back and forth upon the triggers. Jake held the narrow dugout steady by a grip upon a fox-grape tendril.

A little wait and then the finish came. Fishhead emerged from the cabin door and came down the narrow footpath to the water and out upon the water on his log. He was barefooted and bareheaded, his cotton shirt open down the front to show his yellow neck and breast, his dungaree trousers held about his waist by a twisted tow string. His broad splay feet, with the prehensile toes outspread, gripped the polished curve of the log as he moved along its swaying, dipping surface until he came to its outer end and stood there erect, his chest filling, his chinless face lifted up and something of mastership and dominion in his poise. And then—his eye caught what another's eyes might have missed—the round, twin ends of the gun barrels, the fixed gleams of Joel's eyes, aimed at him through the green tracery.

In that swift passage of time, too swift almost to be measured by seconds, realization flashed all through him, and he threw his head still higher and opened wide his shapeless trap of a mouth, and out across the lake he sent skittering and rolling his cry. And in his cry was the laugh of a loon, and the croaking bellow of a frog, and the bay of a hound, all the compounded night noises of the lake. And in it, too, was a farewell and a defiance and an appeal. The heavy roar of the duck gun came.

At twenty yards the double charge tore the throat out of him. He came down, face forward, upon the log and clung there, his trunk twisting distortedly, his legs twitching and kicking like the legs of a speared frog, his shoulders hunching and lifting spasmodically as the life ran out of him all in one swift coursing flow. His head canted up between the heaving shoulders, his eyes looked full on the staring face of his murderer, and then the blood came out of his mouth and Fishhead, in death still as much fish as man, slid flopping, head first, off the end of the log and sank, face downward, slowly, his limbs all extended out. One after another a string of big bubbles came up to burst in the middle of a widening reddish stain on the coffee-colored water.

The brothers watched this, held by the horror of the thing they had done, and the cranky dugout, tipped far

over by the recoil of the gun, took water steadily across its
gunwale; and now there was a sudden stroke from below
upon its careening bottom and it went over and they
were in the lake. But shore was only twenty feet away,
the trunk of the uprooted tree only five. Joel, still holding
fast to his hot gun, made for the log, gaining it with one
stroke. He threw his free arm over it and clung there,
treading water, as he shook his eyes free. Something
gripped him—some great, sinewy, unseen thing gripped
him fast by the thigh, crushing down on his flesh.

He uttered no cry, but his eyes popped out and his
mouth set in a square shape of agony, and his fingers
gripped into the bark of the tree like grapples. He was
pulled down and down, by steady jerks, not rapidly but
steadily, so steadily, and as he went his fingernails tore four
little white strips in the tree bark. His mouth went under,
next his popping eyes, then his erect hair, and finally his
clawing, clutching hand, and that was the end of him.

Jake's fate was harder still, for he lived longer—long
enough to see Joel's finish. He saw it through the water
that ran down his face, and with a great surge of his
whole body he literally flung himself across the log and
jerked his legs up high into the air to save them. He
flung himself too far, though, for his face and chest hit
the water on the far side. And out of this water rose the
head of a great fish, with the lake slime of years on its
flat, black head, its whiskers bristling, its corpsy eyes alight.
Its horny jaws closed and clamped in the front of Jake's
flannel shirt. His hand struck out wildly and was speared
on a poisoned fin, and unlike Joel, he went from sight
with a great yell and a whirling and a churning of the
water that made the cornstalks circle on the edges of a
small whirlpool.

But the whirlpool soon thinned away into widening rings
of ripples and the cornstalks quit circling and became still
again, and only the multiplying night noises sounded about
the mouth of the slough.

The bodies of all three came ashore on the same day
near the same place. Except for the gaping gunshot wound
where the neck met the chest, Fishhead's body was unmarked. But the bodies of the two Baxters were so marred
and mauled that the Reelfooters buried them together on
the bank without ever knowing which might be Jake's and
which might be Joel's.

CAMERA OBSCURA

by Basil Copper

As Mr. Sharsted pushed his way up the narrow, fussily conceived lanes that led to the older part of the town, he was increasingly aware that there was something about Mr. Gingold he didn't like. It was not only the old-fashioned, outdated air of courtesy that irritated the moneylender but the gentle, absent-minded way in which he continually put off settlement. Almost as if money were of no importance.

The moneylender hesitated even to say this to himself; the thought was a blasphemy that rocked the very foundations of his world. He pursed his lips grimly and set himself to mount the ill-paved and flinty roadway that bisected the hilly terrain of this remote part of the town.

The moneylender's narrow, lopsided face was perspiring under his hard hat; lank hair started from beneath the brim, which lent him a curious aspect. This, combined with the green-tinted spectacles he wore, gave him a sinister, decayed look, like someone long dead. The thought may have occurred to the few, scattered passers-by he met in the course of his ascent, for almost to a person they gave one cautious glance and then hurried on as though eager to be rid of his presence.

He turned in at a small courtyard and stood in the shelter of a great old ruined church to catch his breath; his heart was thumping uncomfortably in the confines of his narrow chest and his breath rasped in his throat. Assuredly, he was out of condition, he told himself. Long hours of sedentary work huddled over his accounts were taking their toll; he really must get out more and take some exercise.

The moneylender's sallow face brightened momentarily as he thought of his increasing prosperity, but then he frowned again as he remembered the purpose of his errand. Gingold must be made to toe the line, he told himself, as he set out over the last half-mile of his journey.

If he couldn't raise the necessary cash, there must be many valuables in that rambling old house of his which he could sell and realize on. As Mr. Sharsted forged his way deeper into this forgotten corner of the town, the sun, which was already low in the sky, seemed to have already set, the light was so constricted by the maze of small courts and alleys into which he had plunged. He was panting again when he came at last, abruptly, to a large green door, set crookedly at the top of a flight of time-worn steps.

He stood arrested for a moment or two, one hand grasping the old balustrade, even his mean soul uplifted momentarily by the sight of the smoky haze of the town below, tilted beneath the yellow sky. Everything seemed to be set awry upon this hill, so that the very horizon rushed slanting across the far distance, giving the spectator a feeling of vertigo. A bell pealed faintly as he seized an iron scrollwork pull set into a metal rose alongside the front door. The moneylender's thoughts were turned to irritation again; everything about Mr. Gingold was peculiar, he felt. Even the fittings of his household were things one never saw elsewhere.

Though this might be an advantage if he ever gained control of Mr. Gingold's assets and had need to sell the property; there must be a lot of valuable stuff in this old house he had never seen, he mused. Which was another reason he felt it strange that the old man was unable to pay his dues; he must have a great deal of money, if not in cash, in property, one way or another.

He found it difficult to realize why Mr. Gingold kept hedging over a matter of three hundred pounds; he could easily sell the old place and go to live in a more attractive part of town in a modern, well-appointed villa and still keep his antiquarian interests. Mr. Sharsted sighed. Still, it was none of his business. All he was concerned with was the matter of the money; he had been kept waiting long enough, and he wouldn't be fobbed off any longer. Gingold had got to settle by Monday, or he'd make things unpleasant for him.

Mr. Sharsted's thin lips tightened in an ugly manner as he mused on, oblivious of the sunset staining the upper storeys of the old houses and dyeing the mean streets below the hill a rich carmine. He pulled the bell again impatiently, and this time the door was opened almost immediately.

Mr. Gingold was a very tall, white-haired man with a gentle, almost apologetic manner. He stood slightly stooping in the doorway, blinking as though astonished at the sunlight, half afraid it would fade him if he allowed too much of it to absorb him.

His clothes, which were of good quality and cut, were untidy and sagged loosely on his big frame; they seemed washed-out in the bright light of the sun and appeared to Mr. Sharsted to be all of a part with the man himself; indeed, Mr. Gingold was rinsed to a pale, insipid shade by the sunshine, so that his white hair and face and clothing ran into one another and, somehow, the different aspects of the picture became blurred and indeterminate.

To Mr. Sharsted he bore the aspect of an old photograph which had never been properly fixed and had turned brown and faded with time. Mr. Sharsted thought he might blow away with the breeze that had started up, but Mr. Gingold merely smiled shyly and said, "Oh, there you are, Sharsted. Come on in," as though he had been expecting him all the time.

Surprisingly, Mr. Gingold's eyes were of a marvellous shade of blue and they made his whole face come vividly alive, fighting and challenging the overall neutral tints of his clothing and features. He led the way into a cavernous hall. Mr. Sharsted followed cautiously, his eyes adjusting with difficulty to the cool gloom of the interior. With courteous, old-world motions Mr. Gingold beckoned him forward.

The two men ascended a finely carved staircase, whose balustrades, convoluted and serpentine, seemed to writhe sinuously upwards into the darkness.

"My business will only take a moment," protested Sharsted, anxious to present his ultimatum and depart. But Mr. Gingold merely continued to ascend the staircase.

"Come along, come along," he said gently, as though he hadn't heard Mr. Sharsted's expostulation. "You must take a glass of wine with me. I have so few visitors . . ."

Mr. Sharsted looked about him curiously; he had never been in this part of the house. Usually, Mr. Gingold received occasional callers in a big, cluttered room on the ground floor. This afternoon, for some reason known only to himself, he had chosen to show Mr Sharsted another part of his domain. Mr. Sharsted thought that perhaps Mr. Gingold intended to settle the matter of his repayments. This might be where he transacted business, perhaps kept his money. His thin fingers twitched with nervous excitement.

They continued to ascend what seemed to the moneylender to be enormous distances. The staircase still unwound in front of their measured progress. From the little light which filtered in through rounded windows, Sharsted caught occasional glimpses of objects that aroused his professional curiosity and acquisitive sense. Here a large oil painting swung into view round the bend of the stair; in the necessarily brief glance that Mr. Sharsted caught, he could have sworn it was a Poussin.

A moment later, a large sideboard laden with porcelain slid by the corner of his eye. He stumbled on the stair as he glanced back over his shoulder and in so doing, almost missed a rare suit of Genoese armour which stood concealed in a niche set back from the staircase. The moneylender had reached a state of confused bewilderment when at length Mr. Gingold flung aside a large mahogany door, and motioned him forward.

Mr. Gingold must be a wealthy man and could easily realize enormous amounts on any one of the *objets d'art* Sharsted had seen; why then, thought the latter, did he find it necessary to borrow so frequently, and why was it so difficult to obtain repayment? With interest, the sum owed Sharsted had now risen to a considerable figure; Mr. Gingold must be a compulsive buyer of rare items. Allied to the general shabbiness of the house as seen by the casual visitor, it must mean that his collector's instinct would refuse to allow him to part with anything once bought, which had made him run himself into debt. The moneylender's lips tightened again; well, he must be made to settle his debts, like anyone else.

If not, perhaps Sharsted could force him to part with something—porcelain, a picture—that could be made to realize a handsome profit on the deal. Business was business, and Gingold could not expect him to wait for ever. His musings were interrupted by a query from his host and Sharsted muttered an apology as he saw that Mr. Gingold was waiting, one hand on the neck of a heavy silver and crystal decanter.

"Yes, yes, a sherry, thank you," he murmured in confusion, moving awkwardly. The light was so bad in this place that he felt it difficult to focus his eyes, and objects had a habit of shifting and billowing as though seen under water. Mr. Sharsted was forced to wear tinted spectacles, as his eyes had been weak from childhood. They made these apartments seem twice as dark as they might be. But though Mr. Sharsted squinted over the top of his lenses as Mr. Gingold poured the sherry, he still could not make out objects clearly. He really would have to consult his oculist soon, if this trouble continued.

His voice sounded hollow to his own ears as he ventured a commonplace when Mr. Gingold handed him the glass. He sat down gingerly on a ladderback chair indicated to him by Mr. Gingold, and sipped at the amber liquid in a hesitant fashion. It tasted uncommonly good, but this unexpected hospitality was putting him on a wrong footing with Gingold. He must assert himself and broach the subject of his business. But he felt a curious reluctance and merely sat on in embarrassed silence, one hand round the stem of his goblet, listening to the soothing tick of an old clock, which was the only thing which broke the silence.

He saw now that he was in a large apartment, expensively furnished, which must be high up in the house, under the eaves. Hardly a sound from outside penetrated the windows, which were hung with thick blue-velvet curtains; the parquet floor was covered with exquisitely worked Chinese rugs and the room was apparently divided in half by heavy velvet curtaining to match those which masked the windows.

Mr. Gingold said little, but sat at a large mahogany table, tapping his sherry glass with his long fingers; his bright blue eyes looked with mild interest at Mr. Sharsted as they spoke of everyday matters. At last Mr. Sharsted was moved to broach the object of his visit. He spoke of the long-outstanding sum which he had advanced to Mr. Gingold, of the continued applications for settlement and of the necessity of securing early payment. Strangely, as Mr. Sharsted progressed, his voice began to stammer and eventually he was at a loss for words; normally, as working-class people in the town had reason to know, he was brusque, businesslike, and ruthless. He never hesitated to distrain on debtor's goods, or to evict if necessary and that he was the object of universal hatred in the outside world, bothered him not in the slightest.

In fact, he felt it to be an asset; his reputation in business affairs preceded him, as it were, and acted as an incentive to prompt repayment. If people were fool enough to be poor or to run into debt and couldn't meet their dues, well then, let them; it was all grist to his mill and he could not be expected to run his business on a lot of sentimental nonsense. He felt more irritated with Mr. Gingold than he need have been, for his money was obviously safe; but what continued to baffle him was the man's gentle docility, his obvious wealth, and his reluctance to settle his debts.

Something of this must have eventually permeated his conversation, for Mr. Gingold shifted in his seat, made no comment whatever on Mr. Sharsted's pressing demands and only said, in another of his softly spoken sentences, "Do have another sherry, Mr. Sharsted."

The moneylender felt all the strength going out of him as he weakly assented. He leaned back on his comfortable chair with a swimming head and allowed the second glass to be pressed into his hand, the thread of his discourse completely lost. He mentally cursed himself for a dithering fool and tried to concentrate, but Mr. Gingold's benevolent smile, the curious way the objects in the room shifted and wavered in the heat haze; the general gloom and the discreet curtaining, came more and more to weigh on and oppress his spirits.

So it was with something like relief that Sharsted saw his host rise from the table. He had not changed the topic, but continued to speak as though Mr. Sharsted had never mentioned money to him at all; he merely ignored the whole situation and with an enthusiasm Sharsted found difficult to share, murmured soothingly on about Chinese wall paintings, a subject of which Mr. Sharsted knew nothing.

He found his eyes closing and with an effort opened them again. Mr. Gingold was saying, "I think this will interest you, Mr. Sharsted. Come along . . ."

His host had moved forward and the moneylender, following him down the room, saw that the large expanse of velvet curtaining was in motion. The two men walked through the parted curtains, which closed behind them, and Mr. Sharsted then saw that they were in a semi-circular chamber.

This room was, if anything, even dimmer than the one

they had just left. But the moneylender's interest began to revive; his head felt clearer and he took in a large circular table, some brass wheels and levers which winked in the gloom, and a long shaft which went up to the ceiling.

"This has almost become an obsession with me," murmured Mr. Gingold, as though apologizing to his guest. "You are aware of the principles of the camera obscura, Mr. Sharsted?"

The moneylender pondered slowly, reaching back into memory. "Some sort of Victorian toy, isn't it?" he said at length. Mr. Gingold looked pained, but the expression of his voice did not change.

"Hardly that, Mr. Sharsted," he rejoined. "A most fascinating pursuit. Few people of my acquaintance have been here and seen what you are going to see."

He motioned to the shafting, which passed up through a louvre in the ceiling.

"These controls are coupled to the system of lenses and prisms on the roof. As you will see, the hidden camera, as the Victorian scientists came to call it, gathers a panorama of the town below and transmits it here on to the viewing table. An absorbing study, one's fellow man, don't you think? I spend many hours up here."

Mr. Sharsted had never heard Mr. Gingold in such a talkative mood and now that the wretchedness which had assailed him earlier had disappeared, he felt more suited to tackle him about his debts. First, he would humour him by feigning interest in his stupid toy. But Mr. Sharsted had to admit, almost with a gasp of surprise, that Mr. Gingold's obsession had a valid cause.

For suddenly, as Mr. Gingold moved his hand upon the lever, the room was flooded with light of a blinding clarity and the moneylender saw why gloom was a necessity in this chamber. Presumably, a shutter over the camera obscura slid away upon the rooftop and almost at the same moment, a panel in the ceiling opened to admit a shaft of light directed upon the table before them.

In a second of God-like vision, Mr. Sharsted saw a panorama of part of the old town spread out before him in superbly natural colour. Here were the quaint, cobbled streets dropping to the valley, with the blue hills beyond; factory chimneys smoked in the early evening air; people went about their business in half a hundred roads; distant traffic went noiselessly on its way; once, even, a great white bird soared across the field of vision, so apparently close that Mr. Sharsted started back from the table.

Mr. Gingold gave a dry chuckle and moved a brass wheel at his elbow. The viewpoint abruptly shifted and Mr. Sharsted saw with another gasp, a sparkling vista of the estuary with a big coaling ship moving slowly out to sea. Gulls soared in the foreground and the sullen wash of the tide ringed the shore. Mr. Sharsted, his errand quite forgotten, was fascinated. Half an hour must have passed, each view more enchanting than the last; from this height, the squalor of the town was quite transformed.

He was abruptly recalled to the present, however, by the latest of the views; Mr. Gingold spun the control for the last time and a huddle of crumbling tenements wheeled into view. "The former home of Mrs. Thwaites, I believe," said Mr. Gingold mildly.

Mr. Sharsted flushed and bit his lip in anger. The Thwaites business had aroused more notoriety than he had intended; the woman had borrowed a greater sum than she could afford, the interest mounted, she borrowed again; could he help it if she had a tubercular husband and three children? He had to make an example of her in order to keep his other clients in line; now there was a distraint on the furniture and the Thwaiteses were being turned on to the street. Could he help this? If only people would repay their debts all would be well; he wasn't a philanthropic institution, he told himself angrily.

And at this reference to what was rapidly becoming a scandal in the town, all his smouldering resentment against Mr. Gingold broke out afresh; enough of all these views and childish playthings. Camera obscura, indeed; if Mr. Gingold did not meet his obligations like a gentleman he could sell this pretty toy to meet his debt.

He controlled himself with an effort as he turned to meet Mr. Gingold's gently ironic gaze.

"Ah, yes," said Mr. Sharsted. "The Thwaites business is my affair, Mr. Gingold. Will you please confine yourself to the matter in hand. I have had to come here again at great inconvenience; I must tell you that if the £300, representing the current installment on our loan is not forthcoming by Monday, I shall be obliged to take legal action."

Mr. Sharsted's cheeks were burning and his voice trembled as he pronounced these words; if he expected a violent reaction from Mr. Gingold, he was disappointed. The latter merely gazed at him in mute reproach.

"This is your last word?" he said regretfully. "You will not reconsider?"

"Certainly not," snapped Mr. Sharsted. "I must have the money by Monday."

"You misunderstand me, Mr. Sharsted," said Mr. Gingold, still in that irritatingly mild voice. "I was referring to Mrs. Thwaites. Must you carry on with this unnecessary and somewhat inhuman action? I would . . ."

"Please mind your own business!" retorted Mr. Sharsted, exasperated beyond measure. "Mind what I say . . ."

He looked wildly round for the door through which he had entered.

"That is your last word?" said Mr. Gingold again. One look at the moneylender's set, white face was his mute answer.

"Very well, then," said Mr. Gingold, with a heavy sigh. "So be it. I will see you on your way."

He moved forward again, pulling a heavy velvet cloth over the table of the camera obscura. The louvre in the ceiling closed with a barely audible rumble. To Mr. Sharsted's surprise, he found himself following his host up yet another flight of stairs; these were of stone, fringed with an iron balustrade which was cold to the touch.

His anger was now subsiding as quickly as it had come; he was already regretting losing his temper over the Thwaites business and he hadn't intended to sound so crude and cold-blooded. What must Mr. Gingold think of him? Strange how the story could have got to his ears; surprising how much information about the outside world a recluse could obtain just by sitting still.

Though, on this hill, he supposed Mr. Gingold could be said to be at the centre of things. He shuddered suddenly, for the air seemed to have grown cold. Through a slit in the stone wall he could see the evening sky was already darkening. He really must be on his way; how did the old fool expect him to find his way out when they were still mounting to the very top of the house?

Mr. Sharsted regretted, too, that in antagonizing Mr. Gingold, he might have made it even more difficult to obtain his money; it was almost as though, in mentioning Mrs. Thwaites and trying to take her part, he had been trying a form of subtle blackmail.

He would not have expected it of Gingold; it was not like him to meddle in other people's affairs. If he was so fond of the poor and needy he could well afford to advance the family some money themselves to tide them over their difficulties.

His brain seething with these confused and angry thoughts, Mr. Sharsted, panting and dishevelled, now found himself on a worn stone platform where Mr. Gingold was putting the key into an ancient wooden lock.

"My workshop," he explained, with a shy smile to Mr. Sharsted, who felt his tension eased away by this drop in the emotional atmosphere. Looking through an old, nearly triangular window in front of him, Mr. Sharsted could see that they were in a small, turreted superstructure which towered a good twenty feet over the main roof of the house. There was a sprawl of unfamiliar alleys at the foot of the steep overhang of the building, as far as he could make out through the grimy panes.

"There is a staircase down the outside," explained Mr. Gingold, opening the door. "It will lead you down the other side of the hill and cut over half a mile off your journey."

The moneylender felt a sudden rush of relief at this. He had come almost to fear this deceptively mild and quiet old man who, though he said little and threatened not at all, had begun to exude a faint air of menace to Mr. Sharsted's now over-heated imagination.

"But first," said Mr. Gingold, taking the other man's arm in a surprisingly powerful grip, "I want to show you something else—and this really has been seen by very few people indeed."

Mr. Sharsted looked at the other quickly, but could read nothing in Mr. Gingold's enigmatic blue eyes.

He was surprised to find a similar, though smaller, chamber to the one they had just left. There was another table, another shaft ascending to a domed cupola in the ceiling, and a further arrangement of wheels and tubes.

"This camera obscura," said Mr. Gingold, "is a very rare model, to be sure. In fact, I believe there are only three in existence today, and one of those is in Northern Italy."

Mr. Sharsted cleared his throat and made a non-committal reply.

"I felt sure you would like to see this before you leave,"

said Mr. Gingold softly. "You are quite sure you won't change your mind?" he added, almost inaudibly, as he bent to the levers. "About Mrs. Thwaites, I mean."

Sharsted felt another sudden spurt of anger, but kept his feelings under control.

"I'm sorry . . ." he began.

"No matter," said Mr. Gingold, regretfully. "I only wanted to make sure, before we had a look at this."

He laid his hand with infinite tenderness on Mr. Sharsted's shoulder as he drew him forward.

He pressed the lever and Mr. Sharsted almost cried out with the suddenness of the vision. He was God; the world was spread out before him in a crazy pattern, or at least the segment of it representing the part of the town surrounding the house in which he stood.

He viewed it from a great height, as a man might from an aeroplane; though nothing was quite in perspective.

The picture was of enormous clarity; it was like looking into an old cheval glass which had a faint distorting quality. There was something oblique and elliptical about the sprawl of alleys and roads that spread about the foot of the hill.

The shadows were mauve and violet, and the extremes of the picture were still tinged with the blood red of the dying sun.

It was an appalling, cataclysmic vision, and Mr. Sharsted was shattered; he felt suspended in space, and almost cried out at the dizziness of the height.

When Mr. Gingold twirled the wheel and the picture slowly began to revolve, Mr. Sharsted did cry out and had to clutch at the back of a chair to prevent himself from falling.

He was perturbed, too, as he caught a glimpse of a big, white building in the foreground of the picture.

"I thought that was the old Corn Exchange," he said in bewilderment. "Surely that burned down before the last war?"

"Eigh," said Mr. Gingold, as though he hadn't heard.

"It doesn't matter," said Mr. Sharsted, who now felt quite confused and ill. It must be the combination of the sherry and the enormous height at which he was viewing the vision in the camera obscura.

It was a demoniacal toy and he shrank away from the figure of Mr. Gingold, which looked somewhat sinister in the blood-red and mauve light reflected from the image in the polished table surface.

"I thought you'd like to see this one," said Mr. Gingold, in that same maddening, insipid voice. "It's really special, isn't it? Quite the best of the two . . . you can see all sorts of things that are normally hidden."

As he spoke there appeared on the screen two old buildings which Mr. Sharsted was sure had been destroyed during the war; in fact, he was certain that a public garden and car park had now been erected on the site. His mouth suddenly became dry; he was not sure whether he had drunk too much sherry or the heat of the day had been too much for him.

He had been about to make a sharp remark that the sale of the camera obscura would liquidate Mr. Gingold's current debt, but he felt this would not be a wise comment to make at this juncture. He felt faint, his brow went hot and cold and Mr. Gingold was at his side in an instant.

Mr. Sharsted became aware that the picture had faded from the table and that the day was rapidly turning to dusk outside the dusty windows.

"I really must be going," he said with feeble desperation, trying to free himself from Mr. Gingold's quietly persistent grip.

"Certainly, Mr. Sharsted," said his host. "This way." He led him without ceremony over to a small oval doorway in a corner of the far wall.

"Just go down the stairs. It will bring you on to the street. Please slam the bottom door—it will lock itself." As he spoke, he opened the door and Mr. Sharsted saw a flight of clean, dry stone steps leading downwards. Light still flooded in from windows set in the circular walls.

Mr. Gingold did not offer his hand and Mr. Sharsted stood rather awkwardly, holding the door ajar.

"Until Monday, then," he said.

Mr. Gingold flatly ignored this.

"Good night, Mr. Gingold," said the moneylender with nervous haste, anxious to be gone.

"Goodbye, Mr. Sharsted," said Mr. Gingold with kind finality.

Mr. Sharsted almost thrust himself through the door and nervously fled down the staircase, mentally cursing himself for all sorts of a fool. His feet beat a rapid tattoo that echoed eerily up and down the old tower. Fortunately, there was still plenty of light; this would be a nasty place in the dark. He slowed his pace after a few moments and thought bitterly of the way he had allowed old Gingold to gain the ascendancy over him; and what an impertinence of the man to interfere in the matter of the Thwaites woman.

He would see what sort of man Mr. Sharsted was when Monday came and the eviction went according to plan. Monday would also be a day of reckoning for Mr. Gingold—it was a day they would both remember and Mr. Sharsted felt himself quite looking forward to it.

He quickened his pace again, and presently found himself confronted by a thick oak door.

It gave beneath his hand as he lifted the big, well-oiled catch and the next moment he was in a high-walled alley leading to the street. The door slammed hollowly behind him and he breathed in the cool evening air with a sigh of relief. He jammed his hard hat back onto his head and strode out over the cobbles, as though to affirm the solidity of the outside world.

Once in the street, which seemed somewhat unfamiliar to him, he hesitated which way to go and then set off to the right. He remembered that Mr. Gingold had told him that this way took him over the other side of the hill; he had never been in this part of the town and the walk would do him good.

The sun had quite gone and a thin sliver of moon was showing in the early evening sky. There seemed few people about and when, ten minutes later, Mr. Sharsted came out into a large square which had five or six roads leading off it, he determined to ask the correct way back down to his part of the town. With luck he could catch a tram, for he had now had enough of walking for one day.

There was a large, smoke-grimed chapel on a corner of this square and as Mr. Sharsted passed it, he caught a glimpse of a board with gold-painted letters.

NINIAN'S REVIVALIST BROTHERHOOD, it said. The date, in flaked gold paint, was 1925.

Mr. Sharsted walked on and selected the most important of the roads which faced him. It was getting quite dark and the lamps had not yet been lit on this part of the hill. As he went farther down, the buildings closed in about his head, and the lights of the town below disappeared. Mr. Sharsted felt lost and a little forlorn. Due, no doubt, to the faintly incredible atmosphere of Mr. Gingold's big house.

He determined to ask the next passer-by for the right direction, but for the moment he couldn't see anyone about; the absence of street lights also bothered him. The municipal authorities must have overlooked this section when they switched on at dusk, unless it came under the jurisdiction of another body.

Mr. Sharsted was musing in this manner when he turned the corner of a narrow street and came out opposite a large, white building that looked familiar. For years Mr. Sharsted had a picture of it on the yearly calendar sent by a local tradesman, which used to hang in his office. He gazed at its façade with mounting bewilderment as he approached. The title, CORN EXCHANGE, winked back dully in the moonlight as he got near enough to make out the lettering.

Mr. Sharsted's bewilderment changed to distinct unease as he thought frantically that he had already seen this building once before this evening, in the image captured by the lens of Mr. Gingold's second camera obscura. And he knew with numbing certainty that the old Corn Exchange had burned down in the late thirties.

He swallowed heavily, and hurried on; there was something devilishly wrong, unless he were the victim of an optical illusion engendered by the violence of his thoughts, the unaccustomed walking he had done that day, and the two glasses of sherry.

He had the uncomfortable feeling that Mr. Gingold might be watching him at that very moment, on the table of his camera obscura, and at the thought a cold sweat burst out on his forehead.

He sent himself forward at a smart trot and had soon left the Corn Exchange far behind. In the distance he heard the sharp clopping and the grating rattle of a horse and cart, but as he gained the entrance of an alley he was disappointed to see its shadow disappear round the corner into the next road. He still could not see any people about and again had difficulty in fixing his position in relation to the town.

He set off once more, with a show of determination he was far from feeling, and five minutes later arrived in the middle of a square which was already familiar to him. There was a chapel on the corner and Mr. Sharsted read for the second time that evening the legend: NINIAN'S REVIVALIST BROTHERHOOD.

He stamped his foot in anger. He had walked quite three miles and had been fool enough to describe a complete circle; here he was, not five minutes from Gingold's house, where he had set out, nearly an hour before.

He pulled out his watch at this and was surprised to find it was only a quarter past six, though he could have sworn this was the time he had left Gingold.

Though it could have been a quarter past five; he hardly knew what he was doing this afternoon. He shook it to make sure it was still going and then replaced it in his pocket.

His feet beat the pavement in his fury as he ran down the length of the square. This time he wouldn't make the same silly mistake. He unhesitatingly chose a large, well-kept metalled road that ran fair and square in the direction he knew must take him back to the centre of the town. He found himself humming a little tune under his breath. As he turned the next corner, his confidence increased.

Lights burned brightly on every hand; the authorities must have realized their mistake and finally switched on. But again he was mistaken; there was a little cart parked at the side of the road, with a horse in the shafts. An old man mounted a ladder set against a lamp-post and Mr. Sharsted saw the thin blue flame in the gloom and then the mellow blossoming of the gas lamp.

Now he felt irritated again; what an incredibly archaic part of the town old Gingold lived in. It would just suit him. Gas lamps! And what a system for lighting them; Sharsted thought this method had gone out with the Ark.

Nevertheless, he was most polite.

"Good evening," he said, and the figure at the top of the lamp-post stirred uneasily. The face was in deep shadow.

"Good evening, sir," the lamplighter said in a muffled voice. He started climbing down.

"Could you direct me to the town center?" said Mr. Sharsted with simulated confidence. He took a couple of paces forward and was then arrested with a shock.

There was a strange, sickly stench which reminded him of something he was unable to place. Really, the drains in this place were terrible; he certainly would have to write to the town hall about this backward part of the locality.

The lamplighter had descended to the ground now and he put something down in the back of his cart; the horse shifted uneasily and again Mr. Sharsted caught the charnel stench, sickly sweet on the summer air.

"This is the town center as far as I know, sir," said the lamplighter. As he spoke he stepped forward and the pale lamplight fell on to his face, which had been in shadow before.

Mr. Sharsted no longer waited to ask for any more directions but set off down the road at breakneck speed, not sure whether the green pallor of the man's face was due to a terrible suspicion or the green-tinted glasses he wore.

What he was certain of was that something like a mass of writhing worms projected below the man's cap, where his hair would normally have been. Mr. Sharsted hadn't waited to find out if this Medusa-like supposition were correct; beneath his hideous fear burned a savage anger at Gingold, whom somehow he suspected to be at the back of all these troubles.

Mr. Sharsted fervently hoped that he might soon wake to find himself at home in bed, ready to begin the day that had ended so ignominiously at Gingold's, but even as he formulated the thought, he knew this was reality. This cold moonlight, the hard pavement, his frantic flight, and the breath rasping and sobbing in his throat.

As the mist cleared from in front of his eyes, he slowed to a walk and then found himself in the middle of a square; he knew where he was and he had to force his nerves into a terrible, unnatural calm, just this side of despair. He walked with controlled casualness past the legend, NINIAN'S REVIVALIST BROTHERHOOD, and this time chose the most unlikely road of all, little more than a narrow alley that appeared to lead in the wrong direction.

Mr. Sharsted was willing to try anything which would lead him off this terrifying, accursed hill. There were no lights here and his feet stumbled on the rough stones and flints of the unmade roadway, but at least he was going downhill and the track gradually spiralled until he was in the right direction.

For some little while Mr. Sharsted had heard faint, elusive stirrings in the darkness about him and once he was startled to hear, some way ahead of him, a muffled cough. At least there were other people about, at last, he thought and he was comforted, too, to see, far ahead of him, the dim lights of the town.

As he grew nearer, Mr. Sharsted recovered his spirits and was relieved to see that they did not recede from him, as he had half suspected they might. The shapes about him, too, were solid enough. Their feet rang hollow on the roadway; evidently they were on their way to a meeting.

As Mr. Sharsted came under the light of the first lamp, his earlier panic fear had abated. He still couldn't recognize exactly where he was, but the trim villas they were passing were more reminiscent of the town proper.

Mr. Sharsted stepped up onto the pavement when they reached the well-lit area and in so doing, cannoned into a large, well-built man who had just emerged from a gateway to join the throng in the roadway.

Mr. Sharsted staggered under the impact and once again his nostrils caught the sickly sweet perfume of decay. The man caught him by the front of the coat to prevent him from falling.

"Evening, Mordecai," he said in a thick voice. "I thought you'd be coming, sooner or later."

Mr. Sharsted could not resist a cry of bubbling terror. It was not just the greenish pallor of the man's face or the rotted, leathery lips drawn back from the decayed teeth. He fell back against the fence as Abel Joyce passed on—Abel Joyce, a fellow moneylender and usurer who had died in the nineteen-twenties and whose funeral Mr. Sharsted had attended.

Blackness was about him as he rushed away, a sobbing whistle in his throat. He was beginning to understand Mr. Gingold and that devilish camera obscura; the lost and the damned. He began to babble to himself under his breath.

Now and again he cast a sidelong glimpse at his companions as he ran; there was old Mrs. Sanderson who used to lay out corpses and rob her charges; there Grayson, the estate agent and undertaker; Amos, the war profiteer; Drucker, a swindler, all green of pallor and bearing with them the charnel stench.

All people Mr. Sharsted had business with at one time or another and all of whom had one thing in common. Without exception all had been dead for quite a number of years. Mr. Sharsted stuffed his handkerchief over his mouth to blot out that unbearable odour and heard the mocking laughter as his racing feet carried him past.

"Evening, Mordecai," they said. "We thought you'd be joining us." Mr. Gingold equated him with these ghouls, he sobbed, as he ran on at headlong speed; if only he could make him understand. Sharsted didn't deserve such treatment. He was a businessman, not like these bloodsuckers on society; the lost and the damned. Now he knew why the Corn Exchange still stood and why the town was unfamiliar. It existed only in the eye of the camera obscura. Now he knew that Mr. Gingold had been trying to give him a last chance and why he had said goodbye, instead of goodnight.

There was just one hope; if he could find the door back to Mr. Gingold's perhaps he could make him change his mind. Mr. Sharsted's feet flew over the cobbles as he thought this, his hat fell down and he scraped his hands against the wall. He left the walking corpses far behind, but though he was now looking for the familiar square he seemed to be finding his way back to the Corn Exchange.

He stopped for a moment to regain his breath. He must work this out logically. How had it happened before? Why, of course, by walking away from the desired destination. Mr. Sharsted turned back and set himself to walk steadily towards the lights. Though terrified, he did not despair, now that he knew what he was up against. He felt himself a match for Mr. Gingold. If only he could find the door!

As he reached the warm circle cast by the glow of the street lamps, Mr. Sharsted breathed a sigh of relief. For as he turned a corner there was the big square, with the soot-grimed chapel on the corner. He hurried on. He must remember exactly the turnings he had taken; he couldn't afford to make a mistake.

So much depended on it. If only he could have another chance—he would let the Thwaites family keep their house, he would even be willing to forget Gingold's debt. He couldn't face the possibility of walking these endless streets —for how long? And with the creatures he had seen . . .

Mr. Sharsted groaned as he remembered the face of one old woman he had seen earlier that evening—or what was left of that face, after years of wind and weather. He suddenly recalled that she had died before the 1914 war.

The sweat burst out on his forehead and he tried not to think of it.

Once off the square, he plunged into the alley he remembered. Ah! there it was. Now all he had to do was to go to the left and there was the door. His heart beat higher and he began to hope, with a sick longing, for the security of his well-appointed house and his rows of friendly ledgers. Only one more corner. He ran on and turned up the road towards Mr. Gingold's door. Another thirty yards to the peace of the ordinary world.

The moonlight winked on a wide, well-paved square. Shone, too, on a legend painted in gold leaf on a large board: NINIAN'S REVIVALIST BROTHERHOOD. The date was 1925.

Mr. Sharsted gave a hideous yell of fear and despair and fell to the pavement.

Mr. Gingold sighed heavily and yawned. He glanced at the clock. It was time for bed. He went over once again and stared into the camera obscura. It had been a not altogether unsuccessful day. He put a black velvet cloth over the image in the lens and went off slowly to bed.

Under the cloth, in pitiless detail, was reflected the narrow tangle of streets round Mr. Gingold's house, seen as through the eye of God; there went Mr. Sharsted and his colleagues, the lost and the damned, trapped for eternity, stumbling, weeping, swearing, as they slipped and scrabbled along the alleys and squares of their own private hell, under the pale light of the stars.

A DEATH IN THE FAMILY

by Miriam Allen deFord

At fifty-eight, Jared Sloane had the settled habits of a life-long bachelor. At seven o'clock in summer and six in winter, he put out the lights, locked up and went back to his living quarters. He showered and shaved and put on clothes less formal than his profession demanded, then cooked his supper and cleared it away.

Then he laid the phone extension on the bedroom floor where he would be sure to hear it if it rang, unlocked the tight-fitting door leading from the kitchen, and went downstairs for the evening with his family.

Old Mr. Shallcross, from whom he had bought the building twenty years before, had used the cellar only for storage. But every man who was young and on his own in the big Depression acquired a smattering of many skills, and Jared was no exception; he had sawed and hammered and painted, and what had once been a cellar was now a big, comfortable sitting room, its two small high-up windows always covered with heavy curtains. He was not competent to install electric lights, but he had run a pipe from the kitchen range to the old gas chandelier which, like most of the furniture he had repainted and reupholstered, had come from a glorified junk shop he patronized in McMinnville, the county seat. The room was always cool, and in winter it was so chilly that he had to wear his overcoat, but that was necessary and he no longer noticed it.

They were always there, waiting for him. Dad was in the big easy chair, reading the Middleton *Gazette*. Mother was knitting a sock. Grandma was dozing on the couch—she dozed all the time; she was nearly ninety. Brother Ben and sister Emma were playing whist, sitting in straight chairs at the little table, the cards held cannily against Ben's white shirt and Emma's ruffled foulard print. Gussie, Jared's wife, sat at the piano, her fingers arrested on the keys, her head turned to smile at him as he entered.

Luke, his ten-year-old son, sat on the floor, a half-built model ship before him.

Jared would sit down in the one vacant place, a big comfortable club chair upholstered in plum-colored plush, and would chat with them until bedtime. He told them all the day's doings upstairs, commented on news of the town and of the people they knew, repeated stories and jokes (carefully expurgated) he had heard from salesmen, expressed his views and opinions on any subject that came into his mind. They never argued or contradicted him. They never answered.

Their clothes changed with the seasons and the styles; otherwise the scene never altered. When bedtime came, Jared yawned, stretched, said, "Well, goodnight all—pleasant dreams," turned out the overhead light, climbed the stairs, locked the door behind him and went to bed. For a while he had always kissed his wife on the forehead for goodnight, but he felt that the others might be jealous, and now he showed no favoritism.

The family had not always played their present roles. Once they had all had different names. They had been other people's grandmother and father and mother and sister and brother and wife and son. Now they were his.

He had waited a long time for some of them—for relatives of just the right age, with the right family resemblance. Gussie he had loved, quietly and patiently, for years before she became his wife; she had been Mrs. Ralph Stiegeler then, the wife of the Middleton Drugstore owner, and she had never guessed that Jared Sloane was in love with her. Her name really was Gussie; Ben and Emma and Luke just had names he liked. She was the nucleus of the family; all the others had been added later, one by one. Grandma, strange to say, had been with them the shortest time—little more than a year. All the family needed now to be complete was a daughter, and Jared had already picked her name—she would be called Martha. He liked old-fashioned names; they belonged to the past, to his lonely boyhood in the orphan asylum where he had lived all his life until he was sixteen.

He still remembered bitterly how the others had jeered at him, a foundling whose very name had been given at the whim of the superintendent after he had been found, wrapped in a torn sheet, on the asylum steps. The others were orphans, but they knew who they were; they had

aunts and uncles and cousins who wrote them letters and
came to see them and sent them presents at Christmas and
birthdays, whom they visited sometimes and who often
paid for all or part of their keep. Jared Sloane had nobody.

That was why he had wanted so large a family. Every
evening now he was a man with parents, a brother, a
sister, a wife and child. (Grandma was a lucky fluke;
he had kept an eye on old Mrs. Atkinson and it had paid
off.) There was no more room for another adult member
of the family, but Martha, when he found her, could sit
on a cushion on the floor beside her brother, and play
with a doll he would buy for her or do something else
domestic and childish and feminine. He decided that
she should be younger than Luke—say seven or eight, old
enough to enjoy her father's conversation, not so young
as to need the care called for by a small child.

Every night, in bed, before he set the alarm and put his
teeth in the tumbler, Jared Sloane uttered a grateful little
unvoiced prayer to someone or something—perhaps to
himself—a prayer of thanks for the wonderful, unheard-
of idea that had come to him ten years ago when, in the
middle of a sleepless, mourning night, he had suddenly
realized how he could make Gussie his wife and keep her
with him as long as he himself lived. Ralph Steigeler had
called him only that afternoon. Out of nowhere there had
come to him the daring, frightening scheme, full-fledged
as Pallas Athene from the head of Zeus.

He had gambled on discovery, ruin, imprisonment, disgrace, against the fulfillment of his dearest and most secret
dream—to have a family of his own. And he had won.
After Gussie, the rest had been easy. He could not fore-
see, but he could choose. He blessed Middleton for being
a small town where there was need for only one man of
his profession, and he could get all the business there was.
He had hesitated when first he came here, fresh from
college, fearing there would not be a livelihood for him in
the town and the farms around it. But he was frugal, he
loved quiet, and he dreaded the scramble and competition
of a big city firm; here he would be on his own from the
beginning. When he had learned through a notice in a trade
paper that old Mr. Shallcross wanted to sell his establishment and good will and retire, Jared had answered him.

To his happiness he found that the little nest egg he

had accumulated by hard labor all through his younger years—he had been too young for one war and too old for the other—which had enabled him to be trained in the one profession that had always attracted him, would stretch to cover Mr. Shallcross's modest demands. Within a week the business had changed hands. Now he had long been a settled feature of Middleton; and if he had never been a mixer or made any close friends, he was well-known, respected—and, beyond all, above suspicion.

Everything was always done just as the mourners wished. The funeral was held from the home of the deceased or from his own beautifully redecorated chapel, as they preferred. (That had been his chief terror about Gussie, but everything went his way—Ralph immediately asked for the chapel. He remembered with chagrin how, later on, he had lost a splendid former candidate for brother Ben, because Charles Holden's mother insisted on having the services at the farmhouse.) The deceased, a work of art by a fine embalmer worthy of any big city funeral parlor, lay dressed in his best in the casket, surrounded by flowers and wreaths and set pieces. When the minister had finished, Miss Hattie Blackstock played the organ softly, and then at Jared Sloane's signal the company passed in single file for the last look. The immediate relatives came last. Then they all filed out to enter the waiting cars for the trip to the cemetery. (No one who was to be cremated instead of buried could ever become a member of Jared's family, of course.)

Then came the crucial moment. Most vividly Jared remembered that first time, when it was Gussie, when everything depended on timing and resolution and luck.

The pallbearers waited for him to close the casket, so that they could carry it out to the hearse. In a city funeral, the assistants would have been taking the flowers out, but Jared had no assistant. In that small town, where he knew everybody and everybody knew him, it was natural to say: "Look, fellows, I don't want to hold things up too long; it's hard enough on her folks as it is. I've taken the cards off all the floral offerings; would you mind carrying them to the hearse, all of you, and putting them around the bier? Then by the time you get back I'll have the casket closed and ready for you."

If just one person had said: "I can't get near the roses—they make me sneeze," or "You don't need us all; I'll wait here and rest my bad knee," or "That's not a good idea, Jared—the casket will crush them if we put them in first,"—if that had happened, then the whole desperate gamble would have been lost. Gussie would never have been his wife; the rest of his family would never have come to read and knit and play cards and build model ships in the big sitting room. But from Gussie to Grandma, it had worked.

The instant the last back was turned, bending under its load of flowers, Jared moved like lightning. Quick—lift the body out of the casket. Quick—lay it on the couch concealed behind the heavy velvet curtains. Quick—bring out the life size, carefully weighted dummy prepared and ready, and put it in place. Quick—close the lid and fasten it. It all took between two and three minutes. When the first pallbearer returned, everything was set. Nobody ever knew what rode out to the cemetery, what was lowered into the grave.

He himself drove the hearse, of course. The funeral parlor was safely locked until he returned. Then, with the last sober, sympathetic handshake, he was left alone.

Once inside, he did nothing until closing time. Then, with the office and display room and slumber room and chapel dark, he went behind the velvet curtain and lifted the new member of his family respectfully and tenderly from the couch and took him or her back to the preparation room. Nobody could ever have claimed that the embalming job already done was not as good as anyone could wish for. But now came the last extra refinements of his art—the special preservative he had perfected, the cosmetic changes which increased the resemblances of kindred, the new clothes he had bought in a fast trip to McMinnville. The clothing provided by the "former family"—that was how he always thought of them—he put thriftily away to help stuff the next dummy: if Jared Sloane had been given to frivolity, which he was not, he might have found amusement in the thought that, for instance, the "former" sister Emma's last garments now occupied the coffin of the "former" dad. Last of all, he arranged the new member in the pose which he had decided on for his or her future in the family gathering in the sitting room. Then he carried his newly acquired relative downstairs. No introductions were necessary; it was to be assumed that the Sloane family knew one another. Jared got to bed late on those seven red-letter evenings; it was hard to tear himself away from the companionship of his augmented family circle and go to his lonely room.

As the years went by, he ceased to fret and worry and fear for weeks or months afterward, as he had done at first. After all, he averaged about fifty funerals a year, counting the country around Middleton and occasional Middleton-born people who had left town but were brought home for burial. In ten years that meant some five hundred and out of all these he had taken the big gamble only seven times.

Some day, of course, he himself would die, and then inevitably the discovery would be made. But by that time he would be past caring, and the scandal and excitement and newspaper headlines would be of no concern to him. He was only fifty-eight, and he had never been ill a day in his life; he would count on twenty or twenty-five years more—the only man in Middleton who would never have to dread a lonely old age. He remembered his terribly lonely childhood and youth, and to his grateful little silent prayer he added thanks that by his own efforts he had compensated for it. He was grateful for another thing, too—that the fate that had deprived him of mother-love as a helpless infant had seemed to paralyze his emotional nature; never in his life had he felt or understood what seemed to him the disgusting sexual impulses of other men. Even his long love of Gussie Stiegeler had been made up—as it was now that she was Gussie Sloane— wholly of tenderness and protectiveness and dependency.

Once in a book on psychology he had read about a horrible perversion called necrophilia, and had shuddered. He tried, with an attempt at understanding, to imagine himself taking Gussie—his lovely, precious Gussie, whom he dressed in silk and pearls, for whom he had bought the piano that the "former" Gussie had played so well—away from her piano and into his narrow bed, kissing her embracing her . . . He felt sick. For days thereafter it embarrassed him even to look at Gussie; he blushed at the thought that she might have guessed what foul fancies he had permitted to enter his mind.

He loved his family because they *were* his family, because they were his and no one else's, because with them he could expand and be himself and know that they would always belong to him. He was doing their former selves and their former dear ones no injury. He loved dad and mother and grandma filially, he loved sister Emma and brother Ben as an older brother should, he adored Gussie and little Luke. All he needed now for perfect happiness was a sweet little daughter; it wasn't good for a boy like Luke to be the only child.

Naturally he couldn't look around and pick and choose or even speculate—good heavens, only a ghoul would do that! He must wait, as with all the others, until just the right opportunity came—a seven- or eight-year-old girl, with dark hair (both he and Gussie were dark), a pretty little girl because her mother was pretty, provided for him by good fortune and the kindness of heaven, as all the rest of the family had been. There was no hurry; Luke would always stay ten years old, just as Grandma would always be eighty-nine. Jared would have shrunk from feeling interest or curiosity if he had been told of the illness of somebody's little daughter. He could wait. But his heart gave a little excited jump every time he got a call from a household where there were children, until he learned—as he always did—that it was grandfather or uncle William or old cousin Sarah in whose behalf his services were required. Twice he handled the funerals of little girls, but one was a scrawny, homely blonde brat, and the other had been killed in an auto accident and was dreadfully mangled.

In the early hours of March 31st Jared Sloane was wakened from a sound sleep by a loud knock at the front door. That happened sometimes—people came instead of phoning; like a doctor he was inured to night calls, and he shrugged drowsily into bathrobe and slippers. As he switched on the lights in the front he heard a car driving away; when he opened the door, the street—the main business street of Middleton was part of a state highway—was dark and deserted.

Then his eyes fell to a little bundle, wrapped in a blanket, lying on the porch at his feet. He stooped and picked it up, knowing at once what it must be. Inside, he drew the blanket away from the little corpse.

Even with the head hanging limp on the broken neck, he recognized her at once—the papers had been full of her photographs. It was the Manning child. Manning had disobeyed orders and notified the police, and the kidnappers had brutally made good their threat.

Why they had deposited their victim on the doorstep of a country undertaker two hundred miles away, in another state from the city where the millionaire's child had been snatched, Jared Sloane could not imagine. Probably, making good their escape with the ransom money, they had chanced on the sign as they drove through Middleton, and as a bit of macabre humor had presented him with the body. Much as he disliked the idea of being brought to public notice and having FBI men and police officers and reporters invading his privacy, Jared knew his duty; he must telephone at once to the sheriff's office in McMinnville.

Then he looked down at the blanket and what it held. Diana Manning had been nine, but she was small for her age. She had been a pretty, delicately cared for child. Her hair was long and soft and dark, the blank eyes staring up at him were brown.

He stood for a long time, pondering. Then quietly he lifted Diana and carried her back to the preparation room. Before he returned to bed, he took all her clothing and the thin old blanket out to the incinerator in the back yard, near the garage; he could not arouse suspicion by lighting a fire at three o'clock in the morning, but he burned trash every few days.

The next evening, for the first time since Grandma, Jared dropped in on the family only long enough to tell them the good news. He was moved; he whispered it to Gussie first. After all, Martha was going to be her daughter. He worked till late, then hid Martha carefully away. He had no funeral scheduled for the rest of the week, and there was nobody in the slumber room whom relatives and friends would be coming to visit; he could leave a sign in the door around noon and drive to McMinnville for a wardrobe and a big doll for his little girl. He always did the shopping for the family in McMinnville, which was large enough for him to be a stranger.

There was nothing new in the paper or on the radio about the Manning case. Perhaps the father, poor fool, was still dreaming he could get his daughter back by paying the ransom, and had asked too late for silence and secrecy.

That night Jared Sloane sat in his plum-colored chair and beamed at little Martha, perched on a cushion near her brother, smiling up at her mother at the piano. The family was complete. He was the happiest man on earth.

Three days later, as he worked in his office on accounts, the front door opened and a tall young man entered, carrying a brief case. Jared adjusted his expression to greet a salesman instead of a client.

"Mr. Sloane?" the young man asked amiably. Jared nodded, "Can you spare me a moment?"

"I don't know that there's anything I need right now, thanks."

"Need? Oh," he laughed. "I'm not a salesman."

He opened his wallet and showed a badge and a card. Investigator. His name was Ennis.

Jared slumped in his chair, gripping the arms to hide the sudden shaking of his hands. Ennis seated himself opposite without an invitation.

"About the Manning child's body," he said easily.

Jared had control of himself by now. He stared at Ennis with a puzzled frown.

"The Manning child? The one that was kidnapped? Have they found her?"

"Now, Mr. Sloane—" The man glanced around him at the small, tidy office, at the respectable elderly undertaker in his neat black suit. He seemed disconcerted. Then he leaned forward confidentially.

"Perhaps there's been some mistake," he said. "This isn't for publication yet, but we have a man in custody— a man who's a very hot suspect."

"Good. I hope you nail him. Anybody who would kidnap a child, let alone murder her, killing's too good for him."

"Did I say she was murdered?"

"You said 'the Manning child's body.'"

"So I did. Well, I'll level with you, Mr. Sloane. This man—we've had him for two days now, and he's begun to talk. In fact, to be frank, we have a full confession. And he says that on March 30th he drove through Middleton with the body in his car, and left it on the porch in front of a funeral parlor just off the highway. He told us the name on the sign was Sloane."

"Nobody left any remains or anything else on my porch on the night of March 30th," Jared said steadily. It was perfectly true; it had been quarter to three on the morning of March 31st.

"Now look, Mr. Sloane, please understand we're not

accusing you of anything. Of course concealment of a dead body is a criminal offense, but we're not disposed to be tough about it. I can understand very well what a shock it must have been, and that you might want a little while to make up your mind what to do about it—after all, it isn't pleasant to have a lot of that kind of publicity turned on you through no fault of your own. I'll give you my word—you let us take the child away quietly and we may never have to make public at all where we found the body."

If you had come that very day, Jared thought, I might have done it. Then he had a vision of Martha, in her short pink dress, her dark hair tied with a big pink ribbon, fondling her doll and smiling at her mother. He shook his head stubbornly.

"The man is lying to you," he said. "He must have noticed my sign as he passed through here and sent you on a wild goose chase. I've been in business in Middleton for twenty years, everybody knows me. Do you think I'd be likely to help a kidnapper by hiding the evidence against him? Besides—"

It had been on the tip of his tongue to add that he had a little girl of his own; he stopped himself just in time.

"Besides," he went on, "nobody would know better than a man in my profession that it's a crime to dispose of remains illegally. It's the last thing I'd do."

"Well, you may be right, Mr. Sloane. We'll go over it with him again. So, just for the record, let me have a look around your place so I can report that the body's not here, and we may never have to bother you again. You surely have no objection to that."

Jared felt himself turning pale. He had a sudden swift picture of Ennis, finding the display room and the slumber room and the preparation room and the chapel all empty, asking next to go through his living quarters—and in the kitchen saying: "Where does that door lead to?"

"What are you aiming to do?" he asked sarcastically. "Dig up my back yard to see if I've buried Diana Manning in it for no reason under the sun? Yes, I do object. This is my home as well as my place of business. I know my rights as a citizen. I'm not going to have anybody snooping through my private property without a search warrant—and I take it you haven't got that."

"No, I haven't, Mr. Sloane." The young man's friendly

eyes had turned cold, and his voice was hard. "If that's the way you feel about it, I can go to McMinnville and get one, and be back here with it and the sheriff within an hour. I don't know why a respectable businessman like you should want to obstruct justice and help a dirty rat like the man we've got in custody, but that's what it amounts to.

"Very well. I'll see you an hour from now. And if you've got that body here and make any attempt to hide it or take it away somewhere in your hearse, we'll find that out, too." He paused. His voice grew more conciliatory. "If you want to change your mind—" he said. Jared shook his head again. Ennis picked up his brief case and marched out of the building. Jared watched him climb into the car parked in front and make a U-turn back toward McMinnville.

He stood still for a long minute. Then he picked up the sign which said: "Closed—Be Back Soon," and stuck it in the front door and locked up. He went back to the kitchen and unlocked the door to the sitting room, and this time he took out the key and relocked it on the inside. Then slowly, he walked downstairs to the family.

He reached up and pulled the curtain open on the two windows—the first time they had ever been opened since the room had been furnished for Gussie. It was a risk, though a small one, but it had to be taken for a few moments.

In the white light of day there was something bleak and forlorn about the cozy scene. Dad was reading the paper, Mother knitting, Ben and Emma playing cards, Luke working on his model ship, Gussie at the piano, just as always. Somehow they seemed a little withered, less like living people than like mummies—even darling Gussie, in her new blue dress. Only Martha, the newcomer, looked as fresh and blooming as they all had been in the warm gaslight of his happy evenings.

He sighed deeply. He reached up to the chandelier, and turned on all the jets. Then he sat down in his chair.

He loved them so much. They were his, they belonged to him and he belonged to them. An orphan and a foundling, but he had a family, he had not gone lonely through all his life. A man not made like other men, yet he had loved a woman, and for ten years now she had been his dearly beloved wife.

On an impulse, still half-embarrassed by the eyes of the others on him, he went to the piano bench, put his arms around Gussie, and for the first time kissed her on the lips. Her mouth was cold and dry, but he had never known it warm and moist. Then he went back to sit in his chair.

After a while he began to smell the gas—it was natural gas, but they put something in it to warn people if it was turned on by accident. When waves of giddiness began to flow over him, he knew the room was full. He must not delay until he was too sick and dizzy.

He reached into his coat pocket, ook out a kitchen match and struck it on the sole of his shoe.

THE KNIFE

by Robert Arthur

Edward Dawes stifled his curiosity as long as he could, then he sidled over and lowered his large bulk carefully onto the chair opposite Herbert Smithers. Leaning on the table, he watched the other man clean away rusty mud from the object in his hands. It was a knife, that much was apparent. What was not apparent was why Smithers was so intent upon it, in its present condition. Edward Dawes nursed his glass of half-and-half and waited for Smithers to speak.

When Smithers continued to ignore him, Dawes drained his glass and banged it down with a gesture.

"Doesn't look like much, that there knife doesn't," he remarked disdainfully. " 'Ardly worth cleanin' it, I say."

"Ho!" Herbert Smithers retorted, and continued to work delicately with the point of a fingernail file at the caked dirt on his find.

"What is it?" Gladys, the Three Oaks' buxom barmaid, asked with open curiosity as she collected the empty glasses in front of them.

"It's a knife," Smithers vouchsafed. "A rare antique knife wot belongs to me because I found it."

It was now Mr. Dawes' turn to say, "Ho!"

"Thinks it's valuable, 'e does," he stated to the room at large, though it was empty save for the three of them.

"It don't look valuable to me," Gladys said frankly. "It looks like a nasty rusty old thing that ought to be put back on the rubbish heap it came from."

Smithers' silence was more eloquent than words. Discarding the file, he now moistened the corner of a grimy handkerchief with saliva, and rubbed at a small scarlet spot in the end of the still-obscured hilt. The spot enlarged and emerged from the grime as a faceted stone which glowed redly.

"Why, it's a jool!" Gladys exclaimed with quickened interest. "Look at it shine. Maybe it's real."

"Another half-and-half, if you please!" Smithers said pointedly, and Gladys flounced off. The swing of her well-curved hips disclaimed all interest, but her backward glance revealed what the swinging hips tried to deny.

"A jewel!" There was a hollow quality in Dawes' disdain now, and he leaned forward to stare as Smithers rubbed. "Not likely!"

"And 'ow," Smithers asked, with composed logic, "do you know?"

He breathed upon the red stone, polished it with his sleeve, and held it to admire it. Like a red eye it winked and glittered, seeming to gather into itself every crimson gleam from the tiny grate fire in the corner behind their table.

"Prob'ly," he remarked, with the quiet dignity befitting one who has just come into wealth, "it's a ruby."

"A ruby!" The larger Mr. Dawes seemed to choke on the word. "And wot would a knife with a real ruby in its 'ilt be doin' out in plain sight on the street for you to find?"

"Wasn't," Smithers said succinctly. He picked up the file again and began digging the dirt out of the crevices of the intricately worked handle. "It was in a pile of muck where they're fixin' th' drains, down Dorset street. Prob'ly been in th' drains no tellin' how many years."

His small figure straightened inside its shabby covering of clothes; his thin lips tightened.

"Look at th' rust an' muck on it!" he challenged. "That proves 'ow long it's been lyin' there. Nobody can't claim they lost it in th' blitz."

Reluctantly Mr. Dawes conceded the point.

"It's good steel, though," he added. "Still got a point to it, rust or no rust."

"Only a minute ago," Smithers pointed out, "you said as 'ow it wasn't worth while cleanin'."

Having removed enough of the encrusting dirt to show a slender, ornate hilt and a long tapering blade, he let his fingers close about the weapon. The hilt slipped naturally into the curve of his palm. He swung it a little, made a practice thrust-and-cut.

"It 'andles like it was part of me," he remarked dreamily. "Sends a kind of warm feelin' all up me arm, just to 'old it. Tingles it does, like electricity."

"Let me try," Mr. Dawes suggested, all disdain forgotten. Smithers scowled and drew his hand back.

"It's mine!" he said, a new truculent note in his voice. "Nobody else is touchin' it but me."

He thrust-and-cut again, and the red stone in the hilt flashed fire.

Smithers' thin, pinched face was flushed, as if reflecting the firelight, and he swayed, as though suddenly a little drunk.

"It's worth a 'eap," he said huskily. "This 'ere is a foreign knife, a old one, and it 'as a real ruby in the 'andle. I've made a find, I 'ave."

Gladys set down two glasses and forgot to complete her mechanical wiping of the table top. Smithers held the knife steady, to find the brightest possible glow of the stone in the hilt, and Gladys stared at it with covetous eyes.

"Maybe it is a real ruby at that," she said. "Let me have a look, ducky."

Her moist, outstretched fingers touched Smithers' hand, and the little man whirled, was on his feet.

"No!" he shouted. "It's mine, d'you hear?"

"Just a look," Gladys said eagerly. "I'll give it right back, promise."

She followed him a step, coaxingly, and the flush on Smithers' pinched features deepened.

"I tell you it's mine!" he cried shrilly. "An' no pretty face is gettin' it away from me. D'you hear! D'you hear!"

And then all three of them, even Gladys, were deathly silent, staring transfixed at the winking red eye which now of a sudden stood out some five inches from Gladys' heart, Smithers' fingers still gripped about the hilt.

Gladys' eyes grew wide and wider.

"You stabbed me," she said slowly and distinctly. "You stabbed me!" And then with no other sound but a queer rattling noise in her throat, she crumpled. Her body struck the floor with a crash that seemed to shake the room, and sprawled there emptily. A little red tongue licked across her breast and spread hungrily.

But even that, for a moment, did not change the position of the two men—Smithers standing, the knife left in his hand by Gladys' fall, and Dawes half risen, his hands on the table, his jaw slack.

The power of speech returned first to the little scavenger.

"I didn't do it!" he cried hoarsely. "I never did it! The knife stabbed her! 's truth, it did! And I couldn't stop it."

Then recovering a semblance of self-possession, he flung the knife down. Turning, he stumbled sobbingly toward the door and was gone.

Edward Dawes moved at last. Breathing hard, as if after a long run, he stood up. The knife lay at his feet. He listened. There was no sound, no outcry. He stooped. When he straightened, he held the knife gingerly in his hand. Mechanically, his gaze darting to the door and back, he wiped the blade on half his evening paper. Then he wrapped it in the other half. A moment later he was moving at a shambling run for the door.

His plan, formulated quite without conscious thought, was simple. The lodging house run by his wife was directly across the street. From there he would phone the police. He was taking the knife to protect it as evidence. When the police arrived, he would turn it over to them minus the stone in the hilt. If Smithers, on being caught, mentioned it, he would swear that it must have been knocked out and lost when the knife was thrown to the floor.

Who was to prove different? . . .

Still breathing hard, Edward Dawes pried at the glittering red stone with the blade of a penknife. He was in the kitchen, just outside which was the phone. He had perhaps three minutes before the police got there in response to his call. He worked with the sweat pouring from his brow and his heart thudding as if he was exerting himself to the utmost.

Two minutes more. The prongs that held the stone were stout. His penknife slipped and cut him. He cursed under his breath, and went on working. The blood from his cut made his fingers slippery, and a moment later the the knife shot from between them and clattered to the floor, the steel blade giving out a ringing note.

Dawes stooped, his bulk making the movement difficult, and snatched at the knife. It eluded him and skidded a foot away. A minute left. He followed it, not even taking time to curse now, and had it in his hand when his wife entered and stopped just inside the doorway.

"Edward," she began shrilly, "I heard you at the phone

just now. What nonsense were you talking about a murder at the Three Oaks?"

Then she took in the whole scene as he straightened up —his flushed and furious face, the knife in his hand, the blood staining his fingers.

"Edward!" she shrieked. "You've killed somebody! You've killed somebody!"

He took a step toward her. There was a singing in his ears, and a strange warmth shooting up his arm. A reddish mist floated up before his eyes, hiding his wife from him.

"Shut up, you bloody fool!" he shouted.

His stout wife became silent at that, except for a blubbery gasping through which words seemed to be trying to come.

Then the reddish mist cleared, and Edward Dawes saw that she was lying on the floor, the hilt of the knife standing out from her plump white throat just beneath her chin, the red eye in the end of it winking and blinking up at him, holding him transfixed so that he did not hear the pounding on the outer door. Nor, a moment later, the sound of it opening. Nor the tramp of heavy official feet coming down the hallway . . .

"That's it, sir." Sergeant Tobins' tone was respectful, to a full inspector. "Killed two women inside ten minutes, it did. Two different men used it. Both of them claim they don't know why they did it."

He smiled, as if to say that he for one would never be taken in by such a claim.

"Hmm." The tall, gaunt man turned the knife delicately between his fingers. "Indian workmanship, I see. Sixteenth or seventeenth century."

"Get that, Miss Mapes?"

The plain, middle-aged woman standing at the inspector's elbow nodded. "Yes, sergeant." She made a few squiggles in her notebook.

"It's been cleaned up some, Inspector Frayne," Sergeant Tobins ventured. "No prints on it. Anyway, they both confessed."

"The stone?" The tall man tapped the hilt. "Is it real?"

"It's a ruby, right enough," the thickset sergeant agreed. "Badly flawed, though. Has an air bubble right in the middle of it, shaped like a drop of blood—" he coughed delicately—"like a teardrop, I mean."

Inspector Frayne continued turning the thing. Pencil ready, Miss Mapes waited.

"It's a genuine rarity, all the same," Frayne said. "Glad you asked me to look at it. Probably brought to this country by one of our Tommies after the Sepoy rebellion. Bit of looting done after it was put down, you know."

Miss Mapes' pencil scribbled busily.

"Found in a drain, wasn't it?" the inspector asked. "Been there a long time, that's plain. Which of them found it—Smithers or Dawes?"

"Smithers, sir. Funny thing, that. He was cleaning it, hadn't 'ad . . . had it more than an hour, when he used it on a barmaid. Then Dawes cops it and ten minutes later sticks it in his wife's throat. And both of them said the same thing, when we questioned them."

"They did, eh? Just what did they say?"

"Well, sir, they said they got a warm, tingly feeling just from holding the knife. It came on all of a sudden like when they got angry at the women. They didn't know why they got so angry, they just did . . . and just like that the women were dead! They said—" Sergeant Tobins allowed himself to smile—"that they didn't have anything to do with it. That the knife just sort of moved by itself, with them holding it."

"They said that, eh? . . . Good Lord!" The tall man stared at the knife with a new interest. "Sergeant, just where was the drain in which this thing was found?"

"Dorset street, sir," Sergeant Tobins stated. "Near the corner of Commercial street."

"Dorset street, did you say?" Inspector Frayne's voice was sharp, his eyes alight. "By George, I wonder—"

Neither Tobins nor Miss Mapes interrupted. After a moment, Frayne put the knife back in its box on Sergeant Tobins' desk.

"I was having a brainstorm," he said, smiling. "This knife—well, do you know what happened on Dorset street a good while ago?"

Sergeant Tobins shook his head.

"I seem to remember of reading about it," he said. "But I can't just put my mind on where."

"It's mentioned in one of the largest files in our record department. It happens that in November of 1888 a woman was brutally murdered—with a knife—in Millers Court, off Dorset street. Her name was Marie Kelley."

Sergeant Tobins stared.

"I remember now," he blurted out. "Jack the Ripper!"

"Exactly. His last murder, we believe. The last of twelve. All women. He seemed to have a special, venomous hatred for women. And I was toying with the thought of a murderer hurrying from that spot in the dead of night, with a bloodstained knife in his hand. I could see him dropping it into a drain opening as he fled, to lie there until now . . . Well, as I say, a brainstorm."

Sergeant Tobins watched the door close, then turned.

"The inspector would do great writing thrillers," he said with ponderous humor. "A regular information for it, he has!"

He picked up the knife, gripped it firmly, and struck a pose, winking broadly.

"Be careful, Miss Mapes!" he said. "Jack the Ripper!"

Miss Mapes giggled.

"Well now," she breathed. "Let me look at it, may I Sergeant Tobins, if you don't mind?"

Her fingers touched his, and Sergeant Tobins drew his hand back abruptly. His face flushed, and a fierce anger unaccountably flared up in him at the touch of Miss Mapes' hand. But as he stared into her plain, bewildered face, the anger was soothed by the pleasurable tingling warmth in his right wrist and arm. And as he took a swift step toward her, there was a strange, sweet singing in his ears, high and shrill and faraway.

Or was it the sound of a woman screaming?

CASABLANCA

by Thomas M. Disch

In the morning the man with the red fez always brought them coffee and toast on a tray. He would ask them how it goes, and Mrs. Richmond, who had some French, would say it goes well. The hotel always served the same kind of jam, plum jam. That eventually became so tiresome that Mrs. Richmond went out and bought their own jar of strawberry jam, but in a little while that was just as tiresome as the plum jam. Then they alternated, having plum jam one day, and strawberry jam the next. They wouldn't have taken their breakfasts in the hotel at all, except for the money it saved.

When, on the morning of their second Wednesday at the Belmonte, they came down to the lobby, there was no mail for them at the desk. "You can't really expect them to think of us here," Mrs. Richmond said in a piqued tone, for it had been her expectation.

"I suppose not," Fred agreed.

"I think I'm sick again. It was that funny stew we had last night. Didn't I tell you? Why don't *you* go out and get the newspaper this morning?"

So Fred went, by himself, to the newsstand on the corner. It had neither the *Times* nor the *Tribune*. There weren't even the usual papers from London. Fred went to the magazine store nearby the Marhaba, the big luxury hotel. On the way someone tried to sell him a gold watch. It seemed to Fred that everyone in Morocco was trying to sell gold watches.

The magazine store still had copies of the *Times* from last week. Fred had read those papers already. "Where is today's *Times?*" he asked loudly, in English.

The middle-aged man behind the counter shook his head sadly, either because he didn't understand Fred's question or because he didn't know the answer. He asked Fred how it goes.

"Byen," said Fred, without conviction, "byen."

The local French newspaper, *La Vigie Marocaine,* had black, portentous headlines, which Fred could not decipher. Fred spoke "four languages: English, Irish, Scottish, and American." With only those languages, he insisted, one could be understood anywhere in the free world.

At ten o'clock, Bulova-watch time, Fred found himself, as though by chance, outside his favorite ice cream parlor. Usually, when he was with his wife, he wasn't able to indulge his sweet tooth, because Mrs. Richmond, who had a delicate stomach, distrusted Moroccan dairy products, unless boiled.

The waiter smiled and said, "Good morning, Mr. Richmon." Foreigners were never able to pronounce his name right for some reason.

Fred said, "Good morning."

"How are you?"

"I'm just fine, thank you."

"Good, good," the waiter said. Nevertheless, he looked saddened. He seemed to want to say something to Fred, but his English was very limited.

It was amazing, to Fred, that he had had to come halfway around the world to discover the best damned ice cream sundaes he'd ever tasted. Instead of going to bars, the young men of the town went to ice cream parlors, like this, just as they had in Fred's youth, in Iowa, during Prohibition. It had something to do, here in Casablanca, with the Moslem religion.

A ragged shoeshine boy came in and asked to shine Fred's shoes, which were very well shined already. Fred looked out the plate-glass window to the travel agency across the street. The boy hissed *monsieur, monsieur,* until Fred would have been happy to kick him. The wisest policy was to ignore the beggars. They went away quicker if you didn't look at them. The travel agency displayed a poster showing a pretty young blonde, rather like Doris Day, in a cowboy costume. It was a poster for Pan-American airlines.

At last the shoeshine boy went away. Fred's face was flushed with stifled anger. His sparse white hair made the redness of the flesh seem all the brighter, like a winter sunset.

A grown man came into the ice cream parlor with a bundle of newspapers, French newspapers. Despite his lack

of French, Fred could understand the headlines. He bought
a copy for twenty francs and went back to the hotel, leaving half the sundae uneaten.

The minute he was in the door, Mrs. Richmond cried
out, "Isn't it terrible?" She had a copy of the paper already spread out on her bed. "It doesn't say *anything*
about Cleveland."

Cleveland was where Nan, the Richmonds' married
daughter, lived. There was no point in wondering about
their own home. It was in Florida, within fifty miles of
the Cape, and they'd always known that if there were a
war it would be one of the first places to go.

"The dirty reds!" Fred said, flushing. His wife began
to cry. "God damn them to hell. What did the newspaper
say? How did it start?"

"Do you suppose," Mrs. Richmond asked, "that Billy
and Midge could be at Grandma Holt's farm?"

Fred paged through *La Vigie Marocaine* helplessly,
looking for pictures. Except for the big cutout of a mush-
room cloud on the front page and a stock picture on the
second of the president in a cowboy hat, there were no
photos. He tried to read the lead story but it made no
sense.

Mrs. Richmond rushed out of the room, crying aloud.

Fred wanted to tear the paper into ribbons. To calm
himself he poured a shot from the pint of bourbon he
kept in the dresser. Then he went out into the hall and
called through the locked door to the W.C.: "Well, I'll
bet we knocked hell out of *them* at least."

This was of no comfort to Mrs. Richmond.

Only the day before Mrs. Richmond had written two
letters—one to her granddaughter Midge, the other to
Midge's mother, Nan. The letter to Midge read:

                                                December 2

Dear Mademoiselle Holt,
    Well, here we are in romantic Casablanca, where
the old and the new come together. There are palm
trees growing on the boulevard outside our hotel window, and sometimes it seems that we never left
Florida at all. In Marrakesh we bought presents for
you and Billy, which you should get in time for Christmas if the mails are good. Wouldn't you like to know

what's in those packages! But you'll just have to wait till Christmas!

You should thank God every day, darling, that you live in America. If you could only see the poor Moroccan children, begging on the streets. They aren't able to go to school, and many of them don't even have shoes or warm clothes. And don't think it doesn't get cold here, even if it is Africa! You and Billy don't know how lucky you are!

On the train ride to Marrakesh we saw the farmers plowing their fields in *December*. Each plow has one donkey and one camel. That would probably be an interesting fact for you to tell your geography teacher in school.

Casablanca is wonderfully exciting, and I often wish that you and Billy were here to enjoy it with us. Someday, perhaps! Be good—remember it will be Christmas soon.

> Your loving Grandmother,
> "Grams"

The second letter, to Midge's mother, read as follows:

Dec. 2, Monday afternoon

Dear Nan,

There's no use my pretending any more with *you!* You saw it in my first letter—before I even knew my own feelings. Yes, Morocco has been a terrible disappointment. You wouldn't believe some of the things that have happened. For instance, it is almost impossible to mail a package out of this country; I will have to wait till we get to Spain, therefore, to send Billy and Midge their Xmas presents. Better not tell B & M that however!

Marrakesh was terrible. Fred and I got *lost* in the native quarter, and we thought we'd never escape! The filth is unbelievable, but if I talk about that it will only make me ill. After our experience on "the wrong side of the tracks" I wouldn't leave our hotel. Fred got very angry, and we took the train back to Casablanca the same night. At least there are decent restaurants in Casablanca. You can get a very satisfactory French-type dinner for about $1.00.

After all this you won't believe me when I tell you that we're going to stay here two more weeks. That's when the next boat leaves for Spain. Two more weeks!!! Fred says, take an airplane, but you know me. And I'll be d———d if I'll take a trip on the local railroad with all our luggage, which is the only other way.

I've finished the one book I brought along, and now I have nothing to read but newspapers. They are printed up in Paris and have mostly the news from India and Angola, which I find too depressing, and the political news from Europe, which I can't ever keep up with. Who is Chancellor Zucker and what does he have to do with the war in India? I say, if people would just sit down and try to *understand* each other, most of the world's so-called problems would disappear. Well, that's my opinion, but I have to keep it to myself, or Fred gets an apoplexy. You know Fred! He says, drop a bomb on Red China and to H— with it! Good old Fred!

I hope you and Dan are both fine and *dan*-dy, and I hope B & M are coming along in school. We were both excited to hear about Billy's A in geography. Fred says it's due to all the stories he's told Billy about our travels. Maybe he's right for once!

Love & kisses,
"Grams"

Fred had forgotten to mail these two letters yesterday afternoon, and now, after the news in the paper, it didn't seem worthwhile. The Holts, Nan and Dan and Billy and Midge, were all very probably dead.

"It's so strange," Mrs. Richmond observed at lunch at their restaurant. "I can't believe it really happened. Nothing has changed here. You'd think it would make more of a difference."

"God-damned reds."

"Will you drink the rest of my wine? I'm too upset."

"What do you suppose we should do? Should we try and telephone to Nan?"

"Trans-*Atlantic*? Wouldn't a telegram do just as well?"

So, after lunch, they went to the telegraph office, which was in the main post office, and filled out a form. The message they finally agreed on was: IS EVERYONE WELL QUESTION WAS CLEVELAND HIT QUESTION RETURN REPLY

REQUESTED. It cost eleven dollars to send off, one dollar a word. The post office wouldn't accept a travellers' check, so while Mrs. Richmond waited at the desk, Fred went across the street to the Bank of Morocco to cash it there.

The teller behind the grill looked at Fred's check doubtfully and asked to see his passport. He brought check and passport into an office at the back of the bank. Fred grew more and more peeved, as the time wore on and nothing was done. He was accustomed to being treated with respect, at least. The teller returned with a portly gentleman not much younger than Fred himself. He wore a striped suit with a flower in his buttonhole.

"Are you Mr. Richmon?" the gentleman asked.

"Of course I am. Look at the picture in my passport."

"I'm sorry, Mr. Richmon, but we are not able to cash this check."

"What do you mean? I've cashed checks here before. Look I've noted it down: on November 28, forty dollars; on December 1, twenty dollars."

The man shook his head. "I'm sorry, Mr. Richmon, but we are not able to cash these checks."

"I'd like to see the manager."

"I'm sorry, Mr. Richmon, it is not possible for us to cash your checks. Thank you very much." He turned to go.

"I want to see the manager!" Everybody in the bank, the tellers and the other clients, were staring at Fred, who had turned quite red.

"I am the manager," said the man in the striped suit. "Good-bye, Mr. Richmon."

"These are American Express Travellers' Checks. They're good anywhere in the world!"

The manager returned to his office, and the teller began to wait on another customer. Fred returned to the post office.

"We'll have to return here later, darling," he explained to his wife. She didn't ask why, and he didn't want to tell her.

They bought food to bring back to the hotel, since Mrs. Richmond didn't feel up to dressing for dinner.

The manager of the hotel, a thin, nervous man who wore wire-framed spectacles, was waiting at the desk to see them. Wordlessly he presented them a bill for the room.

Fred protested angrily. "We're paid up. We're paid until the twelfth of this month. What are you trying to pull?"

The manager smiled. He had gold teeth. He explained, in imperfect English, that this was the bill.

"*Nous sommes payée*," Mrs. Richmond explained pleasantly. Then, in a diplomatic whisper to her husband, "Show him the receipt."

The manager examined the receipt. "*Non, non, non*," he said, shaking his head. He handed Fred, instead of his receipt, the new bill.

"I'll take that receipt back, thank you very much." The manager smiled and backed away from Fred. Fred acted without thinking. He grabbed the manager's wrist and pried the receipt out of his fingers. The manager shouted words at him in Arabic. Fred took the key for their room, 216, off its hook behind the desk. Then he took his wife by the elbow and led her up the stairs. The man with the red fez came running down the stairs to do the manager's bidding.

Once they were inside the room, Fred locked the door. He was trembling and short of breath. Mrs. Richmond made him sit down and sponged his fevered brow with cold water. Five minutes later, a little slip of paper slid in under the door. It was the bill.

"Look at this!" he exclaimed. "Forty dirham a day. Eight dollars! That son of a bitch." The regular per diem rate for the room was twenty dirham, and the Richmonds, by taking it for a fortnight, had bargained it down to fifteen.

"Now, Freddy—"

"That bastard!"

"It's probably some sort of misunderstanding."

"He saw that receipt, didn't he? He made out that receipt himself. *You* know why he's doing it. Because of what's happened. Now I won't be able to cash my travellers' checks here either. That son of a bitch!"

"Now, Freddy." She smoothed the ruffled strands of white hair with the wet sponge.

"Don't you now-Freddy me! I know what I'm going to do. I'm going to the American Consulate and register a complaint."

"That's a good idea, but not today, Freddy. Let's stay inside until tomorrow. We're both too tired and upset. Tomorrow we can go there together. Maybe they'll know something about Cleveland by then." Mrs. Richmond was prevented from giving further council by a new onset of her illness. She went out into the hall, but returned almost immediately. "The door into the toilet is padlocked," she said. Her eyes were wide with terror. She had just begun to understand what was happening.

That night, after a frugal dinner of olives, cheese sandwiches, and figs, Mrs. Richmond tried to look on the bright side. "Actually we're very lucky," she said, "to be here, instead of there, when it happened. At least, we're alive. We should thank God for being alive."

"If we'd of bombed them twenty years ago, we wouldn't be in this spot now. Didn't I say way back then that we should have bombed them?"

"Yes, darling. But there's no use crying over spilt milk. Try and look on the bright side, like I do."

"God-damn dirty reds."

The bourbon was all gone. It was dark, and outside, across the square, a billboard advertising Olympic Bleue cigarettes (C'est mieux!) winked on and off, as it had on all the other nights of their visit to Casablanca. Nothing here seemed to have been affected by the momentous event across the ocean.

"We're out of envelopes," Mrs. Richmond complained. She had been trying to compose a letter to her daughter.

Fred was staring out the window, wondering what it had been like: had the sky been filled with planes? Were they still fighting on the ground in India and Angola? What did Florida look like now? He had always wanted to build a bomb shelter in their back yard in Florida, but his wife had been against it. Now it would be impossible to know which of them had been right.

"What time is it?" Mrs. Richmond asked, winding the alarm.

He looked at his watch, which was always right. "Eleven o'clock, Bulova watch time." It was an Accutron that his company, Iowa Mutual Life, had presented to him at retirement.

There was, in the direction of the waterfront, a din of shouting and clashing metal. As it grew louder, Fred could see the head of a ragged parade advancing up the boulevard. He pulled down the lath shutters over the windows till there was just a narrow slit to watch the parade through.

"They're burning something," he informed his wife. "Come see."

"I don't want to watch that sort of thing."

"Some kind of statue, or scarecrow. You can't tell who it's meant to be. Someone in a cowboy hat, looks like. I'll bet they're Commies."

When the mob of demonstrators reached the square over which the Belmonte Hotel looked, they turned to the left, toward the larger luxury hotels, the Marhaba and El Mansour. They were banging cymbals together and beating drums and blowing on loud horns that sounded like bagpipes. Instead of marching in rows, they did a sort of whirling, skipping dance step. Once they'd turned the corner, Walt couldn't see any more of them.

"I'll bet every beggar in town is out there, blowing his horn," Fred said sourly. "Every god-damn watch peddler and shoeshine boy in Casablanca."

"They sound very happy," Mrs. Richmond said. Then she began crying again.

The Richmonds slept together in the same bed that evening for the first time in several months. The noise of the demonstration continued, off and on, nearer or farther away, for several hours. This too set the evening apart from other evenings, for Casablanca was usually very quiet, surprisingly so, after ten o'clock at night.

The office of the American Consul seemed to have been bombed. The front door was broken off its hinges, and Fred entered, after some reluctance, to find all the downstairs rooms empty of furniture, the carpets torn away, the moldings pried from the walls. The files of the consulate had been emptied out and the contents burned in the center of the largest room. Slogans in Arabic had been scrawled on the walls with the ashes.

Leaving the building, he discovered a piece of typing paper nailed to the deranged door. It read: "All Americans in Morocco, whether of tourist or resident status, are advised to leave the country until the present crisis is over. The Consul cannot guarantee the safety of those who choose to remain."

A shoeshine boy, his diseased scalp inadequately concealed by a dirty wool cap, tried to slip his box under Fred's foot.

"Go away, you! *Vamoose!* This is your fault. I know what happened last night. You and your kind did this. Red beggars!"

The boy smiled uncertainly at Fred and tried again to get his shoe on the box. "*Monsieur, monsieur,*" he hissed —or, perhaps, "*Merci, merci.*"

By noonday the center of the town was aswarm with Americans. Fred hadn't realized there had been so many in Casablanca. What were they doing here? Where had they kept themselves hidden? Most of the Americans were on their way to the airport, their cars piled high with luggage. Some said they were bound for England, others for Germany. Spain, they claimed, wouldn't be safe, though it was probably safer than Morocco. They were brusque with Fred to the point of rudeness.

He returned to the hotel, where Mrs. Richmond was waiting for him. They had agreed that one of them must always be in the room. As Fred went up the stairs the manager tried to hand him another bill. "I will call the police," he threatened. Fred was too angry to reply. He wanted to hit the man in the nose and stamp on his ridiculous spectacles. If he'd been ten years younger he might have done so.

"They've cut off the water," Mrs. Richmond announced dramatically, after she'd admitted her husband to the room. "And the man with the red hat tried to get in, but I had the chain across the door, thank heaven. We can't wash or use the bidet. I don't know what will happen. I'm afraid."

She wouldn't listen to anything Fred said about the Consulate. "We've got to take a plane," he insisted. "To England. All the other Americans are going there. There was a sign on the door of the Con—"

"No, Fred. No. Not a plane. You won't make me get into an airplane. I've gone twenty years without that, and I won't start now."

"But this is an emergency. We have to."

"I refuse to talk about it. And don't you shout at *me*, Fred Richmond. We'll sail when the boat sails, and that's that! Now, let's be practical, shall we? The first thing that we have to do is for you to go out and buy some bottled water. Four bottles, and bread, and— No, you'll never remember everything. I'll write out a list."

But when Fred returned, four hours later, when it was growing dark, he had but a single bottle of soda, one loaf of hard bread, and a little box of pasteurized process cheese.

"It was all the money I had. They won't cash my checks. Not at the bank, not at the Marhaba, not anywhere." There were flecks of violet in his red, dirty face, and his voice was hoarse. He had been shouting hours long.

Mrs. Richmond used half the bottle of soda to wash off his face. Then she made sandwiches of cheese and strawberry jam, all the while maintaining a steady stream of conversation, on cheerful topics. She was afraid her husband would have a stroke.

On Thursday the twelfth, the day before their scheduled sailing, Fred went to the travel agency to find out what pier their ship had docked in. He was informed that the sailing had been canceled, permanently. The ship, a Yugoslav freighter, had been in Norfolk on December 4. The agency politely refunded the price of the tickets—in American dollars.

"Couldn't you give me dirham instead?"

"But you paid in dollars, Mr. Richmond." The agent spoke with a fussy, overprecise manner that annoyed Fred more than an honest French accent. "You paid in American Express Traveller's Checks."

"But I'd *rather* have dirham."

"That would be impossible."

"I'll give you one to one. How about that? One dirham for one dollar." He did not even become angry at being forced to make so unfair a suggestion. He had been through this same scene too many times—at banks, at stores, with people off the street.

"The government has forbidden us to trade in American money, Mr. Richmond. I am truly sorry that I cannot help you. If you would be interested to purchase an airplane ticket, however, I can accept money for that. If you have enough."

"You don't leave much choice, do you?" (He thought: *Betty will be furious.*) "What will it cost for two tickets to London?"

The agent named the price. Fred flared up. "That's

highway robbery! Why, that's more than the first-class to New York City!"

The agent smiled. "We have no flights scheduled to New York, sir."

Grimly, Fred signed away his travellers' checks to pay for the tickets. It took all his checks and all but fifty dollars of the refunded money. His wife, however, had her own bundle of American Express checks that hadn't been touched yet. He examined the tickets, which were printed in French. "What does this say here? When does it leave?"

"On the fourteenth. Saturday. At eight in the evening.

"You don't have anything tomorrow?"

"I'm sorry. You should be quite happy that we can sell you these tickets. If it weren't for the fact that our main office is in Paris, and that they've directed that Americans be given priority on all Pan-Am flights, we wouldn't be able to."

"I see. The thing is this—I'm in rather a tight spot. Nobody, not even the banks, will take American money. This is our last night at the hotel, and if we have to stay over Friday night as well . . ."

"You might go to the airport waiting room, sir."

Fred took off his Accutron wristwatch. "In America this watch would cost $120 wholesale. You wouldn't be interested . . ."

"I'm sorry, Mr. Richmond. I have a watch of my own."

Fred, with the tickets securely tucked into his passport case, went out through the thick glass door. He would have liked to have a sundae at the ice cream parlor across the street, but he couldn't afford it. He couldn't afford anything unless he was able to sell his watch. They had lived the last week out on what he'd gotten for the alarm clock and the electric shaver. Now there was nothing left.

When Fred was at the corner, he heard someone calling his name. "Mr. Richmond. Mr. Richmond, sir." It was the agent. Shyly he held out a ten dirham note and three fives. Fred took the money and handed him the watch. The agent put Fred's Accutron on his wrist beside his old watch. He smiled and offered Fred his hand to shake. Fred walked away, ignoring the outstretched hand.

Five dollars, he thought over and over again, *five dollars.* He was too shamed to return at once to the hotel.

Mrs. Richmond wasn't in the room. Instead the man in the red fez was engaged in packing all their clothes and toilet articles into the three suitcases. "Hey!" Fred shouted. "What do you think you're doing? Stop that!"

"You must pay your bill," the hotel manager, who stood back at a safe distance in the hallway, shrilled at him. "You must pay your bill or leave."

Fred tried to prevent the man in the red fez from packing the bags. He was furious with his wife for having gone off—to the W.C. probably—and left the hotel room unguarded.

"Where is my wife?" he demanded of the manager. "This is an outrage." He began to swear. The man in the red fez returned to packing the bags.

Fred made a determined effort to calm himself. He could not risk a stroke. After all, he reasoned with himself, whether they spent one or two nights in the airport waiting room wouldn't make that much difference. So he chased the man in the red fez away and finished the packing himself. When he was done, he rang for the porter, and the man in the red fez returned and helped him carry the bags downstairs. He waited in the dark lobby, using the largest of the suitcases for a stool, for his wife to return. She had probably gone to "their" restaurant, some blocks away, where they were still allowed to use the W.C. The owner of the restaurant couldn't understand why they didn't take their meals there any more and didn't want to offend them, hoping, perhaps, that they would come back.

While he waited, Fred occupied the time by trying to remember the name of the Englishman who had been a supper guest at their house in Florida three years before. It was a strange name that was not pronounced at all the way that it was spelled. At intervals he would go out into the street to try and catch sight of his wife returning to the hotel. Whenever he tried to ask the manager, where she had gone, the man would renew his shrill complaint. Fred became desperate. She was taking altogether too long. He telephoned the restaurant. The owner of the restaurant understood enough English to be able to tell him that she had not visited his W.C. all that day.

An hour or so after sunset, Fred found his way to the police station, a wretched stucco building inside the ancient medina, the non-European quarter. Americans were advised not to venture into the medina after dark.

"My wife is missing," he told one of the gray-uniformed men. "I think she may be the victim of a robbery."

The policeman replied brusquely in French.

"My wife," Fred repeated loudly, gesturing in a vague way.

The policeman turned to speak to his fellows. It was a piece of deliberate rudeness.

Fred took out his passport and waved it in the policeman's face. "This is my passport," he shouted. "My wife is missing. My wife. Doesn't somebody here speak English? Somebody *must* speak English. *Ing-glish!*"

The policeman shrugged and handed Fred back his passport.

"My wife!" Fred screamed hysterically. "Listen to me— my wife, my wife, my wife!"

The policeman, a scrawny, moustached man, grabbed Fred by the neck of his coat and led him forcibly into another room and down a long, unlighted corridor that smelled of urine. Fred didn't realize, until he had been thrust into the room that it was a cell. The door that closed behind him was made not of bars, but of sheet metal nailed over wood. There was no light in the room, no air. He screamed, he kicked at the door and pounded on it with his fists until he had cut a deep gash into the side of his palm. He stopped to suck the blood, fearful of blood-poisoning.

He could, when his eyes had adjusted to the darkness, see a little of the room about him. It was not much larger than Room 216 at the Belmonte, but it contained more people than Fred could count. They were heaped all along the walls, an indiscriminate tumble of rags and filth, old men and young men, a wretched assembly.

They stared at the American gentleman in astonishment.

The police released Fred in the morning, and he returned at once to the hotel, speaking to no one. He was angry but, even more, he was terrified.

His wife had not returned. The three suitcases, for a wonder, were still sitting where he had left them. The manager insisted that he leave the lobby, and Fred did not protest. The Richmonds' time at the hotel had expired, and

Fred didn't have the money for another night, even at the old rate.

Outside, he did not know what to do. He stood on the curbside, trying to decide. His pants were wrinkled, and he feared (though he could not smell it himself) that he stank of the prison cell.

The traffic policeman in the center of the square began giving him funny looks. He was afraid of the policeman, afraid of being returned to the cell. He hailed a taxi and directed the driver to go to the airport.

"*Où?*" the driver asked.

"The airport, the airport," he said testily. Cabbies, at least, could be expected to know English.

But where was his wife? Where was Betty?

When they arrived at the airport, the driver demanded fifteen dirhams, which was an outrageous price in Casablanca, where cabs are pleasantly cheap. Having not had the foresight to negotiate the price in advance, Fred had no choice but to pay the man what he asked.

The waiting room was filled with people, though few seemed to be Americans. The stench of the close air was almost as bad as it had been in the cell. There were no porters, and he could not move through the crowd, so he set the suitcases down just inside the entrance and seated himself on the largest bag.

A man in an olive-drab uniform with a black beret asked, in French, to see his passport. "*Votre passeport,*" he repeated patiently, until Fred had understood. He examined each page with a great show of suspicion, but eventually he handed it back.

"Do you speak English?" Fred asked him then. He thought, because of the different uniform, that he might not be one of the city police. He answered with a stream of coarse Arabic gobbling.

Perhaps, Fred told himself, *she will come out here to look for me.* But why, after all, should she? He should have remained outside the hotel.

He imagined himself safely in England, telling his story to the American Consul there. He imagined the international repercussions it would have. What had been the name of that Englishman he knew. He had lived in London. It began with *C* or *Ch.*

An attractive middle-aged woman sat down on the other end of his suitcase and began speaking in rapid French, making sharp gestures, like karate chops, with her well-groomed hand. She was trying to explain something to him, but of course he couldn't understand her. She broke into tears. Fred couldn't even offer his handkerchief, because it was dirty from last night.

"My wife," he tried to explain. "My—wife—is missing. My wife."

"Bee-yay," the woman said despairingly. "Vote bee-yay." She showed him a handful of dirham notes in large denominations.

"I wish I could understand what it is you want," he said.

She went away from him, as though she were angry, as though he had said something to insult her.

Fred felt someone tugging at his shoe. He remembered, with a start of terror, waking in the cell, the old man tugging at his shoes, trying to steal them but not understanding, apparently, about the laces.

It was only, after all, a shoeshine boy. He had already begun to brush Fred's shoes, which were, he could see, rather dirty. He pushed the boy away.

He had to go back to the hotel to see if his wife had returned there, but he hadn't the money for another taxi and there was no one in the waiting room that he dared trust with the bags.

Yet he couldn't leave Casablanca without his wife. Could he? But if he did stay, what was he to do, if the police would not listen to him?

At about ten o'clock the waiting room grew quiet. All that day no planes had entered or left the airfield. Everyone here was waiting for tomorrow's plane to London. How were so many people, and so much luggage, to fit on one plane, even the largest jet? Did they all have tickets?

They slept anywhere: on the hard benches, on newspapers on the concrete floor, on the narrow window ledges. Fred was one of the luckiest, because he could sleep on his three suitcases.

When he woke the next morning, he found that his passport and the two tickets had been stolen from his breast pocket. He still had his billfold, because he had slept on his back. It contained nine dirham.

Christmas morning, Fred went out and treated himself to an ice cream sundae. Nobody seemed to be celebrating the holiday in Casablanca. Most of the shops in the ancient medina (where Fred had found a hotel room for three dirham a day) were open for business, while in the European quarter one couldn't tell if the stores were closed permanently or just for the day.

Going past the Belmonte, Fred stopped, as was his custom, to ask after his wife. The manager was very polite and said that nothing was known of Mrs. Richmond. The police had her description now.

Hoping to delay the moment when he sat down before the sundae, he walked to the post office and asked if there had been any answer to his telegram to the American Embassy in London. There had not.

When at last he did have his sundae it didn't seem quite as good as he had remembered. There was so little of it! He sat down for an hour with his empty dish, watching the drizzling rain. He was alone in the ice cream parlor. The windows of the travel agency across the street were covered up by a heavy metal shutter, from which the yellow paint was flaking.

The waiter came and sat down at Fred's table. *"Il pleuve, Monsieur Richmon. It rains. Il pleuve."*

"Yes, it does," said Fred. "It rains. It falls. Fall-out."

But the waiter had very little English. "Merry Christmas," he said. *"Joyeuse Nöel.* Merry Christmas."

Fred agreed.

When the drizzle had cleared a bit, Fred strolled to the United Nations Plaza and found a bench under a palm tree that was dry. Despite the cold and damp, he didn't want to return to his cramped hotel room and spend the rest of the day sitting on the edge of his bed.

Fred was by no means alone in the plaza. A number of figures in heavy woolen djelabas, with hoods over their heads, stood or sat on benches, or strolled in circles on the gravel paths. The djelabas made ideal raincoats. Fred had sold his own London Fog three days before for twenty dirham. He was getting better prices for his things now that he had learned to count in French.

The hardest lesson to learn (and he had not yet learned it) was to keep from thinking. When he could do that, he wouldn't become angry, or afraid.

At noon the whistle blew in the handsome tower at the end of the plaza, from the top of which one could see all of Casablanca in every direction. Fred took out the cheese sandwich from the pocket of his suitcoat and ate it, a little bit at a time. Then he took out the chocolate bar with almonds. His mouth began to water.

A shoeshine boy scampered across the graveled circle and sat down in the damp at Fred's feet. He tried to lift Fred's foot and place it on his box.

"No," said Fred. "Go away."

"*Monsieur, monsieur,*" the boy insisted. Or, perhaps, "*Merci, merci.*"

Fred looked down guiltily at his shoes. They were very dirty. He hadn't had them shined in weeks.

The boy kept whistling those meaningless words at him. His gaze was fixed on Fred's chocolate bar. Fred pushed him away with the side of his foot. The boy grabbed for the candy. Fred struck him in the side of his head. The chocolate bar fell to the gravel, not far from the boy's calloused feet. The boy lay on his side, whimpering.

"You little sneak!" Fred shouted at him.

It was a clear-cut case of thievery. He was furious. He had a right to be furious. Standing up to his full height, his foot came down accidentally on the boy's rubbishy shoe shine box. The wood splintered.

The boy began to gabble at Fred in Arabic. He scurried forward on hands and knees to pick up the pieces of the box.

"You asked for this," Fred said. He kicked the boy in the ribs. The boy rolled with the blow, as though he were not unused to such treatment. "Little beggar! Thief!" Fred screamed.

He bent forward and tried to grasp a handhold in the boy's hair, but it was cut too close to his head, to prevent lice. Fred hit him again in the face, but now the boy was on his feet and running.

There was no use pursuing him, he was too fast, too fast.

Fred's face was violet and red, and his white hair, in need of a trim, straggled down over his flushed forehead. He had not noticed, while he was beating the boy, the group of Arabs, or Moslems, or whatever they were, that had gathered around him to watch. Fred could not read the expressions on their dark, wrinkly faces.

"Did you see that?" he asked loudly. "Did you see what that little thief tried to do? Did you see him try to steal . . . my candy bar?"

One of the men, in a tan djelaba striped with brown,

said something to Fred that sounded like so much gargling. Another, younger man, in European dress, struck Fred in the face. Fred teetered backward.

"Now see here!" He had not time to tell them he was an American citizen. The next blow caught him in the mouth, and he fell to the ground. Once he was lying on his back, the older men joined in in kicking him. Some kicked him in the ribs, others in his head, still others had to content themselves with his legs. Curiously, nobody went for his groin. The shoeshine boy watched from a distance, and when Fred was unconscious, came forward and removed his shoes. The young man who had first hit him removed his suitcoat and his belt. Wisely, Fred had left his billfold behind at his hotel.

When he woke he was sitting on the bench again. A policeman was addressing him in Arabic. Fred shook his head uncomprehendingly. His back hurt dreadfully, from when he had fallen to the ground. The policeman addressed him in French. He shivered. Their kicks had not damaged him so much as he had expected. Except for the young man, they had worn slippers instead of shoes. His face experienced only a dull ache, but there was blood all down the front of his shirt, and his mouth tasted of blood. He was cold, very cold.

The policeman went away, shaking his head.

At just that moment Fred remembered the name of the Englishman who had had supper in his house in Florida. It was Cholmondeley, but it was pronounced *Chum-ly*. He was still unable to remember his London address.

Only when he tried to stand did he realize that his shoes were gone. The gravel hurt the tender soles of his bare feet. Fred was mortally certain that the shoeshine boy had stolen his shoes.

He sat back down on the bench with a groan. He hoped to hell he'd hurt the god-damned little son of a bitch. He hoped to hell he had. He grated his teeth together, wishing that he could get hold of him again. The little beggar. He'd kick him this time so that he'd remember it. The god-damn dirty little red beggar. He'd kick his face in.

THE ROAD TO MICTLANTECUTLI

by Adobe James

The ribbon of asphalt—once black, now grey from the years of unrelenting sun—stretched out like a never-ending arrow shaft; in the distance, mirages—like dreams—sprang into life, shimmered, and silently dissolved at the approach of the speeding automobile.

Rivulets of sweat poured down from the face of Hernandez, the driver. Earlier in the day—when they had been in the good land—he had been congenial, expansive, even sympathetic. Now he drove quickly, apprehensively, almost angrily, not wanting to be caught in the bad land after sunset.

"*Semejante los buitres no tienen gordo en este distrito execrable,*" he muttered, squinting his eyes against the glare of the late afternoon sun.

Seated next to him, the man called Morgan smiled at the remark, "Even the vultures are skinny in this lousy land." Hernandez had a sense of humour; for that reason—and that reason, alone—Morgan was sorry that it was going to be necessary to kill him. But Hernandez was a policeman . . . a Mexican Federal cop who was taking him back to the United States border, where Morgan would be handed over to the criminal courts to hang, twitching, at the end of a long Texas rope.

No, Morgan thought, and knew the thought to be true, they won't hang me this time; next time, maybe, but not now. Hernandez was stupid, and it would be only a matter of time before he made a mistake. Completely relaxed, Morgan dozed, his manacled hands lying docilely in his lap . . . waiting . . . waiting . . . waiting.

It was almost five o'clock before Morgan, with all the keen instincts of the hunted, sensed his moment of freedom might be approaching. Hernandez was becoming uncomfortable—the result of two bottles of beer after lunch.

The policeman would be stopping soon. Morgan would make his move then.

On their right, a range of gently sloping foothills gradually had been rising from the flat surface of the desert.

Morgan asked, pretending boredom, "Anything over there?"

Hernandez sighed, *"Quien sabe?"* Who knows? The plateau on the other side of the mountain range is supposed to be worse than this side. *Es imposible!* No one can exist there except a few wild Indians who speak a language that was old before the Aztecs came. It's uncharted, untamed, uncivilized . . . ruled by Mictlantecutli.

Now, slowly, as shadows lengthened, the land was changing all around them. For the first time since leaving Agua Lodoso, they could see some signs of vegetation—mesquite bushes, cactus, shrub brush. Ahead, standing like a lonely outpost sentinel, was a giant Saguaro cactus almost fifty feet high. Hernandez slowed the car and stopped in the shade of the cactus. "Stretch your legs if you want, *amigo,* this is the last stop before Hermosillo."

Hernandez got out, walked around the car, and opened the door for his prisoner. Morgan slipped out and stood, stretching like a cat. While the Mexican was relieving himself against the cactus, Morgan walked over to what had first appeared to be a crude cross stuck in the sand. He peered at it; the cross was only a sign—weatherbeaten and pock-marked by the talons of vultures who had used it as a roosting place.

Hernandez strolled over and joined him. He, too, stared at the sign, his lips pursed in puzzlement under his black moustache. "Linaculan—one hundred twenty kilometres! I did not know there was a road . . ." Then he brightened. "Ah, *si.* I remember now. This must be the old *Real Militar,* the military highway leading from the interior to the east coast."

That was all Morgan needed to know. If Linaculan was on the east coast, then Linaculan meant freedom. He yawned again, his impassive face a portrait of indifference.

"Ready, *amigo?*"

Morgan nodded. "As ready as any man is to be hung."

The Mexican laughed, coughed, and spat in the dust. "Come on then." He led the way towards the car and stood by its open door waiting for his prisoner. Morgan shambled towards him, his shoulders slumped forward as if protecting him from the oppressive heat of late afternoon. When he did move, it was as a snake strikes an unsuspecting victim. His manacled hands came down, viciously, on top of Hernandez's head. The policeman moaned and toppled to the ground. Morgan was on him immediately; his hands seeking, and finding, the gun he knew was in the Mexican's waistband. Then he stood upright—about four paces away from the figure on the ground.

Hernandez shook his head groggily, blinked his eyes, and started to rise. He had struggled to his knees when Morgan's cold voice froze him into immobility.

Morgan said, "Goodbye, Hernandez. No hard feelings."

The Mexican looked up; he saw death. "*Dios . . . dios.* No!" That was as far as he got; the .44 slug caught him above the ridge of the left eye and he was thrown ten feet backwards by the force of the bullet. He shuddered once, his legs beat a small tattoo in the dust, and then he was still.

Morgan walked over, shaking his head mournfully. "I sure had you pegged wrong. You didn't look like a coward who would beg for his life." He sighed at the dead man's lack of dignity—feeling almost as if he had been betrayed by a weak-willed friend.

He squatted and began searching the body. There was a wallet containing a badge, five hundred pesos, and a colour photograph of an overweight Mexican woman surrounded by three laughing small girls and two self-consciously grinning young boys. Morgan grunted non-committally and continued his search.

He found the handcuff keys taped to the calloused white sole of the dead man's foot.

Twilight was beginning to turn the Mexican hills to a red bronze when Morgan loaded Hernandez in the trunk of the car. He strolled back over to the road sign. After the mileage there were the words, "*Cuidado—Peligroso,*" "Take Heed—Dangerous." What a joke, he thought. Could anything be more dangerous than being hung? Or playing the part of a fox hounded by international police? He had been trapped and sentenced to die four different times in his life; and yet, he was still a free man. And . . . there could be nothing, absolutely nothing, ahead of him on this insignificant little dirt road that could match Morgan's wits, Morgan's reactions, Morgan's gun!

He got behind the wheel of the car and turned on to

the road. It was rougher than it had appeared at first, but
none the less, he made good time for the first thirty miles,
and was able to drive fast enough that the dust remained
spread out behind him like the brown tail of a comet
hanging luminously in the fading light.

The sun dropped below the horizon line, but then, as
Morgan began climbing the range of hills, it came back
into sight once more—looking like the malevolent in-
flamed eye of a god angry at being awakened again.

Morgan crested the hill and began a downward ascent
into a valley. Here darkness was embracing the land. He
stopped once, where a *barranca* sloped down from the
road, and threw over Hernandez's body. He watched it,
rolling and tumbling, until it finally disappeared from
sight in the black shadows beneath a strand of mesquite
bushes some hundred feet below at the bottom.

Morgan drove on. He turned on the car lights as night
closed in swiftly around him.

Abruptly, as he reached the valley floor, he began cursing, for the road was really no longer a road—just a
scarred and broken path leading across the wilderness.

The next five kilometres took at least fifteen thousand
miles out of the automobile. Morgan was forced to shift
down to first gear as potholes—deep as wading pools—
wrecked the front-end alignment and suspension system.
Jagged hidden boulders in the middle of the road scraped
at the undercarriage with a thousand steel fingers.

And dust! Dust was everywhere . . . it hung like a
dark ominous cloud all about him; it coated the inside of
the car as though it were beige velvet. It crept into Morgan's nostrils and throat until it became painful to breathe
or swallow.

Minutes later, over the smell of dust, came the odour
of hot water—steam—and he knew the cooling system had
ruptured somewhere. It was then Morgan realized the car
would never make it to Linaculan. By the last barely
perceptible horizon glow, he searched the landscape for
some evidence of life . . . and saw only the grotesque
silhouettes of cactus and stunted desert brush.

The speedometer indicated they had travelled forty-four
miles when his bouncing, weaving headlight picked up the
solitary figure of a priest walking slowly alongside the
road. Morgan's eyes narrowed as he weighed the value of
offering a ride to the padre. That would be stupid, he

thought—the man could be a *bandido* who would produce, and skillfully use, a knife, while Morgan was concentrating on the road.

The padre loomed up larger in the headlights. He did not turn towards the car; it seemed as though he were totally unaware of the car's approach.

Morgan passed without slowing; the figure was lost immediately in the dust and blackness of the Mexican night.

Suddenly, just as though several automatic relays had clicked open somewhere in his brain, all of Morgan's instincts were screaming at him. Something was wrong— terribly wrong. A trap of some sort had been entered. The feeling was familiar; there had been other traps before. He grinned wryly, pulled the gun from his pocket, and laid it on the seat beside him in preparation.

The next three miles seemed endless as he waited, almost eagerly, for the trap to swing shut. When nothing happened, he grew irritable and began cursing his imagination. The smell of hot oil and steam had grown humidly overpowering, and the engine was beginning to labour. Morgan glanced down at the temperature gauge and saw the needle had long since climbed into the red danger zone.

And, it was at this moment, while his attention was distracted, that the left front wheel slammed into a jagged rock which ripped through the tire's sidewall. The vehicle began bucking and weaving from side to side like a wild, enraged, injured animal. Morgan hit his brakes, knowing it was too late. The car skidded sideways on the gravel, swerved to the right, teetered for a second on an embankment, and then—almost as if it were a movie being projected in slow motion—rolled end over end down the incline.

The last thing Morgan saw was a monstrous boulder looking up in the night like some huge basalt fist of God.

For a long time after he regained consciousness, Morgan lay still with his eyes closed. Someone had wiped his forehead and spoken to him. A man! Possibly . . . the priest? He listened to the man's coarse breathing; there was no other sound. They were alone.

Morgan opened his eyes. It was dark, but not as dark as before. A little moonlight was seeping through the high thin clouds. The priest—black of clothes and dark of face—was beside him.

"*Senor,* you are all right?"

Morgan flexed his leg muscles, moved his ankles, moved his shoulders, and turned his head from side to side. There were no aches, no pains; he felt surprisingly good. Well, no sense in letting the other man know; let the priest believe Morgan had injured his back and was incapable of rapid movement . . . then, when he had to move fast, the other would be unprepared.

"I hurt my back."

"Can you stand?"

"Yes . . . I think so. Help me."

The priest reached out; Morgan took the proffered hand, and, groaning audibly, stood erect.

"You are fortunate that I came along."

"Yes. I'm grateful." Morgan felt in his pocket. The wallet was still there; the gun was gone, or had it been in his pocket? Then he remembered, it had been on the seat beside him. Well, no chance of finding it in the darkness . . . and there would be other weapons.

"Where were you going?" the priest asked.

"Linaculan."

"Oh, yes . . . a fine city." The priest was standing quite close to Morgan, staring at the American. The moon slipped in and out of the clouds. There was a moment of light, only a moment, but enough. Suddenly, for the first time in many years, Morgan was afraid . . . frightened by the padre's eyes; they were too black, too piercing, too fierce for a priest.

Morgan stepped back three paces—far enough away from the priest that the other man's eyes were lost in the darkness.

"You need not fear me," the priest said quietly. "I cannot harm you. I can only help you."

It sounded sincere. Some of Morgan's nervousness began to abate. Mentally he sniffed the wind; the odour of the trap was there, but not as strong as before. After a few moments, some of his old cockiness returned. Where do we go from here, he thought. He was at least halfway towards Linaculan, so it would seem prudent to continue on, unless . . . there would be other transportation before then.

Morgan asked, "Is Linaculan the nearest town?"

"Yes."

"Is that where you were going?"

"No."

Hopefully then, "Do you have a church near by?"

"No. But I frequently trod this road."

"For Christ's sake, why walk this miserable road?"

"For the very reason you mentioned, for Christ's sake."

Now Morgan was completely at ease. The padre was harmless. A nut, but harmless. "Well," he said almost jauntily, "I've got a long walk ahead of me. See you."

Morgan thought he saw the priest's expression soften with the remark. "I will walk part way with you."

"Suit yourself, padre. My name's . . . Dan Morgan. I'm an American."

"Yes . . . I know."

The answer surprised Morgan for a moment; then he felt his guard rising again. Obviously the priest had gone through his belongings while he was unconscious . . . and perhaps that was where the gun had gone, too.

They began walking in silence. The moon—that alien globe of cold white light—won its battle with the clouds, and now shone brightly behind them. Long slender shadows raced along the road in front of the two men. The folds of the padre's cassock made whispering noises with each stride he took; his sandals went slap-slap-slap in the thick dust of the road.

In an effort to make conversation, Morgan asked, "How far is Linaculan from here?"

"A great distance."

"But," Morgan exploded, "I thought it was only about another fifty kilometres."

"The candle lights of Linaculan are fifty-four kilometres from the point of your crash."

Well, that was nice to know anyway. With luck, Morgan could make the thirty miles by tomorrow afternoon . . . and then, it would be a simple matter to get another car. He began taking longer strides; the priest kept pace beside him.

In time, the moon was cut off by a range of hills, and their shadows disappeared. The darkness that came in around them now was a tangible thing, warm, disquieting, fearful as the interior of a locked coffin. Morgan glanced at his watch. It had stopped at 8.18, apparently something snapped when the crash occurred. He didn't know how long he had been unconscious, but they had been walking for at least two hours . . . so, perhaps, it was around midnight.

They plodded on, two dark figures—shadows almost—walking a desolate road. They climbed a short hill and were bathed in moonlight again. Morgan liked that. The darkness had been too dark; it seemed to him that there were things—unseen, unreal—out there beyond the moonlight.

They started down the other side of the hill, and the darkness crept back . . .

"Don't you have any lights at all in this God-forsaken place?" Morgan asked irritably.

The padre did not answer. Morgan repeated the question, and his voice was full of frustrated threat.

Still there was no reply. Morgan shrugged and mentally said, "To hell with you, my sullen Catholic friend. I'll take care of you later."

The road led down the far side of the hill. Night—the true horribly oppressive night of the claustrophobiac—closed in menacingly.

They were in a gully for a long time before reaching another hill—this time, no moonlight greeted them; the only illumination was a hollow glow from behind the horizon clouds. It was enough though to show a fork in the road.

Morgan hesitated and asked, "Which one goes to Linaculan?"

The priest stopped. The fierce black pupils of his eyes had grown large; so large, in fact, there seemed to be no longer any white to his eyes at all. He stretched out his arms to adjust his cassock, and at that moment he looked like some evil black praying mantis about to devour a victim. Even in the semi-darkness, he cast a shadow . . . a black, elongated shadow of the cross.

And now, the cornered killer instinct took hold of Morgan. "Answer my question," he snarled. "Which way to Linaculan?"

"Have you so little faith?"

Morgan's voice was shaking in fury. "Listen, you surly bastard! You've refused to answer my questions . . . or even make conversation. What does faith have to do with it? Just tell me how much farther I have to go to get to Linaculan; that's all I want from you. No psalm singing, no preaching. Nothing! Understand?"

"You still have a great distance to go . . ." His voice

trailed off, and Morgan sensed a change in the padre's attitude. A moment later, Morgan heard it too . . . the far-off drumbeat of a horse's hooves.

The moon—as if curious—parted the clouds for the last time. There was only a shadow moving across the landscape at first, but as the horse came nearer, Morgan could see the animal, its mane and tail rippling like black flags straining at their halyards. It was a magnificent beast, quite the largest he had ever seen—coal-black as the midnight and spirited as a thunderhead.

What really took Morgan's breath away, however, was the girl. She rode the animal as though she were an integral part of it. The moonlight played with her, for she was dressed completely in white, from boots and jodhpurs to the form-fitting, long-sleeved blouse and Spanish *grandee* hat. Her hair, though, was black—black as a raven's wing, and it hung like a soft ebony cloud from her shoulders.

Savagely, she reined the stallion to a halt in front of the two men. The horse reared; Morgan jumped back nervously, but the priest stood his ground.

"Well, padre," she said, smiling and—at the same time— slapping her jodhpurs with a riding whip. "I see you have taken another unfortunate under your wing." She put an odd emphasis on the word "unfortunate"; Morgan didn't know whether to be angry or puzzled. He waited, silently watching the dramatic by-play going on between the two people. Perhaps, the entire thing was elaborately staged—all part of the trap. It was of no matter—there was no immediate danger to him. So, for the moment, he was content to merely stand and enjoy the woman's proud body.

In time, the girl became aware of Morgan's stare; her own eyes, answering, were as bold and insolent as the man's. She threw back her head and laughed throatily. "You are in bad hands, my American friend. This *hombre* here"—she nodded contemptuously towards the priest— "is called 'old bad luck' among my people. Each time he is on the road, there is an accident. You have had trouble tonight . . . no?"

Morgan nodded once, then glanced sideways at the priest.

The padre, however, was watching the girl. She laughed under his scrutiny. "Don't look so angry, old man. You can't frighten me. Why don't you run along now; I'll see that our American friend reaches his destination."

The priest held out his hand to Morgan. "You must not go with her. She is evil. Evil personified." He made three crosses in the air.

There was no doubt in Morgan's mind about his decision. The padre had said she was "evil"; coming from a priest, that was a real recommendation. Besides, only an idiot would continue to walk the dark road when there was a chance to ride, a chance for pleasant conversation, a chance—really, a promise if he had correctly interpreted her look—of even more! He hesitated, still a wild, hunted animal wary of the trap.

The girl gently patted the sweating neck of her horse. "Where were you going?"

"Linaculan," Morgan answered.

"That isn't too far away. Come on, I'll give you a ride to Mictlantecutli's ranch . . . you can call for help from there." Her lips were half parted; she seemed almost breathless as she awaited his answer.

Morgan turned to the priest. "Well, thanks for the company, padre. See you around some time."

The priest took two quick steps towards Morgan, and put out his arms, beseeching, "Stay at my side. She is evil, I say."

The girl laughed aloud. "It's two against one, churchman. You've lost another victim."

"Victim?" Morgan's eyes narrowed. He'd been right about the old devil all along. But something was ringing false. Then it came to him . . . if the padre was a thief and a murderer, why hadn't he done the job when Morgan was unconscious?

The priest gazed back over his shoulder towards the setting moon; it would be dark within seconds now. He reached inside his cassock and withdrew an ivory cross about eight or ten inches high. "The night is coming. Hold on to the cross. Believe me. Do not go to Mictlantecutli. I am your last chance."

"Go on, get away from him, you old fool," the girl shouted. "The authorities should take care of you idiots who molest and frighten travellers on this road . . . and prevent them from reaching their destination."

The priest paid no heed to the girl; he implored Morgan once again, and this time his voice was strong as he watched the last red lip of the moon disappear below the hill, "There still is time . . ."

The girl viciously pulled back on the reins and dug her spurs into the horse's flanks; it screamed in rage and reared, its front hooves blotting out the stars. When back on all fours, the stallion was between Morgan and the priest. Her face was a soft glow as she smiled and withdrew a boot from the stirrups. "Come, my friend. Place your foot here. Vault up behind me." She reached out a helping hand, and as she bent over, her blouse gaped open slightly. Morgan grinned, and took her hand. He pulled himself astride the horse. "Put your arms around me and hold on," she ordered. Morgan did so, happily. Her body was supple, delightful to hold, and the faint scent of some exotic perfume wafted back to him from her hair.

He gazed down at the priest; the old man's face was once more unfathomable. "So long, padre. Don't take any wooden *pesos*."

The girl did not wait for an answer. She raked the flank of the horse with her spurs and the beast tore out into the night. "Hold tight," she shouted, "hold tight."

They rode at breakneck speed for almost ten minutes before she reined the stallion to a walk. With their pace slowed, Morgan became aware of the girl's body again, and desire built up rapidly inside him. It had been a long time; there was no one around to stop him . . . and the girl had shown a spirited wantonness that led him to believe she would welcome his advances. They rode with only the hoarse breathing and clip-clop of the horse, and the creak of their saddle breaking the silence. Surreptitiously, his hand began to ride higher and higher on her rib cage. She made no protest, so he became bolder. Finally, he could feel the soft flesh of her breasts beneath the silk blouse.

It was easier than Morgan had ever believed possible. She simply reined in the horse and turned partially around. "We can stop here . . . if you want."

Morgan's voice was guttural, his body pounding in desire, as he said, "Yeh. I want."

She slid from the horse, and Morgan was beside her immediately. Her arms went around his neck; their lips met in a brutal bruising parody of love. Her fingernails dug into his shoulders as his hands sought immediate demanding familiarity with her body. She moaned, deep in her throat as Morgan fumbled with her clothes. And then, with only the disinterested horse grazing near by and the brittle eyes of the stars glittering as they watched, their bodies joined in a violent collusion of hot, implacable lust.

Morgan could feel the lassitude of his body when he awakened. That was his first impression. His second impression was that he was still embracing the girl. The third—an overpowering horrible odour of putrefaction.

He opened his eyes.

And screamed.

It was a scream wrenched involuntarily from his soul, for there, in a faint light of an approaching dawn, he could see that he was holding in his arms the rotting cadaver of a woman—a body from which the flesh was peeling in great huge strips like rotten liver, from which the death grimace revealed crooked brown teeth and eyeless sockets.

Morgan whimpered and jumped to his feet. His heart was hammering as though it were about to fly from his body like some overtaxed runaway machine that explodes into pieces. His breath came in deep animal-like pants of fright. And his eyes darted frantically around like those of a madman tormented by phantoms.

"I . . . I . . . I . . ." he panted. It was all he could say. He began running down the road. He fell twice, painfully ripping open his legs and hands on the rocky surface of the land. "I . . . I . . . I . . ." and then, the words he wanted most to say came spilling out, "Help me . . . someone! Help . . . me!"

He heard the horse's hooves behind him. It was the girl; she was alive . . . and whole! She smiled, reassuringly. "Where did you go?" she asked. And then, she grinned impishly, "Where are your clothes."

"I . . . I . . . I . . ." Morgan could not speak.

"Come," she said.

Morgan shook his head. He could not marshal his thoughts, but this much was certain; he knew he was not going with the girl.

"Come!" And this time it was an imperative command. The girl was no longer amused at his nudity, his frightened inarticulateness.

Morgan willed himself to turn and run away, but his body did not respond to his mental orders. Instead, like a mindless zombie, he mounted the horse.

"That's better," the girl said, soothingly. "Of course, you should have put on your clothes . . . but it doesn't matter." She glanced towards the east, "Night is almost gone. We must hurry. There is something I want you to see before we get to Mictlantecutli's ranch."

She slapped the stallion with her whip, and the animal began chasing the blackness of the sky.

Now, behind them, the sky was definitely beginning to lighten as dawn came to the Mexican desert. In the near light of the new day, Morgan could see a landmark that looked familiar. And then, off the road, at the bottom of the ravine, he saw his car. Gingerly, the horse picked its way down the slope until they were beside the wrecked vehicle.

Ugly, red-necked vultures screamed and flapped their wings as the horse approached. Several were fighting over what appeared to be elongated white ropes hanging out of the car windows. A few of the birds took to the air . . . the rest, arrogant and unafraid, moved over a few reluctant steps away. "But . . . but . . . what are they doing here?" Morgan asked. "There was no one in the car but me."

He could feel the girl's body shaking in silent laughter. She pointed. By squinting his eyes, Morgan could make out the figure impaled on the steering-wheel post. The cold undulating horror he had felt earlier closed in around him again. The body was familiar . . . too familiar! Morgan whimpered as the girl urged the stallion closer. The vultures had gone for the eyes first—as they usually do . . . the entrails of the dead man hung out the open window, and these had been the reason for fighting among the birds.

Morgan saw the clothes. The dead man was dressed the same as he had been. He wore the same shape wristwatch. What terrifying nightmare was this? Awaken . . . wake up . . . wake up, he mentally shouted. But the nightmare, more real than life itself, remained. The dead man was Morgan, there could be no doubt about it.

Morgan's mind was forced in a corner by the realization, his sanity backed away from the fact. He began to lose all control. He screamed, the scream of a demented lunatic.

At his cry, the girl shouted and whipped at the stallion. The horse scrambled up the side of the ravine.

There, in the roadway, stood the priest.

"Help me, Father. Help me. God help me . . ." Morgan mumbled, the saliva trickling slowly from both sides of his lax mouth.

"You made your choice. I am sorry."

"But I did not know what Mictlantecutli was."

"Mictlantecutli is known by many names: Diabolo, Satan, Devil, Lucifer, Mephistopheles. The particular name of evil is never important, for the precepts are the same in every country. You have embraced evil; you have made your last earthly choice. I am powerless now to aid you. Goodbye . . ."

He felt, then heard the girl's laughter—shrill, maniacal, satisfied. Her whip bit into the horse's neck and her spurs drew blood. They tore down the road, galloping, galloping, galloping towards the night. The stench was back again, and shreds of the girl's flesh began sloughing off in the wind.

She turned . . . slowly, this time . . . and Morgan saw the horrible grinning expression of a skeleton.

He twisted around, unable to face the apparition, and cried out once more for the priest. Far back in the distance—as if he were viewing something in another world—Morgan could see the padre's solitary figure at the top of a hill, plodding towards the east, the rising sun, and a new day.

When Morgan turned back again, weeping and knowing now the desperate futility of hope, they had already reached the edge of night . . . and the oppressive darkness reached out to engulf them.

GUIDE TO DOOM

by Ellis Peters

This way down, please. Mind your heads in the doorway, and take care on the stairs, the treads are very worn. And here we are in the courtyard again.

That concludes our tour, ladies and gentlemen. Thank you for your attention. Please keep to the paths as you cross to the gatehouse.

Yes, madam, it *is* a very little castle. Properly speaking, it's a fortified manorhouse. But it's the finest of its kind extant, and in a unique state of repair. That's what comes of being in the hands of the same family for six centuries. Yes, madam, that's how long the Chastelays have been here. And in these very walls until they built the Grace House at the far end of the grounds a hundred and fifty years ago.

The well, sir? You'll see the well as you cross the courtyard there. What was that sir? I didn't quite catch—

Not that well? The *other* one?

Now I wonder, sir, what should put it into your head that a small household like this—

The one where Mary Purcell drowned herself!

Hush, sir, please! Keep your voice down. Mr. Chastelay doesn't like that affair remembered. Yes, sir, I know, but we don't show the well-chamber. He wants it forgotten. No, I can't make exceptions, it's as much as my job's worth. Well, sir—very handsome of you, I'm sure. Were you, indeed? I can understand your being interested, of course, if you were one of the reporters who covered the case. You did say *Mary Purcell?*

Oh, no, sir, I wasn't in this job then. But I read the papers, like everybody else. Look, sir, if you'll wait just a moment, till I see this lot out—

That's better, now we can talk. I'm always glad to get the last party of the day through this old door, and drop the latch on 'em. Nice to hear the cars driving away down the avenue. Notice how the sound vanishes when they reach the turn where the wall begins. Quiet, isn't it? Soon we shall begin to hear the owls.

Now, sir, you want to see the well. The *other* well. The one where the tragedy occurred. I shouldn't do it, really. Mr. Chastelay would be very annoyed if he knew. No, sir, that's right, of course, he never need know.

Very well, sir, it's through here—through the great hall. After you, sir! There, fancy you turning in the right direction without being told! Mind your step, the floor's very uneven in places.

You mustn't be surprised at Mr. Chastelay not wanting that old affair dragged up again. It very nearly wrecked his life. Everybody had him down for the lover, the fellow who drove her to it. Her being his farm foreman's wife, you see, and him having been noticeably took with her, and on familiar terms with the two of them. I daresay it was only natural people should think it was him. If he could have run the rumors to their source he'd have sued, but he never could. For a year it was touch and go whether his wife divorced him, but they're over it now. After all, it's ten years and more. Nobody wants to start the tongues wagging again. No, sir, I'm sure *you* don't, or I wouldn't be doing this.

She was very beautiful, they say, this Mrs. Purcell. Very young, only twenty-one, and fair. They say the photographs didn't do justice to her coloring. Wonderful blue eyes, I believe. *Green,* were they, you say? Not blue? Well, I wouldn't argue with you, sir, you were reporting the affair, you should know. Watch out for the bottom step here, it's worn very hollow. *Green* eyes!

Oh, no, sir, I wouldn't dispute it. Wonderful trained memory you have.

Well, at any rate she was young and very pretty, and I daresay a bit simple and innocent, too, brought up country-style as she was. She was the daughter of one of the gardeners. I don't suppose you ever met him? No, he wouldn't have anything to say to the press, would he? He had a stroke afterwards, and Mr. Chastelay pensioned him off with a light job around the place. But that's neither here nor there. Mind the step into the stone gallery. Here, let me put on the lights.

Yes, gives you quite a turn, doesn't he, that halberdier standing there, with his funny-shaped knife on a stick? I keep him all burnished up like that specially, it gives the kids a thrill. Tell you the truth, when I've been going round here at night, locking up and seeing all's fast after the folks have gone, I've often borrowed his halberd and carried it round with me, just for company like. It gets pretty eerie here after dark. Makes me feel like one of the ghosts myself, trailing this thing. If it's all the same to you, sir, I'll take it along with us now.

They put a heavy cover on the well after that fatality. There's a ring in the middle, and the haft of the halberd makes a very handy lever. You'd like to look inside, I daresay. There are iron rungs down the shaft like a ladder. Her husband went down, you know, and got her out. More than most of us would like to do, but then, he felt responsible, I suppose, poor soul.

Where's her husband now? Did you never hear, sir? He cracked up, poor lad, and they had to put him away. He's still locked up.

The way I heard it, this affair of hers had been going on some time, and when she found she was expecting a child it fairly knocked her over. Made her turn and look again at what she'd let this fellow persuade her into. She went to him, and asked what to do.

And he told her not to be a fool, why should she want to do anything? She'd got a husband, hadn't she? All she had to do was hold her tongue. But he could see she didn't see it that way; she felt bad about her husband and couldn't let him father the child with his eyes shut. She was hating herself, and wanting to be honest, and wanting her lover to stand by her even in that. And wanting her husband back on the old terms, too, because I don't suppose she ever really stopped loving him, she only lost sight of him in the excitement. So this fellow put her off and said they'd talk about it again, after they'd considered it.

And he lit out the next day for I don't know where, and left her.

No, sir, you're right, of course, I wasn't in this job then, how would I know? Just reconstructing in my own mind. Maybe it wasn't like that. No, as you say, if it was Mr. Chastelay he didn't light out for anywhere; he stayed right here and got the muck thrown at him. But a lot of people think now it wasn't him, after all.

Anyhow, she went to her husband and told him the truth. All but the name, she never told anyone that. Very nearly

killed him, I shouldn't wonder, if he was daft about her,
as they say. He didn't rave or anything, just turned his
back on her and went away. And when she followed him,
crying, he couldn't bear it; he turned round and hit her.

Yes, sir, a very vivid imagination I've got, I don't deny
it. So would you have if you lived in this place alone.
I fairly see 'em walking, nights.

And the way I see it, she was too young and inex-
perienced to understand that you don't hit out at somebody
who means nothing to you. She thought he was finished
with her. And if he was gone, everything was gone. She
didn't know enough to wait, and bear it, and hope. She
ran along here, crying, and jumped into the well.

Five minutes, and he was running after her. By that
time it was too late. When he got her out she was dead.
Her fair hair all smeared with scum, and slime in her
beautiful green eyes.

Right here, where we're standing. There's the cover
they've put over it, since. Good and heavy, so's nobody
can shift it easily. But if you'll stand back, sir, and let me
get some leverage on this halberd—

There you are. Nobody knows quite how deep. Let's
have a little more light, shall we? There, now you can
see better. A girl would have to be at the end of her tether,
wouldn't she, to go that way?

My sweet Mary, my little lamb!

No, sir, I didn't say anything. I thought *you* were about
to speak.

What am I doing, sir? Just turning the key in the lock.
Just seeing how smoothly it works. A lot of keys and
wards to look after, you know, and Mr. Chastelay is very
particular about this room being kept closed. No one's been
here for more than three years, except me. Not until tonight. I don't suppose there'll be anyone else for the next
three years, either, and if they did they wouldn't lift the
well-cover. I do all the cleaning myself, you see. I'm a
great one for keeping things in perfect order. Look at this
halberd, now. Sharp as a butcher's knife. Here, look.

Oh, sorry, sir, did I prick you?

Mad, sir? No, sir, not me. That was her husband, remember? They put him away. All that happened to me was
a stroke, and it didn't affect my co-ordination. Pensioned
off with a light job I may be, but you'd be surprised how

strong I still am. So I shouldn't try to rush me, if I were you, sir. It wouldn't do you any good.

It's always a mistake to know too much, sir. *Mary* Purcell, you said. Alice was her first name, the one all the papers used, did you know that? It was only her family and her intimates who called her Mary. And then, *how did you know her eyes were green?* They were shut fast enough before ever the press got near her. But her lover knew.

Yes, sir, I know you now, you were the young man who was staying with the Lovells at the farm that summer. We must have a talk about Mary. Sorry poor Tim Purcell couldn't be here to make up the party; it might have done him a power of good. But we'll spare him a thought, won't we? Now, while there's time.

Funny, isn't it? Providential, when you come to think, you walking out here from the farm, without a car or anything. And I'd stake this key and this halberd—I don't have to tell you how much I value them, do I?—that you never told a soul where you were going.

But you couldn't keep away, could you?

And I don't suppose either you or I will ever really know why you came—never dreaming you'd meet Mary's father. So I can believe it was because I've wanted you so much—*so much!*

Oh, I shouldn't scream like that, if I was you, sir, you'll only do yourself an injury. And nobody'll hear you, you know. There's nobody within half a mile but you and me. And the walls are very thick. Very thick.

THE ESTUARY

by Margaret St. Clair

The best of it was that it wasn't really stealing. Everybody knew that the ships had been moored in the estuary because mooring them was cheaper than cutting them up for scrap metal would have been. There was a guard and a patrol at night, of course, but both were perfunctory and negligent. Evading them was so easy as to make abstractions seem rather more legitimate than they would have if the ships had been unguarded entirely. No wonder Pickard thought of his thefts as a sort of praiseworthy salvaging.

Night after night he scrabbled in the bowels of the rotting Liberty ships and came up with sheets of metal, parts of instruments, and lengths of brass and copper pipe. He had a friend in the boat-building business who bought most of what he appropriated, and who paid him prices which were only a shade below normal. Once in a while pictures of what would happen to him if he were caught bothered Pickard—he rather thought the ships were government property, and carried a proportionate penalty—but those apes on the patrol made so much noise on their rounds that you'd have to be deaf, dumb and blind to get caught.

Business was good. After the first three months Pickard found it expedient to hire a helper, a tall, gangling youth who wore a felt skullcap and was called Gene. He took over with no difficulty at all Pickard's belief that his occupation was, at worst, one of the slight, necessary irregularities which keep the wheels of business lubricated and revolving steadily.

He was a smart boy in other ways, too. After he had worked for Pick for three or four days, he suggested a number of improvements in the salvaging technique. They were well thought of; that week Pickard's receipts were some one hundred and twenty percent above their previous average. A modest prosperity visited the Pickard household. Estelle took to cooking with butter instead of margarine; she read advertisements for fur coats with a puckered brow and a critical eye.

"Say, Pop," Gene said hesitatingly two or three weeks after Estelle had made the down payment on a medium-priced Persian lamb greatcoat, "you ever hear anything on these boats at night? I mean, anything funny?"

Pick looked at him quizzically. The night was hazy and overcast, with a good deal of diffused light in the sky, and he could discern, though dimly, the outline of Gene's head and face beside him in the motorboat. "Don't get cold feet," he said, "that patrol won't bother us none. Those dumb bastards wouldn' know manure if they fell in it."

Gene wriggled. He was still very young. "I don't mean the patrol," he answered, "I mean something, unh, kind of funny. Something on the boats like it was following me."

Pickard laughed. "You got too much imagination, Junior," he said. (The "junior" was his revenge for Gene's calling him "Pop," which he detested.) "Nothing here but a lot of old worn-out boats. You're young and full of—"

"O.K.," Gene said. "I just—O.K."

"See if you can get some more of that little brass tubing," Pick said as they parted. He shoved a hunk of sneuss in his cheek. "Bert told me he could use any amount of it."

"O.K."

Artistically speaking, Gene should have disappeared that night. It was not until Friday, however, that he failed to show up at the motorboat with his load of salvage and scrap.

Pick waited for him impatiently at first, then with anxiety. What could have happened to the kid? He might have got into a tangle with the patrol, of course, but Pick hadn't heard any disturbance, and sound carries well over water. The patrol always went around with lanterns and flashlights, and it made as much noise as a kaffeklatsch. But if Gene hadn't got into trouble with the patrol, where was he? Had he fallen somewhere clambering around in the dark? Was he lying unconscious in the bottom of some hold?

Before the lightening sky forced him home, Pickard hunted for the boy on a handful of ships. He found no sign of him. He hunted the next night and the next and the next (not forgetting, of course, his primary interest in salvage), until he had covered every hull in the slowly-rocking graveyard of them. No Gene. Only, on the third hull he visited on the last night he found the boy's felt skullcap floating brim-up in a sheet of filthy bilge.

Pickard was worried, more worried than he would have cared to admit. If Gene had been hauled off by the patrol, it meant trouble for Pick himself sooner or later. And if the patrol wasn't responsible for his absence, what was?

Estelle noticed his trouble and questioned him until she forced the reason for it from him. At the end of his account, she laughed.

"He was a kind of a jerk, Pick," she said comfortingly. "What happened was he got scared an' ran and then was ashamed to come back and tell you about it afterwards. Just a jerk."

"Yeh. But, what scared him?" Pickard swallowed. "I remember hearing," he said with some difficulty, "about how they was a welder got welded up in one of those ships when they was building them. They launched the ship with him in it. And then there was a man was down in the bottom and his air hose caught fire. An—"

His wife snorted. "That's a lotta horsehair, Pick, and you know it. I never heard such junk. You scared of the patrol?"

"Hunh-unh."

"Well, then! I don't know what's the matter with you. I sure never thought you'd lose your nerve . . . Mabel was telling me they laid off Reese at Selby yesterday." Estelle was thinking, Pickard knew, of the payments on her new fur coat.

Pickard slept in the daytime and worked at night and, though it was a quiet neighborhood, he never slept very well. He had been asleep three or four hours, which brought the time to 11 A.M., when he had his dream.

It started out mildly enough. He was hunting through one of the hulls for a highly salable chunk of everdur he had reason to believe was somewhere about. As he hunted he began to have a feeling, faint at first and then stronger, that something pretty unpleasant was lurking on the periphery of his vision. Two or three times he turned around abruptly, hoping to surprise it, but it moved faster than he could.

He kept on looking for the everdur. He climbed up ladders and down them again, sniffed around in the engine room and the crew's quarters. At last, in the bilge of number three hold, he saw the half-submerged piece of everdur.

As soon as he saw it, he forgot that he had been hunting it. By the strange equivalence of dreams, it was the bilge, the filthy stinking bilge, which became the object of his desire. He knelt down beside it, scooped it up in his hand and, nauseated, sick with disgust and self-loathing, began to drink.

Pick's heart was beating violently when he awoke. Of all the dumb dreams! What did a thing like that mean? What sense was there to it? His pulse was still pounding abnormally when the noon whistles blew.

He hired another helper. Fred wasn't nearly as good as Gene had been, a lazy bum in fact, and he quit after five days, saying he didn't like the noises on the hulls at night. So you can see Pick had plenty of warning before it happened to him.

It was a week later that Gene came up behind him when he was between decks on the *M.S. Blount* and pawed at him with his rotting hands. Pick screamed and screamed and tried to fight him off, but he was wholly unsuccessful. He couldn't hurt Gene; Gene was already dead. And then Pick was floundering around in the sickening stinking loathsome wonderful bilge while Gene stood over him making soft blubbering noises with his peeling, oozing lips and the other one lurked quietly in the background.

Estelle never did get finished paying for her fur coat. After a while she set up housekeeping with a man named Leon Socher who had long admired her. The ships went back to their slow job of rotting at their moorings without bothering the taxpayers. And nowadays, if you are so indiscreet as to go poking at night among the rotting hulls as they roll quietly at anchor in the estuary, you will find that they are populated by a small, select company, a company consisting of Pickard, Gene, and the welder, who is the Oldest Inhabitant.

TOUGH TOWN

by William Sambrot

Ed Dillon hesitated before the neat iron gate that barred the pathway leading to the comfortable home beyond. He shifted his battered sample case, taking no notice of the NO PEDDLERS sign hung prominently near the latch. He was tired, tired as only a door-to-door canvasser can be tired near the end of a day of doors slammed in his face. It was a hard town. A tough town.

He'd seen a constable giving him a long slow stare earlier and he'd walked jauntily on, trying to look like a well-fed tourist just stopping between bus changes, out to look the town over. But the constable hadn't been fooled. He had an eye for the cracked shoes, the shiny serge, the well-worn sample case. It had been a tough town. And only two meager sales.

He glanced at his watch and shrugged his shoulder. Just time to make his pitch here, then hustle down to the bus depot for a bite and the 5:15 on to the next town.

He opened the gate and took two steps when the dog was on him, the red red mouth, the slavering teeth. A strange horrible dog that lurked silently behind a bush and leaped savagely, growling low and deep in its throat. With the instinct of long practice he brought up his sample case and luckily, the dog's teeth only skinned his knuckles. Then the animal was behind and loping away, an eerie long-drawn howl floating back.

Ed watched it go, heart pounding, sucking his knuckles. Out of the corner of his eye he saw the agitated motions of a curtain being dropped at a window, then the door opened and a tall white-haired man stepped out. The man's quick glance raked him from head to foot, and Ed, seeing the set lines, the narrowed piercing eyes, knew there'd be no sale here. He stopped and picking up his case, opened the gate and hurried off.

"Wait!" the white-haired man yelled. "You—come back here you! Stop! Come back here!"

Ed hurried on, without looking back. He knew these towns, these mean bitter people, always anxious to slap a man in jail, to fine him for selling without a license, get his last cent and kick him out like a common bum. He knew them, every miserable sooty burg, every disheveled housewife who listened with flat eyes and contemptuous smile. What was wrong with these people? Why did they hate him, sneer at him, sic their dogs at him? He did them no harm. He brought his few brushes, his kitchen gadgets, his little jokes—and they paid him with insults, threats. Behind him, the man still yelled as he turned the corner and hurried toward the bus depot, his torn knuckles burning.

Over his coffee, with still twenty minutes to go, Ed heard the commotion outside. With caution born of long experience, he picked up a newspaper and held it before his face, then he peered carefully around. There was the tall white-haired old man, talking excitedly to the constable. They walked along the covered ramp outside the depot, looking carefully at the few stragglers waiting for the big silver bus to take on the passengers.

He rose, carrying the paper and his case, walked quietly to the back of the little restaurant and out the door. He had no doubt that the white-haired man wanted him arrested for ignoring his NO PEDDLERS sign. Probably a local merchant, outraged at his unlicensed competition.

His shoulders sagged, he felt tired and empty as he peeked around the corner and watched them enter the restaurant. So they were going to make a production of it.

He picked up his case and glanced quickly around. Down the street was a sad little park filled with straggly trees. In the center was a tiny screened summer-house, leaf-choked, empty-looking.

He started walking quickly. There was a chance, a bare chance, that he could make it to the highway and flag down the bus provided he could get out of town without being seen by the constable. He simply couldn't afford a fine—or thirty days in jail—or both. He barely had bus fare and room rent for tonight. And tomorrow, if the next town wasn't better—

He entered the park and walked along a disused path toward the summer-house. In the distance, the bus burst into sound and staccato backfires. He hesitated. Too late now.

He peered into the summer-house, at the littered floor, the dust-covered benches. He could stay there, wait until dark and then head out to catch the ten o'clock. It wasn't a pleasant prospect, but then, it was better than running into the eager-beaver constable.

He looked beyond the park, at the snug little homes, the tree-lined streets, and a vague sadness came over him. He was the eternal wanderer, peddler, an itinerant whose trade was old when the pyramids were built.

He sighed and settled himself on the bench. Tough town. Tough people. Even the damn dogs bit without warning. His knuckles hurt. He flipped open the paper and scanned the headlines quickly. LOCAL GIRL VAN-ISHES. The subhead said: "Judy Howell Feared Victim of Foul Play." He grunted, squinting in the dimness, gave up, tucked the paper under his head and in a minute was asleep. When he awoke, it was dark.

His tongue felt thick, his head throbbed and his knuckles burned like consuming fire. He examined his watch. He just had time to ease out of town and flag down the 10:15 if he hurried. He rose and suddenly the room whirled, there was a huge roaring in his ears. He waited, strangely frightened, until his head cleared. He'd been hungry and tired before but nothing like that had ever happened. He picked up his case, wincing at the stiff pain in his scraped knuckles, cursing again the town, the dog, the white-haired man who pursued him, even through his uneasy slumber.

Unless he wanted to cut across fields, climb through or under barbed wire, he had to walk through a well-lighted section in order to get to the highway. He hesitated, but his throbbing hand gave him no choice. He was in no mood to climb fences.

Head down, clutching the rolled-up newspaper, he strode along, trying to look like a well-fed tourist out to see the town between bus stops. His feet were killing him and deep behind his eyes strange flashes came and went. It had been a long time since he'd eaten lunch, but still—

He stiffened as a man approached, staring curiously at him as most small-towners stare at strangers. The man's steps slowed as Ed approached and finally stopped, frankly waiting for Ed to come closer. With the skill born of long practice Ed sized up the stranger. Not a constable, or even a deputy. Just a local out for a stroll—and yet, the way he stared, the sudden look as of recognition—

Ed pulled his hat brim down farther and brushed by

the man, forcing his aching legs to move briskly, the handle of his sample case wet in his palm.

Ed crossed the street hurriedly, glancing back. He saw the man stand irresolutely for a moment and then rush up a walk and begin pounding on the door of a house.

Suddenly he was soaked in perspiration. That man had acted as though he'd recognized him, as though his picture had been plastered all over the papers or something. Little nightmare thoughts pushed and darted about the edges of his mind. That white-haired man. Talking, telling people about him until the whole town was out to get him.

Ridiculous. For what? People in a town, even a tough town like this, didn't concern themselves about a little thing like canvassing without a license.

He averted his face as a group of laughing young girls came out of a brightly lit soda fountain. He heard one sing a brief snatch of a popular song, clear and sweet, as he passed them. And another gasped, a choked little sound that tightened his hand convulsively on the case handle.

"Did you see that man? Isn't that—it's him!"

He faltered. It was crazy. Even the kids—

"Gray suit and brown hat, carrying a suitcase—"

"It is! It is!"

Their little squeals and gasps pursued him as he crossed the street again, rounded the corner and stopped in a darkened doorway. Through the broad window opening on the street he could see them. The girls were clustered about the door of the drugstore, talking and pointing in his direction. A tall young man dressed in whites had joined them. A small boy leaped on his bike and peddled furiously up and rounded the corner, not seeing him flattened in the doorway.

The tiny bicycle light dimmed and vanished up the street, and Ed felt a terrible tremor in his neck, an uncontrollable jerking. The spasm passed and he leaned limply in the doorway, looking through the window to across the street. The man who had pounded on the door came up with several others. Cars converged on the spot. The little knot before the drugstore grew, the babble of their voices reaching him, an ominous murmur. The crowd grew, the noises it made swelled. Then they started to cross the street.

He began walking hurriedly, his head remote, the

roaring returning. The street stretched endlessly, growing dim, receding into an infinite distance. Behind, he heard running footsteps, hurried explanations as others joined the group.

Something horrible had happened to this town, the people. The word of him had spread like a crown fire in a forest and they were out to get him. Why? He was no criminal. What could he possibly have done to start them off? He shifted his sample case, trying to think. And then he remembered the newspaper he'd read. The little girl. Missing. Foul-play suspected. Good God! Could it be they—?

He hurried. He realized his danger. He was The Stranger. Outsider. Beyond the sacred community pale.

He broke into a shambling staggering run. Across the street, through an empty lot, down an embankment and up the other side. There was no choice now. He had to cut across the fields, running heavily, the case banging against him, clutching the newspaper, while behind, the shouts rose. He tried to duck behind a huge oak tree but already they'd spotted him. The pursuit became bedlam. He ran. He was every frightened man ever pursued. The night surrounded him, hideous with piercing calls. He moved spasmodically, a man in a nightmare. The town was after him, baying, slavering, with red red mouth. He should never have ignored that gigantic neon-lit NO PEDDLERS that burned and flared behind his eyes.

From all about they converged, seeing beyond the flimsy camouflage of his jaunty carriage, seeing the cracked shoes, the shining serge, the battered sample case. They knew. Canvasser. Peddler. Keep out. This is a tough town.

Suddenly he was down and they were on him, shouting, hands pulling at him.

"It's him. The guy the radio described—"

"He's the one the sheriff's after—"

"He did it. *Killer. Rapist!*"

Killer. Rapist. The words roared and crashed against his body from all angles, leaving great hurting welts. Dimly he heard a siren approaching, wailing thin and clear above the surf-sounds of the mob. Brakes squealed. There was an obscure scuffle, and still the mob pounded and pulled at him alternately.

"—not wanted for the girl!" a voice roared. "Let him go!" The voice was swallowed up in the huge murmuring.

"He's been bitten by a mad dog. Stand back. In the name of the law, stand back or I'll shoot!"

Mad dog! The words swept through the mob like a tremendous wave, battering and buffeting, surging back again.

"He's a mad dog!"

One voice, howling, horrible to hear rising above the others: "You heard the sheriff. He's a mad dog killer! You know what he did to Julie Howell. *What are we waiting for?*"

Another voice, lost, remote: "Stop! In the name of—"

There were shots, the mob shouted in unison, then swept forward like one kill-crazy animal. He was picked up. Hands plucked and tore at him. Faces, red, sweaty, glaring-eyed, came and went. Sounds swelled and swelled. This couldn't be real. This must be delirium, the result of the venom the mad dog had introduced into his blood. He'd heard the sheriff's words. He understood at last. It would be all right. This was fever. Soon, they'd put him between cool sheets and kind nurses would bathe his hot forehead.

He tried to move his broken mouth, to tell them this. He'd misjudged the people, the town. They weren't tough. Not really. It was just that he'd been bitten by a mad dog and they'd wanted to find him, to help him. They meant him no harm. All this, the noises, the battering blows, the mob—this wasn't really happening. Not really. It was the delirium.

Brilliant lights flared in his face. He opened his swollen eyes, squinting against the glare. Above was the massive outline of a great tree. An oak tree. Something moved up there, then came dropping toward him, alien, sinuous, like a brown hairy snake.

It dangled before his face and he smiled at it while lights flared and diminished in his eyes. It looked like a rope, it felt harsh when they put it around his neck, but it couldn't be a rope. Not really. The crowd screamed, a strangely feminine sound that lifted him up, up on a shrill crest of unbelievable sound, then suddenly he felt himself dropping, dropping.

It was just part of the nightmare. They meant him no harm. Soon they'd put him between cool sheets and kind nur—

THE TROLL

by T. H. White

"My father," said Mr. Marx, "used to say that an experience like the one I am about to relate was apt to shake one's interest in mundane matters. Naturally he did not expect to be believed, and he did not mind whether he was or not. He did not himself believe in the supernatural, but the thing happened, and he proposed to tell it as simply as possible. It was stupid of him to say that it shook his faith in mundane affairs, for it was just as mundane as anything else. Indeed the really frightening part about it was the horribly tangible atmosphere in which it took place. None of the outlines wavered in the least. The creature would have been less remarkable if it had been less natural. It seemed to overcome the usual laws without being immune to them.

"My father was a keen fisherman, and used to go to all sorts of places for his fish. On one occasion he made Abisko his Lapland base, a comfortable railway hotel, one hundred and fifty miles within the Arctic circle. He travelled the prodigious length of Sweden (I believe it is as far from the South of Sweden to the North, as it is from the South of Sweden to the South of Italy) in the electric railway, and arrived tired out. He went to bed early, sleeping almost immediately, although it was bright daylight outside; as it is in those parts throughout the night at that time of the year. Not the least shaking part of his experience was that it should all have happened under the sun.

"He went to bed early, and slept, and dreamt. I may as well make it clear at once, as clear as the outlines of that creature in the northern sun, that his story did not turn out to be a dream in the last paragraph. The division between sleeping and waking was abrupt, although the feeling of both was the same. They were both in the same sphere of horrible absurdity, though in the former he was asleep and in the latter almost terribly awake. He tried to be asleep several times.

"My father always used to tell one of his dreams, because it somehow seemed of a piece with what was to follow. He believed that it was a consequence of the thing's presence in the next room. My father dreamed of blood.

"It was the vividness of the dreams that was impressive, their minute detail and horrible reality. The blood came through the keyhole of a locked door which communicated with the next room. I suppose the two rooms had originally been designed *en suite*. It ran down the door panel with a viscous ripple, like the artificial one created in the conduit of Trumpingdon Street. But it was heavy, and smelt. The slow welling of it sopped the carpet and reached the bed. It was warm and sticky. My father woke up with the impression that it was all over his hands. He was rubbing his first two fingers together, trying to rid them of the greasy adhesion where the fingers joined.

"My father knew what he had got to do. Let me make it clear that he was now perfectly wide awake, but he knew what he had got to do. He got out of bed, under this irresistible knowledge, and looked through the keyhole into the next room.

"I suppose the best way to tell the story is simply to narrate it, without an effort to carry belief. The thing did not require belief. It was not a feeling of horror in one's bones, or a misty outline, or anything that needed to be given actuality by an act of faith. It was as solid as a wardrobe. You don't have to believe in wardrobes. They are there, with corners.

"What my father saw through the keyhole in the next room was a Troll. It was eminently solid, about eight feet high, and dressed in brightly ornamented skins. It had a blue face, with yellow eyes, and on its head there was a woolly sort of nightcap with a red bobble on top. The features were Mongolian. Its body was long and sturdy, like the trunk of a tree. Its legs were short and thick, like the elephant's feet that used to be cut off for umbrella stands, and its arms were wasted: little rudimentary members like the forelegs of a kangaroo. Its head and neck were very thick and massive. On the whole, it looked like a grotesque doll.

"That was the horror of it. Imagine a perfectly normal

golliwog (but without the association of a Christie min-
strel) standing in the corner of a room, eight feet high.
The creature was as ordinary as that, as tangible, as stuffed,
and as ungainly at the joints: but it could move itself
about.

"The Troll was eating a lady. Poor girl, she was tightly
clutched to its breast by those rudimentary arms, with her
head on a level with its mouth. She was dressed in a nightdress which had crumpled up under her armpits, so that
she was a pitiful naked offering, like a classical picture of
Andromeda. Mercifully, she appeared to have fainted.

"Just as my father applied his eye to the keyhole, the
Troll opened its mouth and bit off her head. Then, holding the neck between the bright blue lips, he sucked the
bare meat dry. She shrivelled, like a squeezed orange, and
her heels kicked. The creature had a look of thoughtful
ecstasy. When the girl seemed to have lost succulence as
an orange she was lifted into the air. She vanished in two
bites. The Troll remained leaning against the wall, munch-
ing patiently and casting its eyes about it with a vague
benevolence. Then it leant forward from the low hips,
like a jack-knife folding in half, and opened its mouth to
lick the blood up from the carpet. The mouth was incan-
descent inside, like a gas fire, and the blood evaporated
before its tongue, like dust before a vacuum cleaner. It
straightened itself, the arms dangling before it in patient
uselessness, and fixed its eyes upon the keyhole.

"My father crawled back to bed, like a hunted fox after
fifteen miles. At first it was because he was afraid that the
creature had seen him through the hole, but afterwards it
was because of his reason. A man can attribute many night-
time appearances to the imagination, and can ultimately
persuade himself that creatures of the dark did not exist.
But this was an appearance in a sunlit room, with all the
solidity of a wardrobe and unfortunately almost none of
its possibility. He spent the first ten minutes making sure
that he was awake, and the rest of the night trying to
hope that he was asleep. It was either that, or else he was
mad.

"It is not pleasant to doubt one's sanity. There are no
satisfactory tests. One can pinch oneself to see if one is
asleep, but there are no means of determining the other
problem. He spent some time opening and shutting his
eyes, but the room seemed normal and remained unaltered.

He also soused his head in a basin of cold water, without result. Then he lay on his back, for hours, watching the mosquitoes on the ceiling.

"He was tired when he was called. A bright Scandinavian maid admitted the full sunlight for him and told him that it was a fine day. He spoke to her several times, and watched her carefully, but she seemed to have no doubts about his behaviour. Evidently, then, he was not badly mad: and by now he had been thinking about the matter for so many hours that it had begun to get obscure. The outlines were blurring again, and he determined that the whole thing must have been a dream or a temporary delusion, something temporary, anyway, and finished with; so that there was no good in thinking about it longer. He got up, dressed himself fairly cheerfully, and went down to breakfast.

"These hotels used to be run extraordinary well. There was a hostess always handy in a little office off the hall, who was delighted to answer any questions, spoke every conceivable language, and generally made it her business to make the guests feel at home. The particular hostess at Abisko was a lovely creature into the bargain. My father used to speak to her a good deal. He had an idea that when you had a bath in Sweden one of the maids was sent to wash you. As a matter of fact this sometimes used to be the case, but it was always an old maid and highly trusted. You had to keep yourself under water and this was supposed to confer a cloak of invisibility. If you popped your knee out she was shocked. My father had a dim sort of hope that the hostess would be sent to bathe him one day: and I daresay he would have shocked her a good deal. However, this is beside the point. As he passed through the hall something prompted him to ask about the room next to his. Had anybody, he enquired, taken number 23?

" 'But, yes,' said the lady manager with a bright smile, '23 is taken by a doctor professor from Upsala and his wife, such a charming couple!'

"My father wondered what the charming couple had been doing, whilst the Troll was eating the lady in the nightdress. However, he decided to think no more about it. He pulled himself together, and went in to breakfast. The Professor was sitting in an opposite corner (the manageress had kindly pointed him out), looking mild and shortsighted, by himself. My father thought he would go out for a long climb on the mountains, since exercise was evidently what his constitution needed.

"He had a lovely day. Lake Torne blazed a deep blue below him, for all its thirty miles, and the melting snow made a lacework of filigree round the tops of the surrounding mountain basin. He got away from the stunted birch trees, and the mossy bogs with the reindeer in them, and the mosquitoes, too. He forded something that might have been a temporary tributary of the Abiskojokk, having to take off his trousers to do so and tucking his shirt up round his neck. He wanted to shout, bracing himself against the glorious tug of the snow water, with his legs crossing each other involuntarily as they passed, and the boulders turning under his feet. His body made a bow wave in the water, which climbed and feathered on his stomach, on the upstream side. When he was under the opposite bank a stone turned in earnest, and he went in. He came up, shouting with laughter, and made out loud a remark which has since become a classic in my family, 'Thank God,' he said, 'I rolled up my sleeves.' He wrung out everything as best he could, and dressed again in the wet clothes, and set off up the shoulder of Niakatjavelk. He was dry and warm again in half a mile. Less than a thousand feet took him over the snow line, and there, crawling on hands and knees, he came face to face with what seemed to be the summit of ambition. He met an ermine. They were both on all fours, so that there was a sort of equality about the encounter, especially as the ermine was higher up than he was. They looked at each other for a fifth of a second, without saying anything, and then the ermine vanished. He searched for it everywhere in vain, for the snow was only patchy. My father sat down on a dry rock, to eat his well-soaked luncheon of chocolate and rye bread.

"Life is such unutterable hell, solely because it is sometimes beautiful. If we could only be miserable all the time, if there could be no such things as love or beauty or faith or hope, if I could be absolutely certain that my love would never be returned: how much more simple life would be. One could plod through the Siberian salt mines of existence without being bothered about happiness. Unfortunately the happiness is there. There is always the chance (about eight hundred and fifty to one) that another heart will come to mine. I can't help hoping, and keeping faith, and loving beauty. Quite frequently I am not so miserable as it would be wise to be. And there, for my poor father sitting on his boulder above the snow, was stark happiness beating at the gates.

"The boulder on which he was sitting had probably never been sat upon before. It was a hundred and fifty miles within the Arctic circle, on a mountain five thousand feet high, looking down on a blue lake. The lake was so long that he could have sworn it sloped away at the ends, proving to the naked eye that the sweet earth was round. The railway line and the half-dozen houses of Abisko were hidden in the trees. The sun was warm on the boulder, blue on the snow, and his body tingled smooth from the spate water. His mouth watered for the chocolate, just behind the tip of his tongue.

"And yet, when he had eaten the chocolate—perhaps it was heavy on his stomach—there was the memory of the Troll. My father fell suddenly into a black mood, and began to think about the supernatural. Lapland was beautiful in the summer, with the sun sweeping round the horizon day and night, and the small tree leaves twinkling. It was not the sort of place for wicked things. But what about the winter? A picture of the Arctic night came before him, with the silence and the snow. Then the legendary wolves and bears snuffled at the far encampments, and the nameless winter spirits moved on their darkling courses. Lapland had always been associated with sorcery, even by Shakespeare. It was at the outskirts of the world that the Old Things accumulated, like driftwood round the edges of the sea. If one wanted to find a wise woman, one went to the rims of the Hebrides; on the coast of Brittany one sought the mass of St. Secaire. And what an outskirt Lapland was! It was an outskirt not only of Europe, but of civilisation. It had no boundaries. The Lapps went with the reindeer, and where the reindeer were was Lapland. Curiously indefinite region, suitable to the indefinite things. The Lapps were not Christians. What a fund of power they must have had behind them, to resist the march of mind. All through the missionary centuries they had held to something: something had stood behind them, a power against Christ. My father realised with a shock that he was living in the age of the reindeer, a period contiguous to the mammoth and the fossil.

"Well, this was not what he had come out to do. He dismissed the nightmares with an effort, got up from his boulder, and began the scramble back to his hotel. It was impossible that a professor from Abisko could become a troll.

"As my father was going in to dinner that evening the manageress stopped him in the hall.

" 'We have had a day so sad,' she said. 'The poor Dr. Professor has disappeared his wife. She has been missing since last night. The Dr. Professor is inconsolable.'

"My father then knew for certain that he had lost his reason.

"He went blindly to dinner, without making any answer, and began to eat a thick sour-cream soup that was taken cold with pepper and sugar. The Professor was still sitting in his corner, a sandy-headed man with thick spectacles and a desolate expression. He was looking at my father, and my father, with the soup spoon half-way to his mouth, looked at him. You know that eye-to-eye recognition, when two people look deeply into each other's pupils, and burrow to the soul? It usually comes before love. I mean the clear, deep, milk-eyed recognition expressed by the poet Donne. Their eyebeams twisted and did thread their eyes upon a double string. My father recognised that the Professor was a Troll, and the Professor recognised my father's recognition. Both of them knew that the Professor had eaten his wife.

"My father put down his soup spoon, and the Professor began to grow. The top of his head lifted and expanded, like a great loaf rising in an oven; his face went red and purple, and finally blue; the whole ungainly upperworks began to sway and topple towards the ceiling. My father looked about him. The other diners were eating unconcernedly. Nobody else could see it, and he was definitely mad at last. When he looked at the Troll again, the creature bowed. The enormous superstructure inclined itself towards him from the hips, and grinned seductively.

"My father got up from his table experimentally, and advanced towards the Troll, arranging his feet on the carpet with excessive care. He did not find it easy to walk, or to approach the monster, but it was a question of his reason. If he was mad, he was mad; and it was essential that he should come to grips with the thing, in order to make certain.

"He stood before it like a small boy, and held out his hand, saying, 'Good-evening.'

"'Ho! Ho!' said the Troll, "little mannikin. And what shall I have for my supper to-night?'

"Then it held out its wizened furry paw and took my father by the hand.

"My father went straight out of the dining-room, walking on air. He found the manageress in the passage and held out his hand to her.

"'I am afraid I have burnt my hand,' he said. 'Do you think you could tie it up?'

"The manageress said, 'But it is a very bad burn. There are blisters all over the back. Of course, I will bind it up at once.'

"He explained that he had burnt it on one of the spirit lamps at the sideboard. He could scarcely conceal his delight. One cannot burn oneself by being insane.

"'I saw you talking to the Dr. Professor,' said the manageress, as she was putting on the bandage. 'He is a sympathetic gentleman, is he not?'

"The relief about his sanity soon gave place to other troubles. The Troll had eaten its wife and given him a blister, but it had also made an unpleasant remark about its supper that evening. It proposed to eat my father. Now very few people can have been in a position to decide what to do when a troll earmarks them for its next meal. To begin with, although it was a tangible Troll in two ways, it had been invisible to the other diners. This put my father in a difficult position. He could not, for instance, ask for protection. He could scarcely go to the manageress and say, 'Professor Skål is an odd kind of werewolf, ate his wife last night, and proposes to eat me this evening.' He would have found himself in a looney-bin at once. Besides, he was too proud to do this, and still too confused. Whatever the proofs and blisters, he did not find it easy to believe in professors that turned into Trolls. He had lived in the normal world all his life, and, at his age, it was difficult to start learning afresh. It would have been quite easy for a baby, who was still co-ordinating the world, to cope with the Troll situation: for my father, not. He kept trying to fit it in somewhere, without disturbing the universe. He kept telling himself that it was nonsense: one did not get eaten by professors. It was like having a fever, and telling oneself that it was all right, really, only a delirium, only something that would pass

"There was that feeling on the one side, the desperate assertion of all the truths that he had learned so far, the tussle to keep the world from drifting, the brave but intimidated refusal to give in or to make a fool of himself.

"On the other side there was stark terror. However much one struggled to be merely deluded, or hitched up momentarily in an odd pocket of space-time, there was panic. There was the urge to go away as quickly as possible, to flee the dreadful Troll. Unfortunately the last train had left Abisko, and there was nowhere else to go.

"My father was not able to distinguish these trends of thought. For him they were at the time intricately muddled together. He was in a whirl. A proud man, and an agnostic, he stuck to his muddled guns alone. He was terribly afraid of the Troll, but he could not afford to admit its existence. All his mental processes remained hung up, whilst he talked on the terrace, in a state of suspended animation, with an American tourist who had come to Abisko to photograph the midnight sun.

"The American told my father that the Abisko railway was the northernmost electric railway in the world, that twelve trains passed through it every day travelling between Upsala and Narvik, that the population of Abo was 12,000 in 1862, and that Gustavus Adolphus ascended the throne of Sweden in 1611. He also gave some facts about Greta Garbo.

"My father told the American that a dead baby was required for the mass of St. Secaire, that an elemental was a kind of mouth in space that sucked at you and tried to gulp you down, that homeopathic magic was practised by the aborigines of Australia, and that a Lapland woman was careful at her confinement to have no knots or loops about her person, lest these should make the delivery difficult.

"The American, who had been looking at my father in a strange way for some time, took offense at this and walked away; so that there was nothing for it but to go to bed.

"My father walked upstairs on will power alone. His faculties seemed to have shrunk and confused themselves. He had to help himself with the banister. He seemed to be navigating himself by wireless, from a spot about a foot above his forehead. The issues that were involved had ceased to have any meaning, but he went on doggedly up the stairs, moved forward by pride and contrariety. It was physical fear that alienated him from his body, the same fear that he had felt as a boy, walking down long corridors to be beaten. He walked firmly up the stairs.

"Oddly enough, he went to sleep at once. He had climbed all day and been awake all night and suffered emotional extremes. Like a condemned man, who was to be hanged in the morning, my father gave the whole business up and went to sleep.

"He was woken at midnight exactly. He heard the American on the terrace below his window, explaining excitedly that there had been a cloud on the last two nights at 11:58, thus making it impossible to photograph the midnight sun. He heard the camera click.

"There seemed to be a sudden storm of hail and wind. It roared at his window-sill, and the window curtains lifted themselves taut, pointing horizontally into the room. The shriek and rattle of the tempest framed the window in a crescendo of growing sound, an increasing blizzard directed towards himself. A blue paw came over the sill.

"My father turned over and hid his head in the pillow. He could feel the domed head dawning at the window and the eyes fixing themselves upon the small of his back. He could feel the places physically, about four inches apart. They itched. Or else the rest of his body itched, except those places. He could feel the creature growing into the room, glowing like ice, and giving off a storm. His mosquito curtains rose in its afflatus, uncovering him, leaving him defenceless. He was in such an ecstasy of terror that he almost enjoyed it. He was like a bather plunging for the first time into freezing water and unable to articulate. He was trying to yell, but all he could do was to throw a series of hooting noises from his paralysed lungs. He became a part of the blizzard. The bedclothes were gone. He felt the Troll put out its hands.

"My father was an agnostic, but, like most idle men, he was not above having a bee in his bonnet. His favourite bee was the psychology of the Catholic Church. He was ready to talk for hours about psycho-analysis and the confession. His greatest discovery had been the rosary.

"The rosary, my father used to say, was intended solely as a factual occupation which calmed the lower centres of the mind. The automatic telling of the beads liberated the higher centres to meditate upon the mysteries. They were a sedative, like knitting or counting sheep. There was no better cure for insomnia than a rosary. For several years he had given up deep breathing or regular counting. When he was sleepless he lay on his back and told his beads, and there was a small rosary in the pocket of his pyjama coat.

"The Troll put out its hands, to take him round the waist. He became completely paralysed, as if he had been winded. The Troll put its hand upon the beads.

"They met, the occult forces, in a clash above my father's heart. There was an explosion, he said, a quick creation of power. Positive and negative. A flash, a beam. Something like the splutter with which the antenna of a tram meets its overhead wires again, when it is being changed about.

"The Troll made a high squealing noise, like a crab being boiled, and began rapidly to dwindle in size. It dropped my father and turned about, and ran wailing, as if it had been terribly burnt, for the window. Its colour waned as its size decreased. It was one of those air-toys now, that expire with a piercing whistle. It scrambled over the window-sill, scarcely larger than a little child, and sagging visibly.

"My father leaped out of bed and followed it to the window. He saw it drop on the terrace like a toad, gather itself together, stumble off, staggering and whistling like a bat, down the valley of the Abiskojokk.

"My father fainted.

"In the morning the manageress said, 'There has been such a terrible tragedy. The poor Dr. Professor was found this morning in the lake. The worry about his wife had certainly unhinged his mind.'

"A subscription for a wreath was started by the American, to which my father subscribed five shillings; and the body was shipped off next morning, on one of the twelve trains that travel between Upsala and Narvik every day."

EVENING AT THE BLACK HOUSE

by Robert Somerlott

His eyes widened and his big hands holding the sherry bottle trembled slightly, causing a brown trickle to run down the side of the goblet.

"Are you certain, Eric?"

"Yes," I said. "I've been around enough to know when something's up."

"Tell me exactly what happened. It may be important."

"It was just getting dark when I left the hotel. I walked along, thinking how good Frieda's sauerbraten was going to taste after eating tortillas and chili most of the week. I didn't pay any attention to the pair when I passed them in the plaza. It was three blocks before I realized they were following me."

Henry Black's hands were under control as he offered me the sherry. He sat quietly in the leather chair opposite me, his face calm, but the pale blue eyes glancing uneasily toward the living room windows with their drawn drapes and barred shutters. He tilted his close-cropped head, as though listening for some unfamiliar sound outside. I heard nothing but a patter of rain and the whining of Inga, the more nervous of his two Doberman pinschers. I pictured the restless dogs prowling between the house and the barb-topped fence that encircled it. Loki, the male, was more powerful. But Inga was tautly alert, tense with suspicion. Months before, during my first evenings at Henry Black's, I had felt like an explorer sitting down with cannibals. Would the dogs lunge for my throat if I reached for a fork? They were completely unused to strangers. In the house, they never left Henry's side. It had taken two months and a dozen visits before they would trust me to walk across the room. Now, patrolling in the yard, they probed the night for a warning scent, a muffled footfall.

"What did these men look like?" Henry asked.

"Like a couple of Mexican drunks," I said. "When I realized they were following me, I figured they were out to sandbag and roll an American tourist. Then I felt—I don't know—they just didn't *walk* like Mexicans. I suppose that's ridiculous, but—"

"No, Eric, it's not!" His sudden excitement carried him to his feet. "Every race, every nationality moves differently. Like breeds of dogs—each has its own gait. Some people would never notice the difference, but you and I would."

"Anyway," I said, "there was something odd about them. I decided if I was going to have trouble, I'd better have it in the village instead of on this deserted country road. So I stopped and waited. They didn't pass me, but turned into one of those courtyards. I would have forgotten the whole thing if I hadn't seen them later near your gate."

"What were they doing?"

"This black car was parked in the road and they were talking to the driver. They watched me for a minute, and when they saw me turn toward your gate, they got in the car. They took off down the road heading away from town. Oh, yes, the car had an American license."

Henry slammed his hard fist into his palm. "Took off for where? That road leads to a couple of adobe huts and a pig farm three miles away. You should have told me at once, Eric."

I chuckled, trying to ease the tension in the room. "Did you want me to ruin Frieda's dinner with a story about being watched by mysterious strangers? Besides, nothing happened. They just looked peculiar, and I can't figure out how they got here ahead of me without my seeing them on the road. Oh, hell, I think they just wanted to grab a few American dollars and changed their minds."

"Perhaps. Perhaps."

Frieda entered so suddenly that I had a feeling she had been standing just outside the dining room archway, listening.

"Nutses," she announced, displaying a carved wooden tray. "*Und* cheeses."

"*And* cheeses," Henry corrected.

"*Ja.*" Frieda's round face had a dumpling-fed smile, but there was a strained look around her eyes. Her plump fingers, weighted by gold rings, were fidgety as she set the tray on the coffee table. The dishes brimmed with after-dinner tidbits.

"When I break down and get married—Lord help me
—it's going to be a German girl like Frieda."

"*Ja*," she smiled, "but a younger."

"She's a good wife," said Henry. A long look passed
between them, a half smile of devotion and appreciation—
but at the same time there was sadness.

"You have been a good husband," she said. Every syl-
lable carried a weight of doom, making her words sound
like a good-bye whispered beside a new grave. Henry
patted her hand, his fingers touching the beautiful gold
bracelet she wore proudly. Frieda was so plain, so house-
wifely, that her fascination with gold ornaments seemed
like a child's. She delighted equally in the really lovely
bracelet and the cheap, gypsy hoops that dragged at the
lobes of her pierced ears.

Outside, Inga barked sharply. Henry crossed the room
in three strides. Jerking back the drapes, he flung open the
window and pressed his face against the shutter slats. He
was well past fifty, but he moved like a tiger, power and
balance in every step.

"What is it?" I asked.

His tense body slowly relaxed. "Nothing. I heard Inga
bark."

"I'll go out to take a look around."

Before I could take a step toward the door, he stopped
me with a snapped military command. "No, Eric!"

I faced him. "Look, Henry, all evening you've acted like
you expected a bomb to come through the window. It
started long before I mentioned being followed. At dinner you were jumpy as a cat. It's not like you. Now you
think something's outside. Well, I'm going to find out."

"Go ahead. It's better to know."

At the door, the dogs raced to me. "Good boy, Loki,"
I said, petting him. I did not touch Inga. Together, we
slowly circled the house.

The place was a fortress, or perhaps more like a concen-
tration camp, with the high wire fence and cleared strip
between it and the surrounding jungle. The fence, power-
fully electrified, claimed a daily toll of birds which perched
on its deadly strands. Even in this remote part of Mexico,
where the rich always topped their walls with jagged
glass and kept guard dogs, such precautions as Henry
Black had taken were extraordinary.

I had met Henry five months before, shortly after my

arrival in the village of San Xavier. He was an arresting figure, striding through the plaza with Inga at his side and Hugo, the square-faced valet, at his heels. For a second, he paused to glance at the painting I was struggling with. Nodding curtly to me, he moved on, his back as military as the revolver holstered at his side.

During the next two weeks he passed me every morning on his way to and from the post office, never speaking, but always glancing curiously. Finally, his fascination with painting and his love of the flowers that were my constantly repeated subject overcame his aloofness.

After the first brief conversation our friendship developed rapidly, since he was an amateur painter himself. We played chess together; we were evenly matched. Our similar backgrounds overcame the twenty-year difference in our ages. I had seen a lot of the world during my thirty years. Henry and I had both fought in wars, knew odd countries and remembered certain twisting streets in Singapore or Barcelona.

"What a relief to talk to an intelligent man again!" he said. "How did you happen to come to this hellhole?"

"No accident," I said. "I'd made inquiries from friends and connections in Mexico for three years before I decided on this town. For me, it's ideal."

I did not question him about his reasons for choosing San Xavier as a retirement spot. Something about Henry warded off inquiry.

A week later, I met Frieda. "I found her in Germany," he said, "when I was on a military mission. Eric, you should have seen her thirty years ago!"

Henry was always on guard. But his watchfulness had increased during the last six weeks. I became aware of new shadows under his eyes, a tension in his manner. He took to glancing over his shoulder in the street. I realized one day that he was deliberately varying his arrival time at the post office.

Now, as the dogs and I turned the fourth corner of the house and were once again in the front yard, I felt that he was close to a breaking point. Through the shutter slits I could see him watching me, straining to see into the night.

Reaching the window, I stopped suddenly, my shoulders stiffening. Loki barked as my hand touched him. The dogs, sensing an uneasiness in me, growled viciously, sniffing as near the fence as they dared go.

I returned quickly to the house.

"What was it?" Henry asked.

"Nothing."

"No, Eric! You saw something. I watched through the shutter. You were startled by something in the jungle."

"Just a light," I said. "It came on twice, then vanished. For a moment I thought it was some kind of signal, but probably it was just some Mexican carrying an open lantern that the rain put out. It's plenty wet out there."

Henry looked doubtful. I felt uncomfortable as he stared at me without speaking.

"What is this?" I asked, taking off my dampened coat. "Why did Hugo come this morning and ask me to come here tonight instead of Friday as usual? It's not like you to change plans suddenly."

He continued to stare at me, inner conflict apparent on his face.

"I'm your friend," I told him. "You and Frieda have meant a lot to me in the past months. Sometime I hope I can show you how much. If you need help, I'm here, and I'm not easy to scare. But I have to know what it's all about."

"Sit down, Eric." He took a long time lighting cigarettes for himself and me. "I once swore I'd never speak to a living soul. But now I need help. I have to protect Frieda no matter what the risk is." His eyes were intent on my face, boring into me. "Eric, will you swear before God that no matter what I tell you—no matter what you think of me afterward—you'll guard her for twenty-four hours, if I'm not around to do it?"

I hesitated, then made up my mind. "Of course I will. You knew I would before you asked."

"You swear?"

"Yes," I said. "But with a condition. Whatever you tell me, make it the truth. Otherwise, don't count on me."

"Always a chess player," he said. "I agree. It is an oath between friends. First, you tell me some things. How much have you figured out about me?"

"All right," I said. "Don't blame me if I'm wrong. To start with, you're not really an American. Your accent's almost perfect, but wrong in little ways. Then there's the way you sit at the dinner table, the way you reach out when you move a chess piece. Right so far?"

"Exactly," he said. "You're sharp, and I think there's a

ruthless streak in you. Perhaps that's why I trust you."

"I know you're hiding from something," I continued. "This house is ready for a siege. Yet you're not a crook and I don't think you've ever been one."

Frieda was in the archway. "Come in, *Liebchen*," he said. She knelt beside his chair. "You're correct on all counts, Eric. Now, it's my turn to speak."

"*Nein, nein,*" came Frieda's terrified whisper. "No one—"

"We must have help, Frieda." It was the curt tone he used when speaking to Inga. Frieda stifled a sob and was silent.

"My name is Heinrich Schwartz," he said. "I am in Mexico illegally, passing myself off as a retired American, which is not difficult for me. As a child I lived for eight years in the town of Milwaukee. Later I had training in 'American' at a German military establishment."

Outside, the rain increased. I could hear the wind begin to rise as Black left his chair, moving slowly across the room, twisting his hands together.

"I was a major in the German Army. Young for the assignments they gave me, but I come from an important family. We were not Nazis! No matter what they say, we were not! True, we had Party connections. Frieda had important contacts. Who didn't have? But I was an Army man, decorated three times, once in Poland, twice in Africa."

Hugo entered, carrying a wooden box that I took to be a gun chest. Henry did not seem to notice him.

"I went to the school in Bavaria where we learned to impersonate Americans, to create disorder, to sabotage. Then a shrapnel wound from Africa began to cripple me again. They took me from active duty and put me in charge of a transport depot near the Belgian border. Hugo was my orderly then. He still is." The valet bowed his head dumbly.

"Part of my job was transportation of Jew fugitives caught in Holland, but it was a small part of my work. Just providing guards, clearing facilities for removal to the interior. There weren't many of them. Less than a hundred a week. It was a nuisance, but I never paid much attention. Dull, routine work. But at least Frieda could be with me there.

"Then everything started to collapse. I had fourteen

prisoners on my hands and the Americans were almost upon us. There was no more transport." His fist crashed down on the coffee table. "What was I to do? Turn the prisoners loose to sabotage what was left of our Army?" His voice rose to a shout. *"I had orders!* I was a soldier. Hugo and I carried them out." His eyes wandered to the windows. "It was raining that night," he said. "Just like this."

I tried to see the pictures that were before the eyes of my three companions. Did they see a pitiful procession of captives, starved faces hardly more than skin-covered skulls? I pictured Hugo and Henry standing near a stalled boxcar, waiting for the final line to be formed. Was Frieda, in her mind, now hearing methodical, evenly spaced Luger shots? The last whimpers of the victims? No, she was listening for a nearer danger. Something outside in the night.

"Later they tried me at Nuremberg," Henry said dully. "They proved nothing. There was a rumor that two children with that group had escaped. So they kept me in jail for months while they searched for imaginary witnesses. They failed. They even dragged poor Frieda into it, accusing her of being a ghoul who robbed the dead bodies. *Mein Gott!* Horrible! They proved nothing, but I spent five years in Landsberg prison.

"The week after they released me, we fled here. We knew as long as we could be found, vengeance would follow. At last, they have caught up with us. Look." Reaching into his pocket, he drew out an envelope with a Mexico City postmark.

Inside was a page from a desk calendar, bearing today's date. The drawing on it was crude, almost childish. Three bodies, one in a skirt, dangled grotesquely from a tree. *Tonight, Major* was scribbled across the bottom in German.

"Other things came before," he said. "Starting six weeks ago. First a package with a gold bracelet—like the one Frieda wears. The devils had wrapped a rubber snake around it. That time the note said, *Soon, Major, but not too soon.*"

Frieda's breathing was harsh, rapid. "Then the toy gun," she cried. "With red paint—like on it was blood. Another time a book it was."

"Yes," said Henry. "A book about Adolf Eichmann. They wrote, *You will join him this month,* on the inside."

I looked at the three of them on the opposite side of the room. "That's why you asked me here tonight," I said. "You think they won't strike if there's a stranger in the house."

"I don't know, Eric," he said. "They won't harm you. You're an American, and it would cause trouble for them. They're careful. Read the Eichmann story!" A deep frown crossed his face. "Yet this isn't like it was with Eichmann. These warnings that have come to torture us. It's personal somehow. Fiendish!" Henry put his hand on my shoulder. "Hugo and I can take care of ourselves. We've got guns and plenty of ammunition. But I've got to get Frieda to Mexico City. You swore you'd do it."

I couldn't look into his eyes. "I promised," I said. "I'll do it. Whatever you've done, it isn't her fault. And if things get rough here tonight, I'll help you. No matter what I think of your story, I won't stand by while you're shot by some cowards out there in the dark."

"Thank you, Eric." His voice almost broke. Frieda came to my side. Standing on tiptoe, she kissed my cheek.

As the wind drove rain against the shutters, there was a *rata-tat-tat* outside. Inga, Loki barked wildly. *Rata-tat*. The noise was high-pitched, metallic. We seized guns from the box that Hugo opened. I checked the Luger in my hand, finding it ready for action.

"Frieda!" She came to attention at Henry's command. "The lights. *Aus.*"

Moving militarily, trained by long drill, Frieda took her assigned place at the light switches. She reversed the first two, plunging the house into darkness but lighting up the yard as much as was possible in the driving rain. *Rata-tat!* It seemed closer. "Stay by the door," I told Henry. "Hugo and I'll go out back and circle around through the cane."

"Ja." The terror in the brief word told me that Henry was trembling in the darkness. We slipped through the kitchen door, Hugo reaching to the left to switch off the current to the back gate. The dogs found us instantly, but Hugo silenced them with a soft command. As a gust of wind bearing a sheet of water struck our faces, we heard the metallic noise again.

The blinding rain and tangled jungle of cane shoots and banana palms battled against us as we tried to move carefully over concealed roots and fallen branches. At this season in San Xavier, a windborne storm came almost every night at the same hour. Obviously this was part of the plan —to strike during the worst of it. Nothing had been left to chance.

Fifty yards from the house we found the source of the noise—a simple device attached to a tree trunk operated by the wind like a schoolboy's tick-tack, a wooden beater striking a metal pan. Cursing, Hugo ripped it from the tree. "A trick," I said, "to get us to this side. Get back fast." We started for the house, even more cautious now, neither of us knowing exactly what lay ahead.

We were almost to the rear gate when Hugo seemed to sense something. He halted abruptly. I suddenly realized what he saw. "Hugo!" I yelled as he threw himself to the ground—too late. A shot rang out in the darkness. There was no cry from the dead valet.

Crouching low, I raced through the gate, pushing aside the yelping dogs, now roused to frenzy by the gunshot. For a terrible second I thought Inga would attack me in her confusion, but she let me pass.

Slamming open the kitchen door, I stumbled through the dark interior. "Henry!" I yelled. "They got Hugo. He's dead."

"*Mein Gott!* Where are they now? How many?"

"Coming round front, I think. I couldn't tell how many. Maybe three. Maybe four."

In the streaked light between the shutter slats, I saw Frieda still at her post near the switches. Henry's revolver dangled at his side as he peered into the yard. With one swift movement, I knocked it from his hand and shoved Frieda aside. Light flooded the room.

"There's only one, Major," I said. "And he's not out there. He's here. It was stupid of you to let those two children escape."

The terror on their faces was all I had dreamed it would be. It was worth waiting for through all those years, then through the last months when, finally, I had found them. I stood quietly a moment, enjoying it, letting every detail stamp itself on my memory. I would have to recall every expression, every pleading look for my sister who was waiting in Mexico City.

"It's raining tonight, Major," I said in German. "Just as it was then."

I killed Frieda first, so he would be alive to see it happen. Then I shot Heinrich through the head as he lunged for the revolver on the floor. The few minor things I had to do in the house—planting the death gun on Heinrich, removing the other guns and disposing of my sherry glass—did not take much time. Besides, no one would miss the trio for a couple of days. By then, my sister and I would be happily back in New York.

Before leaving, I took the gold bracelet from Frieda's wrist. On the back I found my mother's initials—as I knew I would. I remembered the bracelet so clearly. It had been the last of our wealth and we had thought someday we might barter it for our lives. I remember how, as I lay in the mud pretending death, Frieda had ripped it from its hiding place on my mother's wet, lifeless body.

The time I took doing these things gave the dogs a chance to quiet down. Their greeting was almost friendly as I went toward the gate.

"*Shalom,* Loki," I said. "*Shalom,* Inga."

ONE OF THE DEAD

by William Wood

We couldn't have been more pleased. Deep in Clay Canyon we came upon the lot abruptly at a turn in the winding road. There was a crudely lettered board nailed to a dead tree which read, LOT FOR SALE—$1500 OR BEST OFFER, and a phone number.

"Fifteen hundred dollars—in Clay Canyon? I can't believe it," Ellen said.

"Or best offer," I corrected.

"I've heard you can't take a step without bumping into some movie person here."

"We've come three miles already without bumping into one. I haven't seen a soul."

"But there are the houses." Ellen looked about breathlessly.

There indeed were the houses—to our left and our right, to our front and our rear—low, ranch-style houses, unostentatious, prosaic, giving no hint of the gay and improbable lives we imagined went on inside them. But as the houses marched up the gradually climbing road there was not a single person to be seen. The cars—the Jaguars and Mercedeses and Cadillacs and Chryslers—were parked unattended in the driveways, their chrome gleaming in the sun; I caught a glimpse of one corner of a pool and a white diving board, but no one swam in the turquoise water. We climbed out of the car, Ellen with her rather large, short-haired head stooped forward as if under a weight. Except for the fiddling of a cicada somewhere on the hill, a profound hush lay over us in the stifling air. Not even a bird moved in the motionless trees.

"There must be something wrong with it," Ellen said.

"It's probably already been sold, and they just didn't bother to take down the sign. . . . There was something here once, though." I had come across several ragged chunks of concrete that lay about randomly as if heaved out of the earth.

"A house, do you think?"

"It's hard to say. If it was a house it's been gone for years."

"Oh, Ted," Ellen cried. "It's perfect! Look at the view!" She pointed up the canyon toward the round, parched hills. Through the heat shimmering on the road they appeared to be melting down like wax.

"Another good thing," I said. "There won't be much to do to get the ground ready except for clearing the brush away. This place has been graded once. We save a thousand dollars right there."

Ellen took both my hands. Her eyes shone in her solemn face. "What do you think, Ted? What do you think?"

Ellen and I had been married four years, having both taken the step relatively late—in our early thirties—and in that time had lived in two different places, first an apartment in Santa Monica, then, when I was promoted to office manager, in a partly furnished house in the Hollywood Hills, always with the idea that when our first child came we would either buy or build a larger house of our own. But the child had not come. It was a source of anxiety and sadness to us both and lay between us like an old scandal for which each of us took on the blame.

Then I made an unexpected killing on the stock market and Ellen suddenly began agitating in her gentle way for the house. As we shopped around she dropped hints along the way—"This place is really too small for us, don't you think?" or "We'd have to fence off the yard of course"— that let me know that the house had become a talisman for her; she had conceived the notion that perhaps, in some occult way, if we went ahead with our accommodations for a child the child might come. The notion gave her happiness. Her face filled out, the gray circles under her eyes disappeared, the quiet gaiety, which did not seem like gaiety at all but a form of peace, returned.

As Ellen held on to my hands, I hesitated. I am convinced now that there was something behind my hesitation —something I felt then only as a quality of silence, a fleeting twinge of utter desolation. "It's so safe," she said. "There's no traffic at all."

I explained that. "It's not a through street. It ends somewhere up in the hills."

She turned back to me again with her bright, questioning eyes. The happiness that had grown in her during our months of house-hunting seemed to have welled into near rapture.

"We'll call the number," I said, "but don't expect too much. It must have been sold long ago."

We walked slowly back to the car. The door handle burned to the touch. Down the canyon the rear end of a panel truck disappeared noiselessly around a bend.

"No," Ellen said, "I have a feeling about this place. I think it was meant to be ours."

And she was right, of course.

Mr. Carswell Deeves, who owned the land, was called upon to do very little except take my check for $1500 and hand over the deed to us, for by the time Ellen and I met him we had already sold ourselves. Mr. Deeves, as we had suspected from the unprofessional sign, was a private citizen. We found his house in a predominantly Mexican section of Santa Monica. He was a chubby, pink man of indeterminate age dressed in white ducks and soft white shoes, as if he had had a tennis court hidden away among the squalid, asphalt-shingled houses and dry kitchen gardens of his neighbors.

"Going to live in Clay Canyon, are you?" he said. "Ros Russell lives up there, or used to." So, we discovered, did Joel McCrea, Jimmy Stewart and Paula Raymond, as well as a cross-section of producers, directors and character actors. "Oh, yes," said Mr. Deeves, "it's an address that will look extremely good on your stationery."

Ellen beamed and squeezed my hand.

Mr. Deeves turned out to know very little about the land other than that a house had been destroyed by fire there years ago and that the land had changed hands many times since. "I myself acquired it in what may strike you as a novel way," he said as we sat in his parlor—a dark, airless box which smelled faintly of camphor and whose walls were obscured with yellowing autographed photographs of movie stars. "I won it in a game of hearts from a makeup man on the set of *Quo Vadis*. Perhaps you remember me. I had a close-up in one of the crowd scenes."

"That was a number of years ago, Mr. Deeves," I said. "Have you been trying to sell it all this time?"

"I've nearly sold it dozens of times," he said, "but something always went wrong somehow."

"What kind of things?"

"Naturally, the fire-insurance rates up there put off a lot of people. I hope you're prepared to pay a high premium——"

"I've already checked into that."

"Good. You'd be surprised how many people will let details like that go till the last minute."

"What other things have gone wrong?"

Ellen touched my arm to discourage my wasting any more time with foolish questions.

Mr. Deeves spread out the deed before me and smoothed it with his forearm. "Silly things, some of them. One couple found some dead doves. . . ."

"Dead doves?" I handed him the signed article. With one pink hand Mr. Deeves waved it back and forth to dry the ink. "Five of them, if I remember correctly. In my opinion they'd sat on a wire and were electrocuted somehow. The husband thought nothing of it, of course, but his wife became so hysterical that we had to call off the transaction."

I made a sign at Mr. Deeves to drop this line of conversation. Ellen loves animals and birds of all kinds with a devotion that turns the loss of a household pet into a major tragedy, which is why, since the death of our cocker spaniel, we have had no more pets. But Ellen appeared not to have heard; she was watching the paper in Mr. Deeve's hand fixedly, as if she were afraid it might vanish.

Mr. Deeves sprang suddenly to his feet. "Well!" he cried. "It's all yours now. I know you'll be happy there."

Ellen flushed with pleasure. "I'm sure we will," she said, and took his pudgy hand in both of hers.

"A prestige address," called Mr. Deeves from his porch as we drove away. "A real prestige address."

Ellen and I are modern people. Our talk in the evenings is generally on issues of the modern world. Ellen paints a little and I do some writing from time to time—mostly on technical subjects. The house that Ellen and I built mirrored our concern with present-day aesthetics. We worked closely with Jack Salmanson, the architect and a friend, who designed a steel module house, low and compact and private, which could be fitted into the irregularities of our patch of land for a maximum of space. The interior *décor* we left largely up to Ellen, who combed the home magazines and made sketches as if she were decorating a dozen homes.

I mention these things to show that there is nothing Gothic about my wife and me: We are as thankful for our common sense as for our sensibilities, and we flattered ourselves that the house we built achieved a balance between the aesthetic and the functional. Its lines were simple and clean; there were no dark corners, and it was surrounded on three sides by houses, none of which were more than eight years old.

There were, however, signs from the very beginning, ominous signs which can be read only in retrospect, though it seems to me now that there were others who suspected but said nothing. One was the Mexican who cut down the tree.

As a money-saving favor to us, Jack Salmanson agreed to supervise the building himself and hire small, independent contractors to do the labor, many of whom were Mexicans or Negroes with dilapidated equipment that appeared to run only by some mechanical miracle. The Mexican, a small, forlorn workman with a stringy moustache, had already burned out two chain-saw blades and still had not cut halfway through the tree. It was inexplicable. The tree, the same one on which Ellen and I had seen the original For Sale sign, had obviously been dead for years, and the branches that already lay scattered on the ground were rotted through.

"You must have run into a batch of knots," Jack said. "Try it again. If the saw gets too hot, quit and we'll pull it down with the bulldozer." As if answering to its name, the bulldozer turned at the back of the lot and lumbered toward us in a cloud of dust, the black shoulders of the Negro operator gleaming in the sun.

The Mexican need not have feared for his saw. He had scarcely touched it to the tree when it started to topple of its own accord. Startled, he backed away a few steps. The tree had begun to fall toward the back of the lot, in the direction of his cut, but now it appeared to arrest itself, its naked branches trembling as if in agitation; then with an awful rending sound it writhed upright and fell back on itself, gaining momentum and plunging directly at the bulldozer. My voice died in my throat, but Jack and the Mexican shouted, and the operator jumped and rolled on the ground just as the tree fell high on the hood, sh tter-ing the windshield to bits. The bulldozer, out of control and knocked off course, came directly at us, gears whin-ing and gouging a deep trough in the earth. Jack and I jumped one way, the Mexican the other; the bulldozer lurched between us and ground on toward the street, the Negro sprinting after it.

"The car!" Jack shouted. "The car!"

Parked in front of the house across the street was a car, a car which was certainly brand-new. The bulldozer headed straight for it, its blade striking clusters of sparks from the pavement. The Mexican waved his chain saw over his head like a toy and shouted in Spanish. I cov-ered my eyes with my hands and heard Jack grunt softly, as if he had been struck in the mid-section, just before the crash.

Two woman stood on the porch of the house across the street and gaped. The car had caved in at the center, its steel roof wrinkled like tissue paper; its front and rear ends were folded around the bulldozer as if embracing it. Then, with a low whoosh, both vehicles were enveloped in creeping blue flame.

"Rotten luck," Jack muttered under his breath as we ran into the street. From the corner of my eye I caught the curious sight of the Mexican on the ground, praying, his chain saw lying by his knees.

In the evening Ellen and I paid a visit to the Sheffits', Sondra and Jeff, our neighbors across the canyon road, where we met the owner of the ruined car, Joyce Castle, a striking blonde in lemon-colored pants. The shock of the accident itself wore off with the passing of time and cock-tails, and the three of them treated it as a tremendous joke.

Mrs. Castle was particularly hilarious. "I'm doing bet-ter," she rejoiced. "The Alfa-Romeo only lasted two days, but I held on to this one a whole six weeks. I even had the permanent plates on."

"But you mustn't be without a car, Mrs. Castle," Ellen said in her serious way. "We'd be glad to loan you our Plymouth until you can—"

"I'm having a new car delivered tomorrow afternoon. Don't worry about me. A Daimler, Jeff, you'll be inter-ested to know. I couldn't resist after riding in yours. What about the poor bulldozer man? Is he absolutely wiped out?"

"I think he'll survive," I said. "In any case he has two other 'dozers."

"Then you won't be held up," Jeff said.

"I wouldn't think so."

Sondra chuckled softly. "I just happened to look out the window," she said. "It was just like a Rube Goldberg cartoon. A chain reaction."

"And there was my poor old Cadillac at the end of it," Mrs. Castle sighed.

Suey, Mrs. Castle's dog, who had been lying on the floor beside his mistress glaring dourly at us between dozes, suddenly ran to the front door barking ferociously, his red mane standing straight up.

"Suey!" Mrs. Castle slapped her knee. "Suey! Come here!"

The dog merely flattened its ears and looked from his mistress toward the door again as if measuring a decision. He growled deep in his throat.

"It's the ghost," Sondra said lightly. "He's behind the whole thing." Sondra sat curled up in one corner of the sofa and tilted her head to one side as she spoke, like a very clever child.

Jeff laughed sharply. "Oh, they tell some very good stories."

With a sigh Mrs. Castle rose and dragged Suey back by his collar. "If I didn't feel so self-conscious about it I'd take him to an analyst," she said. "Sit, Suey! Here's a cashew nut for you."

"I'm very fond of ghost stories," I said, smiling.

"Oh, well," Jeff murmured, mildly disparaging.

"Go ahead, Jeff," Sondra urged him over the rim of her glass. "They'd like to hear it."

Jeff was a literary agent, a tall, sallow man with dark oily hair that he was continually pushing out of his eyes with his fingers. As he spoke he smiled lopsidedly as if defending against the probability of being taken seriously. "All I know is that back in the late seventeenth century the Spanish used to have hangings here. The victims are supposed to float around at night and make noises."

"Criminals?" I asked.

"Of the worst sort," said Sondra. "What was the story Guy Relling told you, Joyce?" She smiled with a curious inward relish that suggested she knew the story perfectly well herself.

"Is that Guy Relling, the director?" I asked.

"Yes," Jeff said. "He owns those stables down the canyon."

"I've seen them," Ellen said. "Such lovely horses."

Joyce Castle hoisted her empty glass into the air. "Jeff, love, will you find me another?"

"We keep straying from the subject," said Sondra gently. "Fetch me another too, darling"—she handed her glass to Jeff as he went by—"like a good boy. . . . I didn't mean to interrupt, Joyce. Go on." She gestured toward us as the intended audience. Ellen stiffened slightly in her chair.

"It seems that there was one *hombre* of outstanding depravity," Joyce Castle said languidly. "I forgot the name. He murdered, stole, raped . . . one of those endless Spanish names with a 'Luis' in it, a nobleman I think Guy said. A charming sort. Mad, of course, and completely unpredictable. They hanged him at last for some unsavory escapade in a nunnery. You two are moving into a neighborhood rich with tradition."

We all laughed.

"What about the noises?" Ellen asked Sondra. "Have you heard anything?"

"Of course," Sondra said, tipping her head prettily. Every inch of her skin was tanned to the color of coffee from afternoons by the pool. It was a form of leisure that her husband, with his bilious coloring and lank hair, apparently did not enjoy.

"Everywhere I've ever lived," he said, his grin growing crookeder and more apologetic, "there were noises in the night that you couldn't explain. Here there are all kinds of wildlife—foxes, coons, possums—even coyotes up on the ridge. They're all active after sundown."

Ellen's smile of pleasure at this news turned to distress as Sondra remarked in her offhand way, "We found our poor kitty-cat positively torn to pieces one morning. He was all blood. We never did find his head."

"A fox," Jeff put in quickly. Everything he said seemed hollow. Something came from him like a vapor. I thought it was grief.

Sondra gazed smugly into her lap as if hugging a secret to herself. She seemed enormously pleased. It occurred to me that Sondra was trying to frighten us. In a way it relieved me. She was enjoying herself too much, I thought, looking at her spoiled, brown face, to be frightened herself.

After the incident of the tree everything went well for some weeks. The house went up rapidly. Ellen and I visited it as often as we could, walking over the raw ground and making our home in our mind's eye. The fireplace would go here, the refrigerator here, our Picasso print there. "Ted," Ellen said timidly, "I've been thinking. Why don't we fix up the extra bedroom as a children's room?"

I waited.

"Now that we'll be living out here our friends will have to stay overnight more often. Most of them have young children. It would be nice for them."

I slipped my arm around her shoulders. She knew I understood. It was a delicate matter. She raised her face and I kissed her between her brows. Signal and countersignal, the keystones of our life together—a life of sensibility and tact.

"Hey, you two!" Sondra Sheffits called from across the street. She stood on her front porch in a pink bathing suit, her skin brown, her hair nearly white. "How about a swim?"

"No suits!"

"Come on, we've got plenty."

Ellen and I debated the question with a glance, settled it with a nod.

As I came out onto the patio in one of Jeff's suits, Sondra said, "Ted, you're pale as a ghost. Don't you get any sun where you are?" She lay in a chaise longue behind huge elliptical sunglasses encrusted with glass gems.

"I stay inside too much, writing articles," I said.

"You're welcome to come here any time you like"—she smiled suddenly, showing me a row of small, perfect teeth—"and swim."

Ellen appeared in her borrowed suit, a red one with a short, limp ruffle. She shaded her eyes as the sun, glittering metallically on the water, struck her full in the face.

Sondra ushered her forward as if to introduce my wife to me. "You look much better in that suit than I ever did." Her red nails flashed on Ellen's arm. Ellen smiled guardedly. The two women were about the same height, but Ellen was narrower in the shoulders, thicker through the waist and hips. As they came toward me it seemed to me that Ellen was the one I did not know. Her familiar body became strange. It looked out of proportion. Hairs that on Sondra were all but invisible except when the sun turned them to silver, lay flat and dark on Ellen's pallid arm.

As if sensing the sudden distance between us, Ellen took my hand. "Let's jump in together," she said gaily. "No hanging back."

Sondra retreated to the chaise longue to watch us, her eyes invisible behind her outrageous glasses, her head on one side.

Incidents began again and continued at intervals. Guy Relling, whom I never met but whose pronouncements on the supernatural reached me through others from time to time like messages from an oracle, claims that the existence of the living dead is a particularly excruciating one as they hover between two states of being. Their memories keep the passions of life forever fresh and sharp, but they are able to relieve them only at a monstrous expense of will and energy which leaves them literally helpless for months or sometimes even years afterward. This was why materializations and other forms of tangible action are relatively rare. There are of course exceptions, Sondra, our most frequent translator of Relling's theories, pointed out one evening with the odd joy that accompanied all of her remarks on the subject; some ghosts are terrifically active—particularly the insane ones who, ignorant of the limitations of death as they were of the impossibilities of life, transcend them with the dynamism that is exclusively the property of madness. Generally, however, it was Relling's opinion that a ghost was more to be pitied than feared. Sondra quoted him as having said, "The notion of a haunted house is a misconception semantically. It is not the house but the soul itself that is haunted."

On Saturday, August 6, a workman laying pipe was blinded in one eye by an acetylene torch.

On Thursday, September 1, a rockslide on the hill behind us dumped four tons of dirt and rock on the half-finished house and halted work for two weeks.

On Sunday, October 9—my birthday, oddly enough—while visiting the house alone, I slipped on a stray screw and struck my head on a can of latex paint which opened up a gash requiring ten stitches. I rushed across to the

Sheffits'. Sondra answered the door in her bathing suit and a magazine in her hand. "Ted?" She peered at me. "I scarcely recognized you through the blood. Come in, I'll call the doctor. Try not to drip on the furniture, will you?"

I told the doctor of the screw on the floor, the big can of paint. I did not tell him that my foot had slipped because I had turned too quickly and that I had turned too quickly because the sensation had grown on me that there was someone behind me, close enough to touch me, perhaps, because something hovered there, fetid and damp and cold and almost palpable in its nearness; I remember shivering violently as I turned, as if the sun of this burning summer's day had been replaced by a mysterious star without warmth. I did not tell the doctor this nor anyone else.

In November Los Angeles burns. After the long drought of summer the sap goes underground and the baked hills seem to gasp in pain for the merciful release of either life or death—rain or fire. Invariably fire comes first, spreading through the outlying parts of the country like an epidemic, till the sky is livid and starless at night and overhung with dun-colored smoke during the day.

There was a huge fire in Tujunga, north of us, the day Ellen and I moved into our new house—handsome, severe, aggressively new on its dry hillside—under a choked sky the color of earth and a muffled, flyspeck sun. Sondra and Jeff came over to help, and in the evening Joyce Castle stopped by with Suey and a magnum of champagne.

Ellen clasped her hands under her chin. "What a lovely surprise!"

"I hope it's cold enough. I've had it in my refrigerator since four o'clock. Welcome to the canyon. You're nice people. You remind me of my parents. God, it's hot. I've been weeping all day on account of the smoke. You'll have air conditioning I suppose?"

Jeff was sprawled in a chair with his long legs straight in front of him in the way a cripple might put aside a pair of crutches. "Joyce, you're an angel. Excuse me if I don't get up. I'm recuperating."

"You're excused, doll, you're excused."

"Ted." Ellen said softly. "Why don't you get some glasses?"

Jeff hauled in his legs. "Can I give you a hand?"

"Sit still, Jeff."

He sighed. "I hadn't realized I was so out of shape." He looked more cadaverous than ever after our afternoon of lifting and shoving. Sweat had collected in the hollows under his eyes.

"Shall I show you in the house, Joyce? While Ted is in the kitchen?"

"I love you, Ellen," Joyce said. "Take me on the whole tour."

Sondra followed me into the kitchen. She leaned against the wall and smoked, supporting her left elbow in the palm of her right hand. She didn't say a word. Through the open door I could see Jeff's outstretched legs from the calves down.

"Thanks for all the help today," I said to Sondra in a voice unaccountably close to a whisper. I could hear Joyce and Ellen as they moved from room to room, their voices swelling and dying: "It's all steel? You mean everything? Walls and all? Aren't you afraid of lightning?"

"Oh, we're all safely grounded, I think."

Jeff yawned noisily in the living room. Wordlessly Sondra put a tray on the kitchen table as I rummaged in an unpacked carton for the glasses. She watched me steadily and coolly, as if she expected me to entertain her. I wanted to say something further to break a silence which was becoming unnatural and oppressive. The sounds around us seemed only to isolate us in a ring of intimacy. With her head on one side Sondra smiled at me. I could hear her rapid breathing.

"What's this, a nursery? Ellen, love!"

"No, no! It's only for our friends' children."

Sondra's eyes were blue, the color of shallow water. She seemed faintly amused, as if we were sharing in a conspiracy—a conspiracy I was anxious to repudiate by making some prosaic remark in a loud voice for all to hear, but a kind of pain developed in my chest as the words seemed dammed there, and I only smiled at her foolishly. With every passing minute of silence, the more impossible it became to break through and the more I felt drawn in to the intrigue of which, though I was ignorant, I was surely guilty. Without so much as a touch she had made us lovers.

Ellen stood in the doorway, half turned away as if her first impulse had been to run. She appeared to be deep in thought, her eyes fixed on the steel, cream-colored door-jamb.

Sondra began to talk to Ellen in her dry, satirical voice. It was chatter of the idlest sort, but she was destroying, as I had wished to destroy, the absurd notion that there was something between us. I could see Ellen's confusion. She hung on Sondra's words, watching her lips attentively, as if this elegant, tanned woman, calmly smoking and talking of trifles, were her savior.

As for myself, I felt as if I had lost the power of speech entirely. If I joined in with Sondra's carefully innocent chatter I would only be joining in the deception against my wife; if I proclaimed the truth and ended everything by bringing it into the open. . . . but what truth? What was there in fact to bring into the open? What was there to end? A feeling in the air? An intimation? The answer was nothing, of course. I did not even like Sondra very much. There was something cold and unpleasant about her. There was nothing to proclaim because nothing had happened. "Where's Joyce?" I asked finally, out of a dry mouth. "Doesn't she want to see the kitchen?"

Ellen turned slowly toward me, as if it cost her a great effort. "She'll be here in a minute," she said tonelessly, and I became aware of Joyce's and Jeff's voices from the living room. Ellen studied my face, her pupils oddly dilated under the pinkish fluorescent light, as if she were trying to penetrate to the bottom of a great darkness that lay beneath my chance remark. Was it a code of some kind, a new signal for her that I would shortly make clear? What did it mean? I smiled at her and she responded with a smile of her own, a tentative and formal upturning of her mouth, as if I were a familiar face whose name escaped her for the moment.

Joyce came in behind Ellen. "I hate kitchens. I never go into mine." She looked from one to the other of us. "Am I interrupting something?"

At two o'clock in the morning I sat up in bed, wide awake. The bedroom was bathed in the dark red glow of the fire which had come closer in the night. A thin, autumnal veil of smoke hung in the room. Ellen lay on her side, asleep, one hand cupped on the pillow next to her face as if waiting for something to be put in it. I had no idea why I was so fully awake, but I threw off the covers and went to the window to check on the fire. I could see no flame, but the hills stood out blackly against a turgid sky that belled and sagged as the wind blew and relented.

Then I heard the sound.

I am a person who sets store by precision in the use of words—in the field of technical writing this is a necessity. But I can think of no word to describe that sound. The closest I can come with a word of my own invention is "vlump." It came erratically, neither loud nor soft. It was, rather, pervasive and without location. It was not a *solid* sound. There was something vague and whispering about it, and from time to time it began with the suggestion of a sigh—a shuffing dissipation in the air that seemed to take form and die in the same instant. In a way I cannot define, it was mindless, without will or reason, yet implacable. Because I could not explain it immediately I went to seek an explanation.

I stepped into the hall and switched on the light, pressing the noiseless button. The light came down out of a fixture set flush into the ceilings and diffused through a milky plastic-like Japanese rice paper. The clean, indestructible walls rose perpendicularly around me. Through the slight haze of smoke came the smell of the newness, sweet and metallic—more like a car than a house. And still the sound went on. It seemed to be coming from the room at the end of the hall, the room we had designed for our friends' children. The door was open and I could see a gray patch that was a west window. Vlump . . . vlump . . . vlumpvlump. . . .

Fixing on the gray patch, I moved down the hall while my legs made themselves heavy as logs, and all the while I repeated to myself, "The house is settling. All new houses settle and make strange noises." And so lucid was I that I believed I was not afraid. I was walking down the bright new hall of my new steel house to investigate a noise, for the house might be settling unevenly, or an animal might be up to some mischief—raccoons regularly raided the garbage cans, I had been told. There might be something wrong with the plumbing or with the radiant-heating system that warmed our steel and vinyl floors. And now, like the responsible master of the house, I had located the apparent center of the sound and was going responsibly toward it. In a second or two, very likely, I would know.

Vlump vlump. The gray of the window turned rosy as I came near enough to see the hillside beyond it. That black was underbrush and that pink the dusty swath cut by the bulldozer before it had run amok. I had watched the accident from just about the spot where I stood now, and the obliterated hole where the tree had been, laid firmly over with the prefabricated floor of the room whose darkness I would eradicate by touching with my right hand the light switch inside the door.

"Ted?"

Blood boomed in my ears. I had the impression that my heart had burst. I clutched at the wall for support. Yet of course I knew it was Ellen's voice, and I answered her calmly. "Yes, it's me."

"What's the matter?" I heard the bedclothes rustle.

"Don't get up, I'm coming right in." The noise had stopped. There was nothing. Only the almost inaudible hum of the refrigerator, the stirring of the wind.

Ellen was sitting up in bed. "I was just checking on the fire," I said. She patted my side of the bed and in the instant before I turned out the hall light I saw her smile.

"I was just dreaming about you," she said softly, as I climbed under the sheets. She rolled against me. "Why, you're trembling."

"I should have worn my robe."

"You'll be warm in a minute." Her fragrant body lay against mine, but I remained rigid as stone and just as cold, staring at the ceiling, my mind a furious blank. After a moment she said, "Ted?" It was her signal, always hesitant, always tremulous, that meant I was to roll over and take her in my arms.

Instead I answered, "What?" just as if I had not understood.

For a few seconds I sensed her struggling against her reserve to give me a further sign that would pierce my peculiar distraction and tell me she wanted love. But it was too much for her—too alien. My coldness had created a vacuum she was too unpracticed to fill—a coldness sudden and inexplicable, unless . . .

She withdrew slowly and pulled the covers up under her chin. Finally she asked, "Ted, is there something happening that I should know about?" She had remembered Sondra and the curious scene in the kitchen. It took, I knew, great courage for Ellen to ask that question, though she must have known my answer.

"No, I'm just tired. We've had a busy day. Good-night, dear." I kissed her on the cheek and sensed her eyes, in the shadow of the fire, searching mine, asking the question she could not give voice to. I turned away, somehow ashamed because I could not supply the answer that would fulfill her need. Because there was no answer at all.

The fire was brought under control after burning some eight hundred acres and several homes, and three weeks later the rains came. Jack Salmanson came out one Sunday to see how the house was holding up, checked the foundation, the roof and all the seams and pronounced it tight as a drum. We sat looking moodily out the glass doors onto the patio—a flatland of grayish mud which threatened to swamp with a thin ooze of silt and gravel the few flagstones I had set in the ground. Ellen was in the bedroom lying down; she had got into the habit of taking a nap after lunch, though it was I, not she, who lay stark awake night after night explaining away sounds that became more and more impossible to explain away. The gagging sound that sometimes accompanied the vlump and the strangled expulsion of air that followed it were surely the result of some disturbance in the water pipes; the footsteps that came slowly down the hall and stopped outside our closed door and then went away again with something like a low chuckle were merely the night contracting of our metal house after the heat of the day. Through all this Ellen slept as if in a stupor; she seemed to have become addicted to sleep. She went to bed at nine and got up at ten the next morning; she napped in the afternoon and moved about lethargically the rest of the time with a Mexican shawl around her shoulders, complaining of the cold. The doctor examined her for mononucleosis but found nothing. He said perhaps it was her sinuses and that she should rest as much as she wanted.

After a protracted silence Jack put aside his drink and stood up. "I guess I'll go along."

"I'll tell Ellen."

"What the hell for? Let her sleep. Tell her I hope she feels better." He turned to frown at the room of the house he had designed and built. "Are you happy here?" he asked suddenly.

"Happy?" I repeated the word awkwardly. "Of course

we're happy. We love the house. It's . . . just a little noisy at night, that's all." I stammered it out, like the first word of a monstrous confession, but Jack seemed hardly to hear it. He waved a hand. "House settling." He squinted from one side of the room to the other. "I don't know. There's something about it. . . . It's not right. Maybe it's just the weather . . . the light. . . . It could be friendlier, you know what I mean? It seems cheerless."

I watched him with a kind of wild hope, as if he might magically fathom my terror—do for me what I could not do for myself, and permit it to be discussed calmly between two men of temperate mind. But Jack was not looking for the cause of the gloom but the cure for it. "Why don't you try putting down a couple of orange rugs in this room?" he said.

I stared at the floor as if two orange rugs were an infallible charm. "Yes," I said, "I think we'll try that."

Ellen scuffed in, pushing back her hair, her face puffy with sleep. "Jack," she said, "when the weather clears and I'm feeling livelier, you and Anne and the children must come and spend the night."

"We'd like that. After the noises die down," he added satirically to me.

"Noises? What noises?" A certain blankness came over Ellen's face when she looked at me now. The expression was the same, but what had been open in it before was now merely empty. She had put up her guard against me; she suspected me of keeping things from her.

"At night," I said. "The house is settling. You don't hear them."

When Jack had gone, Ellen sat with a cup of tea in the chair where Jack had sat, looking out at the mud. Her long purple shawl hung all the way to her knees and made her look armless. There seemed no explanation for the two white hands that curled around the teacup in her lap. "It's a sad thing," she said tonelessly. "I can't help but feel sorry for Sondra."

"Why is that?" I asked guardedly.

"Joyce was here yesterday. She told me that she and Jeff have been having an affair off and on for six years." She turned to see how I would receive this news.

"Well, that explains the way Joyce and Sondra behave toward each other," I said, with a pleasant glance straight into Ellen's eyes; there I encountered only the reflection of the glass doors, even to the rain trickling down them, and I had the eerie sensation of having been shown a picture of the truth, as if she were weeping secretly in the depths of a soul I could no longer touch. For Ellen did not believe in my innocence; I'm not sure I still believed in it myself; very likely Jeff and Joyce didn't either. It is impossible to say what Sondra believed. She behaved as if our infidelity were an accomplished fact. In its way it was a performance of genius, for Sondra never touched me except in the most accidental or impersonal way; even her glances, the foundation on which she built the myth of our liaison, had nothing soft in them; they were probing and sly and were always accompanied by a furtive smile, as if we merely shared some private joke. Yet there was something in the way she did it—in the tilt of her head perhaps—that plainly implied that the joke was at everyone else's expense. And she had taken to calling me "darling."

"Sondra and Jeff have a feebleminded child off in an institution somewhere," Ellen said. "That set them against each other, apparently."

"Joyce told you all this?"

"She just mentioned it casually as if it were the most natural thing in the world—she assumed we must have known. . . . But I don't want to know things like that about my friends."

"That's show biz, I guess. You and I are just provincials at heart."

"Sondra must be a very unhappy girl."

"It's hard to tell with Sondra."

"I wonder what she tries to do with her life. . . . If she looks for anything—outside."

I waited.

"Probably not," Ellen answered her own question. "She seems very self-contained. Almost cold . . ."

I was treated to the spectacle of my wife fighting with herself to delay a wound that she was convinced would come home to her sooner or later. She did not want to believe in my infidelity. I might have comforted her with lies. I might have told her that Sondra and I rendezvoused downtown in a cafeteria and made love in a second-rate hotel on the evenings when I called to say that I was working late. Then the wound would be open and could be cleaned and cured. It would be painful of course, but I would have confided in her again and our old system would be restored. Watching Ellen torture herself with doubt, I was tempted to tell her those lies. The truth never tempted me: To have admitted that I knew what she was thinking would have been tantamount to an admission of guilt. How could I suspect such a thing unless it were true? And was I to explain my coldness by terrifying her with vague stories of indescribable sounds which she never heard?

And so the two of us sat on, dumb and chilled, in our watertight house as the daylight began to go. And then a sort of exultation seized me. What if my terror were no more real than Ellen's? What if both our ghosts were only ghosts of the mind which needed only a little common sense to drive them away? And I saw that if I could drive away my ghost, Ellen's would soon follow, for the secret that shut me away from her would be gone. It was a revelation, a triumph of reason.

"What's that up there?" Ellen pointed to something that looked like a leaf blowing at the top of the glass doors. "It's a tail, Ted. There must be some animal on the roof."

Only the bushy tip was visible. As I drew close to it I could see raindrops clinging as if by a geometrical system to each black hair. "It looks like a raccoon tail. What would a coon be doing out so early?" I put on a coat and went outside. The tail hung limply over the edge, ringed with white and swaying phlegmatically in the breeze. The animal itself was hidden behind the low parapet. Using the ship's ladder at the back of the house I climbed up to look at it.

The human mind, just like other parts of the anatomy, is an organ of habit. Its capabilities are bounded by the limits of precedent; it thinks what it is used to thinking. Faced with a phenomenon beyond its range it rebels, it rejects, sometimes it collapses. My mind, which for weeks had steadfastly refused to honor the evidence of my senses that there was Something Else living in the house with Ellen and me, something unearthly and evil, largely on the basis of insufficient evidence, was now forced to the subsequent denial by saying, as Jeff had said, "fox." It was of course, ridiculous. The chances of a fox's winning a battle with a raccoon were very slight at best, let alone what had been done to this raccoon. The body lay on the far side of the roof. I didn't see the head at all until I had stumbled against it and it had rolled over and over to come to rest against the parapet where it pointed its masked, ferret face at me.

Only because my beleaguered mind kept repeating, like a voice, "Ellen mustn't know, Ellen mustn't know," was I able to take up the dismembered parts and hurl them with all my strength onto the hillside and answer when Ellen called out, "What is it, Ted?" "Must have been a coon. It's gone now," in a perfectly level voice before I went to the back of the roof and vomited.

I recalled Sondra's mention of their mutilated cat and phoned Jeff at his agency. "We will discuss it over lunch," I told myself. I had a great need to talk, an action impossible within my own home, where every day the silence became denser and more intractable. Once or twice Ellen ventured to ask, "What's the matter, Ted?" but I always answered, "Nothing." And there our talk ended. I could see it in her wary eyes: I was not the man she had married; I was cold, secretive. The children's room, furnished with double bunks and wallpaper figured with toys, stood like a rebuke. Ellen kept the door closed most of the time though once or twice, in the late afternoon, I had found her in there moving about aimlessly, touching objects as if half in wonder that they should still linger on after so many long, sterile months; a foolish hope had failed. Neither did our friends bring their children to stay. They did not because we did not ask them. The silence had brought with it a profound and debilitating inertia. Ellen's face seemed perpetually swollen, the features cloudy and amorphous, the eyes dull; her whole body had become bloated, as if an enormous cache of pain had backed up inside her. We moved through the house in our orbits like two sleepwalkers, going about our business out of habit. Our friends called at first, puzzled, a little hurt, but soon stopped and left us to ourselves. Occasionally we saw the Sheffitses. Jeff was looking seedier and seedier, told bad jokes, drank too much and seemed always ill at ease. Sondra did most of the talking, chattering blandly on indifferent subjects and always hinting by gesture, word or glance at our underground affair.

Jeff and I had lunch at the Brown Derby on Vine Street under charcoal caricatures of show folk. At a table next to ours an agent was eulogizing an actor in a voice hoarse with trumped-up enthusiasm to a large, purple-faced man who was devoting his entire attention to a bowl of vichyssoise.

"It's a crazy business," Jeff said to me. "Be glad you're not in it."

"I see what you mean," I replied. Jeff had not the faintest idea of why I had brought him there, nor had I given him any clue. We were "breaking the ice." Jeff grinned at me with that crooked trick of his mouth, and I grinned back. "We are friends"—presumably that is the message we were grinning at each other. Was he my friend? Was I his friend? He lived across the street; our paths crossed perhaps once a week; we joked together; he sat always in the same chair in our living room twisting from one sprawl to another; there was a straight white chair in his living room that I preferred. Friendships have been founded on less, I suppose. Yet he had an idiot child locked off in an asylum somewhere and a wife who amused herself with infidelity by suggestion; I had a demon loose in my house and a wife gnawed with suspicion and growing remote and old because of it. And I had said, "I see what you mean." It seemed insufferable. I caught Jeff's eye. "You remember we talked once about a ghost?" My tone was bantering; perhaps I meant to make a joke.

"I remember."

"Sondra said something about a cat of yours that was killed."

"The one the fox got."

"That's what you said. That's not what Sondra said."

Jeff shrugged. "What about it?"

"I found a dead raccoon on our roof."

"Your roof!"

"Yes. It was pretty awful."

Jeff toyed with his fork. All pretense of levity was at an end. "No head?"

"Worse."

For a few moments he was silent. I felt him struggle with himself before he spoke. "Maybe you'd better move out, Ted," he said.

He was trying to help—I knew it. With a single swipe he had tried to push through the restraint that hung between us. He was my friend; he was putting out his hand to me. And I suppose I must have known what he'd suggest. But I could not accept it. It was not what I wanted to hear.

"Jeff, I can't do that," I said tolerantly, as if he had missed my point. "We've only been living there five months. It cost me twenty-two thousand to build that place. We have to live in it at least a year under the GI loan."

"Well, you know best, Ted." The smile dipped at me again.

"I just wanted to talk," I said, irritated at the ease with which he had given in. "I wanted to find out what you knew about this ghost business."

"Not very much. Sondra knows more than I do."

"I doubt that you would advise me to leave a house I had just built for no reason at all."

"There seems to be some sort of jinx on the property, that's all. Whether there's a ghost or not I couldn't tell you," he replied, annoyed in his turn at the line the conversation was taking. "How does Ellen feel about this?"

"She doesn't know."

"About the raccoon?"

"About anything."

"You mean there's more?"

"There are noises—at night. . . ."

"I'd speak to Sondra if I were you. She's gone into this business much more deeply than I. When we first moved in, she used to hang around your land a good deal . . . just snooping . . . particularly after that cat was killed. . . ." He was having some difficulty with his words. It struck me that the conversation was causing him pain. He was showing his teeth now in a smiling grimace. Dangling an arm over the back of his chair he seemed loose to the point of collapse. We circled warily about his wife's name.

"Look, Jeff," I said, and took a breath, "about Sondra . . ."

Jeff cut me off with a wave of his hand. "Don't worry, I know Sondra."

"Then you know there's nothing between us?"

"It's just her way of amusing herself. Sondra's a strange girl. She does the same thing with me. She flirts with me but we don't sleep together." He picked up his spoon and stared at it unseeingly. "It started when she became pregnant. After she had the boy, everything between us stopped. You knew we had a son? He's in a sanitarium in the Valley."

"Can't you do anything?"

"Sure. Joyce Castle. I don't know what I'd have done without her."

"I mean divorce."

"Sondra won't divorce me. And I can't divorce her. No grounds." He shrugged as if the whole thing were of no concern at all to him. "What could I say? I want to divorce my wife because of the way she looks at other men? She's scrupulously faithful."

"To whom, Jeff? To you? To whom?"

"I don't know—to herself, maybe," he mumbled.

Whether with encouragement he might have gone on I don't know, for I cut him off. I sensed that with the enigmatic remark he was giving me my cue and that if I had chosen to respond to it he would have told me what I had asked him to lunch to find out—and all at once I was terrified; I did not want to hear it; I did not want to hear it at all. And so I laughed in a quiet way and said, "Undoubtedly, undoubtedly," and pushed it behind the closed door of my mind where I had stored all the impossibilities of the last months—the footsteps, the sounds in the night, the mutilated raccoon—or else, by recognizing them, go mad.

Jeff suddenly looked me full in the face; his cheeks were flushed, his teeth clamped together. "Look, Ted," he said, "can you take the afternoon off? I've got to go to the sanitarium and sign some papers. They're going to transfer the boy. He has fits of violence and does . . . awful things. He's finally gotten out of hand."

"What about Sondra?"

"Sondra's signed already. She likes to go alone to visit him. She seems to like to have him to herself. I'd appreciate it, Ted—the moral support. . . . You don't have to come in. You can wait in the car. It's only about thirty miles from here, you'd be back by dinnertime. . . ." His voice shook, tears clouded the yellow-stained whites of his eyes He looked like a man with fever. I noticed how shrunken his neck had become as it revolved in his collar, how his head caved in sharply at the temples. He fastened one hand on my arm, like a claw. "Of course I'll go, Jeff," I said. "I'll call the office. They can get along without me for one afternoon."

He collected himself in an instant. "I'd appreciate it, Ted. I promise you it won't be so bad."

The sanitarium was in the San Fernando Valley, a com-

plex of new stucco buildings on a newly seeded lawn.
Everywhere there were signs that read, PLEASE KEEP OFF,
FOLKS. Midget saplings stood in discs of powdery earth
along the cement walks angling white and hot through the
grass. On these walks, faithfully observing the signs, the inmates strolled. Their traffic, as it flowed somnolently from
one avenue to another, was controlled by attendants sta-
tioned at intersections, conspicuous in white uniforms and
pith helmets.

After a time it became unbearably hot in the car, and
I climbed out. Unless I wished to pace in the parking lot
among the cars, I had no choice but to join the inmates
and their visitors on the walks. I chose a nearly deserted
walk and went slowly toward a building that had a yard
attached to it surrounded by a wire fence. From the slide
and the junglegym in it I judged it to be for the children.
Then I saw Jeff come into it. With him was a nurse pushing a kind of cart railed around like an oversized toddler.
Stropped into it was "the boy."

He was human, I suppose, for he had all the equipment
assigned to humans, yet I had the feeling that if it were not
for the cart the creature would have crawled on his belly
like an alligator. He had the eyes of an alligator too—
sleepy, cold and soulless—set in a swarthy face and a head
that seemed to run in a horizontal direction rather than
the vertical, like an egg lying on its side. The features
were devoid of any vestige of intelligence; the mouth hung
open and the chin shone with saliva. While Jeff and the
nurse talked, he sat under the sun, inert and repulsive.

I turned on my heel and bolted, feeling that I had in-
truded on a disgrace. I imagined that I had been given a
glimpse of a diseased universe, the mere existence of
which constituted a threat to my life; the sight of th t
monstrous boy with his cold, bestial eyes made me feel
as if, by stumbling on this shame I somehow shared in it
with Jeff. Yet I told myself that the greatest service I
could do him was to pretend that I had seen nothing, know
nothing, and not place on him the hardship of talking
about something which obviously caused him pain.

He returned to the car pale and shaky and wanting a
drink. We stopped first at a place called Joey's on Hollywood Way. After that it was Cherry Lane on Vine Street,
where a couple of girls propositioned us, and then a stop
at the Brown Derby again, where I had left my car. Jeff

downed the liquor in a joyless, businesslike way and talked to me in a rapid, confidential voice about a book he had just sold to Warner Brothers Studio for an exorbitant sum of money—trash in his opinion, but that was always the way—the parasites made it. Pretty soon there wouldn't be any good writers left: "There'll only be competent parasites and incompetent parasites." This was perhaps the third time we had had this conversation. Now Jeff repeated it mechanically, all the time looking down at the table where he was painstakingly breaking a red swizzle stick into ever tinier pieces.

When we left the restaurant, the sun had gone down, and the evening chill of the desert on which the city had been built had settled in. A faint pink glow from the vanished sun still lingered on the top of the Broadway Building. Jeff took a deep breath, then fell into a fit of coughing. "Goddam smog," he said. "Goddam city. I can't think of a single reason why I live here." He started toward his Daimler, tottering slightly.

"How about driving home with me?" I said. "You can pick your car up tomorrow."

He fumbled in the glove compartment and drew out a packet of small cigars. He stuck one between his teeth where it jutted unlit toward the end of his nose. "I'm not going home tonight, Ted friend," he said. "If you'll just drop me up the street at the Cherry Lane I'll remember you for life."

"Are you sure? I'll go with you if you want."

Jeff shook a forefinger at me archly. "Ted, you're a gentleman and a scholar. But my advice to you is to go home and take care of your wife. No, seriously. Take care of her, Ted. As for myself I shall go quietly to seed in the Cherry Lane Café." I had started toward my car when Jeff called out to me again. "I just want to tell you, Ted friend. . . . My wife was once just as nice as your wife. . . ."

I had gone no more than a mile when the last glimmer of light left the sky and night fell like a shutter. The sky above the neon of Sunset Boulevard turned jet black, and a sickly half-moon rose and was immediately obscured by thick fog that lowered itself steadily as I traveled west, till at the foot of Clay Canyon it began to pat my windshield with little smears of moisture.

The house was dark, and at first I thought Ellen must have gone out, but then seeing her old Plymouth in the driveway I felt the grip of a cold and unreasoning fear. The events of the day seemed to crowd around and hover at my head in the fog; and the commonplace sight of that car, together with the blackness and silence of the house, sent me into a panic as I ran for the door. I pushed at it with my shoulder as if expecting it to be locked, but it swung open easily and I found myself in the darkened living room with no light anywhere and the only sound the rhythm of my own short breathing. "Ellen!" I called in a high, querulous voice I hardly recognized. "Ellen!" I seemed to lose my balance; my head swam; it was as if this darkness and silence were the one last iota that the chamber of horrors in my mind could not hold, and the door snapped open a crack, emitting a cloudy light that stank of corruption, and I saw the landscape of my denial, like a tomb. It was the children's room. Rats nested in the double bunks, mold caked the red wallpaper, and in it an insane Spanish don hung by his neck from a dead tree, his heels vlumping against the wall, his foppish clothes rubbing as he revolved slowly in invisible currents of bad air. And as he swung toward me, I saw his familiar reptile eyes open and stare at me with loathing and contempt.

I conceded: It is here and It is evil, and I have left my wife alone in the house with It, and now she has been sucked into that cold eternity where the dumb shades store their plasms against an anguished centenary of speech—a single word issuing from the petrified throat, a scream or a sigh or a groan, syllables dredged up from a lifetime of eloquence to slake the bottomless thirst of living death.

And then a light went on over my head, and I found myself in the hall outside the children's room. Ellen was in her nightgown, smiling at me. "Ted? Why on earth are you standing here in the dark? I was just taking a nap. Do you want some dinner? Why don't you say something? Are you all right?" She came toward me; she seemed extraordinarily lovely; her eyes, a deeper blue than Sondra's, looked almost purple; she seemed young and slender again; her old serenity shone through like a restored beacon.

"I'm all right," I said hoarsely. "Are you sure you are?"

"Of course I am," she laughed. "Why shouldn't I be? I'm feeling much, much better." She took my hand and kissed it gaily. "I'll put on some clothes and then we'll have our dinner." She turned and went down the hall to our bedroom, leaving me with a clear view into the children's room. Though the room itself was dark, I could see by the hall light that the covers on the lower bunk had been turned back and that the bed had been slept in. "Ellen," I said. "Ellen, were you sleeping in the children's room?"

"Yes," she said, and I heard the rustle of a dress as she carried it from the closet. "I was in there mooning around, waiting for you to come home. I got sleepy and lay down on the bunk. What were *you* doing, by the way? Working late?"

"And nothing happened?"

"Why? What should have happened?"

I could not answer; my head throbbed with joy. It was over—whatever it was, it was over. All unknowing Ellen had faced the very heart of the evil and had slept through it like a child, and now she was herself again without having been tainted by the knowledge of what she had defeated; I had protected her by my silence, by my refusal to share my terror with this woman whom I loved. I reached inside and touched the light button; there was the brave red wallpaper scattered over with toys, the red-and-white curtains, the blue-and-red bedspreads. It was a fine room. A fine, gay room fit for children.

Ellen came down the hall in her slip. "Is anything wrong, Ted? You seem so distraught. Is everything all right at the office?"

"Yes, yes," I said. "I was with Jeff Sheffits. We went to see his boy in the asylum. Poor Jeff; he leads a rotten life." I told Ellen the whole story of our afternoon, speaking freely in my house for the first time since we had moved there. Ellen listened carefully as she always did, and wanted to know, when I had finished, what the boy was like.

"Like an alligator," I said with disgust. "Just like an alligator."

Ellen's face took on an unaccountable expression of private glee. She seemed to be looking past me into the children's room, as if the source of her amusement lay there. At the same moment I shivered in a breath of profound cold, the same clammy draft that might have warned me on my last birthday had I been other than what I am. I had a sense of sudden dehydration, as if all the blood had vanished from my veins. I felt as if I were shrinking. When I spoke, my voice seemed to come from a throat rusty and dry with disuse. "Is that funny?" I whispered.

And my wife replied, "Funny? Oh, no, it's just that I'm feeling so much better. I think I'm pregnant, Ted." She tipped her head to one side and smiled at me.

THE REAL THING

by Robert Specht

They took Charlie Atkinson and Tad Winters off to the madhouse on the same day. Charlie went real quiet—being a half-wit, one place to sleep was just as good as another to him. Not Tad, though. When they took him away he was howling like a run-over dog.

Every small town has its village idiot and its practical joker. And it seems that the first is always going to be made a fool of by the second. That was Charlie and Tad. Charlie never seemed to mind, though. No matter what kind of trick Tad played on him, he'd smile that fool's smile of his and say, "That Tad's funny. He's sure funny."

Charlie slept in a little room in back of Mr. Eakins' funeral parlor. He kept the place neat and swept up once in a while. Mister Eakins let him do little chores like that so Charlie wouldn't feel he was getting charity. Charlie liked his little room, not minding at all that most of the time there was somebody dead lying out in the parlor.

Came April, though, the main water line that led into town burst. The seepage turned the graveyard into pure mud, and until the water could be pumped out, Eakins' Funeral Parlor had three people laid out and waiting to make the final trip. Charlie was forced to share his little room with the Dayton girl, who'd died of pneumonia a few days before.

As soon as Tad heard about it he couldn't resist ribbing Charlie. "Hear you got company, Charlie, is that right?"

Charlie looked at him quizzically.

"I mean that pretty little girl you got stayin' with you."

"Shucks, Tad, that's the Dayton girl. You know that." Charlie looked around at Tad's cronies to see if they were smiling. He still wasn't sure his leg was being pulled.

"You mean she ain't your wife?"

"Tad, that girl's *dead*. She couldn't be nobody's wife. You sure are a card you are."

Some of the fellows were ready to laugh, but Tad gave

them a quick look that shut them up. He had an idea. "Charlie . . . you ever see that girl get up and wander around at night?"

"Now I know you're foolin'."

"I ain't foolin' you at all," Tad said darkly. "All I can tell you is you better make sure that lid's on tight."

The faces around Charlie took on serious expressions. "Why should I better make sure?" he asked.

"Talk's around town that girl was bitten by a wolf before she died." Tad put his face close to Charlie's. "But not by no *ordinary* wolf. A werewolf. You know what that makes her, don't you?"

"A vampire?"

Charlie had got his legends mixed, but Tad let it go. "That's right. Sure enough you're going to be asleep some night and the next thing you know that gal's teeth'll be in your throat, suckin' you dry as a bone." With that, Tad walked away with his friends, leaving Charlie to think about it alone.

Later Charlie asked Mr. Eakins about vampires and Mr. Eakins told him all he knew. Before he could ask Charlie why he wanted to know, a customer came in and Eakins forgot about it.

It was too bad he did, because that same night Tad and his pals were gathered at the back of the funeral parlor outside of Charlie's room. A few of the merchants in town paid Charlie fifty cents a week to check their doors before he went to sleep, and that's what the group outside his room were waiting for him to do.

Tad turned to Susan, the one girl among them. He was due to be married to her shortly, but the way her face was made up that night even Tad couldn't help but be a little frightened looking at it. Her eyes were ringed in black and her lips were painted scarlet. The rest of her face was painted chalk-white, except for some streaks of black that hollowed her cheeks. "Tad, I don't like doing this," she whispered.

"Now, honey, it's all in fun . . ."

"Yeah, but I don't like the idea of gettin' into that casket."

"You won't be in there but for a few minutes until Charlie gets back. Like I said, we're gonna put you in the one Eakins keeps in the front room for a sample, then switch it with the one in Charlie's room. When he comes back you give out with a few moans, open the casket, and it's all a laugh."

"Suppose he gets a heart attack or something?"

"Aw, he's too dumb for that. He'll let out a yell and high-tail it for the county line—be there in two minutes."

Susan giggled.

"Sshh," a voice said. It belonged to someone who was peering around the edge of the building, towards the front. "He's gone. Let's go."

The group stole forward, and when Charlie disappeared up the street they hurried through the unlocked door of the shop. A few minutes later, when Charlie returned, the men were once more waiting outside the back of the shop.

"Give me a boost," Tad said. With one man holding each of his legs Tad was slowly raised until he could see into Charlie's room through a little transom-like window. "He's comin' in," Tad whispered to the men below. "He's settin' down on the cot takin' his shoes off."

Tad didn't have to report what happened next, for even from where they were the moan that came from the wicker casket could be heard. Within the little room Charlie sat bolt upright. Another moan issued from the casket and Charlie gripped the edge of his cot. At the same time Tad held onto the edge of the window sill with one hand while he tried to stifle his laughter with the other.

"What's happening?" a voice below him asked.

"Wait." He giggled. "The casket's opening. She's comin' up. God, she looks like the real thing! I think Charlie's gon—" He broke off as Charlie suddenly came to life. He moved swiftly—not for the door as Tad thought he would, but straight for the casket. Susan, too, was surprised, Tad saw. She offered no resistance as in almost one motion Charlie sprang, pushed her back in the casket and shoved the lid down on her.

"What's goin' on, Tad?" someone hissed.

Tad was almost too amazed to answer. "I don't know. . . . He locked her in. Now he's gettin' somethin' out from under his cot. Looks like— Oh my God! *Oh my God, NO!*"

The horror in his voice cut through the suppressed laughter of his friends. One of the men holding his legs shifted suddenly and Tad fell to the ground, yelling. Before the men could untangle themselves an unearthly shriek came from within Charlie's room, cutting through Tad's frantic cries and freezing everyone where he stood. It was the shriek of a woman in mortal agony, and it was followed by another, louder than the first.

Tad scrambled to his feet and dashed around the building. When his friends caught up with him he was already hurling himself against the heavy front door in a frenzy. One of the men kept his wits about him. Warning the others away, he picked up a chair that stood in front of the plateglass window and heaved it. Tad was the first one through when the glass stopped falling. The shrieks from Charlie's room had reached a peak. They died suddenly as the men reached his door.

Tad was the first one in the room, and what he saw forced a groan from him. The wicker casket still straddled the two sawhorses on which it had been placed only a few minutes before. Charlie stood before it with a mallet in his hand. A soft gurgling sound came from the casket and the long wooden stake that had been driven through its woven fibres moved a little as the remains of the woman within shuddered once and then were still. Blood had begun to drip to the floor.

Tad began to scream.

Later on, after the authorities took Tad and Charlie away everybody agreed it was Tad's fault. Everybody except Mister Eakins. He stayed drunk for a week, saying that he was the damn fool who told Charlie that the way to kill a vampire was with a stake through its heart.

JOURNEY TO DEATH

by Donald E. Westlake

Although ocean voyages are not new to me, I have never grown accustomed to the sway and roll of ships, especially at night. For that reason, I normally get very little sleep while crossing the Atlantic, not being able to close my eyes until I have reached such a point of exhaustion that it is no longer possible for me to keep them open. Since business often makes it necessary for me to journey to America, my wife has urged me, from time to time, to go by air, but I'm afraid I'm much too cowardly for that. The rolling of a ship at sea causes uneasiness in both my stomach and mind, but the mere thought of traveling through the air terrifies me. A sea voyage, then, is the lesser of two evils, and I face my insomnia, after all these years, with the calm of old resignation.

And yet, it is impossible to merely lie in bed awake, eyes staring at the ceiling, through all the long rolling nights between Dover and New York, and even reading begins, at last, to pall. On so many voyages, I have been reduced to aimless pacing of the deck, watching the million moons reflected in the waves surrounding me.

I was delighted, therefore, on this last and latest crossing, to discover, the third night out, a fellow-sufferer, an insomniac like myself, named Cowley. Cowley was an American, a businessman, younger than me, perhaps forty-five or fifty. A direct and sensible man I found him, and enjoyed his company, late at night, when all the other passengers slept and we were alone in an empty and silent sea. I found no fault in him at all, save for an occasional example of rather grim and tasteless humor, a reference to the decaying bodies in Davy Jones's locker, or some such thing.

The nights were spent in conversation, in strolls about the decks, or in billiards, a game which we both loved but which neither had ever mastered. Being of equal incompetence in the sport, we contentedly wiled away many hours in the large billiard room located on the same deck as my cabin.

The eighth night of the voyage was spent in this room, where we puffed happily at cigars, played with our normal lack of skill, and waited patiently for dawn. It was a brisk and chilly night, with a cold wet wind scampering across the waves like a chilled and lonely ghost searching for land, and we had closed every door and window in the room, preferring an atmosphere polluted by cigar smoke to being chilled to the bone.

It was only fifteen minutes after thus sealing ourselves into the room that the catastrophe struck. I don't know what it could have been, an explosion in the huge and mysterious engines somewhere in the bowels of the ship, perhaps unexpected contact with a mine still unreclaimed from the Second World War. Whatever it was, the silence of the night was suddenly torn apart by a tremendous and powerful *sound,* a roar, a crash that dulled the senses and paralyzed the body, and the whole ship, the *Aragon,* shuddered and trembled with a violent jerking spasm. Cowley and I were both thrown to the floor, and on all the tables, the billiard balls clacked and rolled, as though their hysteria and fear were equal to our own.

And then the ship seemed to poise, to stop and hold itself immobile while time flashed by, and I struggled to my feet, hearing the hum of absolute silence, of a broken world suddenly without time or movement.

I turned toward the main door, leading out to the deck, and saw there, staring in, a wild and terrified face, a woman, still in her nightgown, whose mouth was open and who was screaming. I started toward her, staring at her through the glass in the door, and time began again. The ship lurched, bent, and as I struggled to keep my balance, I saw her torn away, out to the emptiness, and eager waves dashed against the window panes.

It was like an elevator gone mad, hurtling down from the uppermost story. The water boiled and fumed outside the window, and I clung to the wall, sick and terrified, knowing that we were sinking, we were sinking, and in a matter of seconds I would surely be dead.

A final jolt, and all movement stopped. The ship lay at a slight angle, the floor was at a slant, and we were at the bottom of the sea.

A part of my mind screamed in horror and fear, but another part of me was calm, as though outside myself, separate, a brain not dependent upon this frail and doomed body. It—this part of my mind that I had never known before—it thought, it conjectured, it reasoned. The ship was lying on the sea floor, that much was obvious. But how far down, how far from the surface? Not too far, surely, or the pressure of the water would have burst the glass of the windows. Was the surface close enough for me to dare to leave the ship, this room, this pocket of trapped air? Could I hope to fight my way to the surface before my lungs burst, before my need for air drove open my mouth and let the water in to kill me?

I couldn't take the chance. We had fallen for so long, and I was not a young man. I couldn't take the chance.

A groan reminded me of Cowley. I turned and saw him lying on the floor against one wall, apparently rolled there when the ship sank. He moved now, feebly, and touched his hand to his head.

I hurried to him and helped him to his feet. At first, he had no idea what had happened. He had heard the explosion, had stumbled, his head had hit the edge of a billiard table, that was all he knew. I told him of our situation, and he stared at me, unbelieving.

"Underwater?" His face was pale with shock, pale and stiff as dry clay. He turned and hurried to the nearest window. Outside, the feeble light from our prison faintly illuminated the swirling waters around us. Cowley faced me again. "The lights—" he said.

I shrugged. "Perhaps there are other rooms still sealed off," I said, and as I finished speaking, the lights flickered and grew dim.

I had expected Cowley to panic, as I had done, but he smiled instead, sardonically, and said, "What a way to die."

"We may not die," I told him. "If there were survivors—"

"Survivors? What if there were? We aren't among them."

"They'll be rescued," I said, suddenly full of hope. "They'll know where the ship went down. And divers will come."

"Divers? Why?"

"They always do. At once. To salvage what they can, to determine the cause of the sinking. They'll send divers. We may yet be saved."

"If there were survivors," said Cowley. "And, if not?"

I sat down, heavily. "Then we are dead men."

"You suggest we wait, is that it?"

I looked at him, surprised. "What else can we do?"

"We can get it over with. We can open the door."

I stared at him. He seemed calm, the faint smile was still on his lips. "Can you give up so easily?"

The smile broadened. "I suppose not," he said, and once more the lights flickered. We looked up, staring at the dimming bulbs. Yet a third time they flickered, and all at once they went out. We were in the dark, in pitch blackness, alone beneath the sea.

In the blackness, Cowley said, "I suppose you're right. There's nothing to lose but our sanity. We'll wait."

I didn't answer him. I was lost in my own thoughts, of my wife, of my children and their families, of my friends on both continents, of land and air and life. We were both silent. Unable to see one another, unable to see anything at all, it seemed impossible to converse.

How long we sat there I don't know, but suddenly I realized that it was not quite so dark any more. Vaguely, I could make out shapes within the room, I could see the form of Cowley sitting in another chair.

He stirred. "It must be daylight," he said. "A sunny day. On the surface."

"How long," I asked him, "how long do you suppose the air will last?"

"I don't know. It's a large room, there's only two of us. Long enough for us to starve to death, I suppose."

"Starve?" I realized, all at once, just how hungry I was. This was a danger I hadn't thought about. Keeping the water out, yes. The amount of air we had, yes. But it hadn't occurred to me, until just now, that we were completely without food.

Cowley got to his feet and paced about the dim room, stretching and roaming restlessly. "Assuming survivors," he said, as though our earlier conversation were still going on, as though there had been no intervening silence, "assuming survivors, and assuming divers, how long do you suppose it will take? Perhaps the survivors will be resc ed today. When will the divers come? Tomorrow? Next week? Two months from now?"

"I don't know."

Cowley laughed suddenly, a shrill and harsh sound in the

closed room, and I realized that he wasn't as calm as he had seemed. "If this were fiction," he said, "they would come at the last minute. In the nick of time. Fiction is wonderful that way. It is full of last minutes. But in life there is only one last minute. The minute before death."

"Let's talk about other things," I said.

"Let's not talk at all," said Cowley. He stopped by one of the tables and picked up a billiard ball. In the gloom, I saw him toss the ball into the air, catch it, toss it and catch it, and then he said, "I could solve our problem easily. Merely throw this ball through the window there."

I jumped to my feet. "Put it down! If you care nothing for your own life, at least remember that *I* want to live!"

Again he laughed, and dropped the ball onto the table. He paced again for a while, then sank at last into a chair. "I'm tired," he said. "The ship is very still now. I think I could sleep."

I was afraid to go to sleep, afraid that Cowley would wait until I was dozing and would then open the door after all, or throw the billiard ball through the window. I sat and watched him for as long as I could, but my eyelids grew heavy and at last, in spite of my fears, my eyes closed and I slept.

When I awoke, it was dark again, the dark of a clouded midnight, the dark of blindness. I stirred, stretched my cramped limbs, then subsided. I could hear Cowley's measured breathing. He slumbered on.

He woke as it was again growing light, as the absolute blackness was once again dispelled by a gray and murky gloom, the look of late evening, a frustrating half-light that made the eyes strain to see details where there were only shapes and vague forms and half-seen mounds.

Cowley grumbled and stirred and came slowly to consciousness. He got to his feet and moved his arms in undefined and meaningless arcs. "I'm hungry," he muttered. "The walls are closing in on me."

"Maybe they'll come today," I said.

"And maybe they'll never come." Once more, he paced around the room. At length, he stopped. "I once read," he said, as though to himself, "that hunger is always the greatest after the first meal missed. That after a day or two without food, the hunger pains grow less."

"I think that's right. I don't think I'm as hungry now as I was yesterday."

"I am," he said, petulantly, as though it were my fault. "I'm twice as hungry. My stomach is full of cramps. And I'm thirsty." He stood by a window, looking out. "I'm thirsty," he said again. "Why don't I open the window and let some water in?"

"Stay away from there!" I hurried across the room and pulled him away from the window. "Cowley, for God's sake get hold of yourself! If we're calm, if we're patient, if we have the self-reliance and strength to wait, we may yet be saved. Don't you *want* to live?"

"Live?" He laughed at me. "I died the day before yesterday." He flung away from me, hurled himself into his chair. "I'm dead," he said bitterly, "dead and my stomach doesn't know it. Oh, *damn* this pain! Martin, believe me, I could stand anything, I could be as calm and solid as a rock, except for these terrible pains in my stomach. I have to eat, Martin. If I don't get food soon, I'll go out of my mind. I know I will."

I stood watching him, helpless to say or do a thing.

His moods changed abruptly, instantaneously, without rhyme or reason. Now, he suddenly laughed again, that harsh and strident laugh that grated on my spine, that was more terrible to me than the weight of the water outside the windows. He laughed, and said, "I have read of men, isolated, without food, who finally turned to the last solution to the problem of hunger."

I didn't understand him. I said, "What is that?"

"Each other."

I stared at him, and a chill breath of terror touched my throat and dried it. I tried to speak, but my voice was hoarse, and I could only whisper, "Cannibalism? Good God, Cowley, you can't mean—"

Again, he laughed. "Don't worry, Martin. I don't think I could. If I could *cook* you, I might consider it. But raw? No, I don't believe I'll ever get *that* hungry." His mood changed again, and he cursed. "I'll be eating the rug soon, my own clothing, anything!"

He grew silent, and I sat as far from him as I could get. I meant to stay awake now, no matter how long it took, no matter what happened. This man was insane, he was capable of anything. I didn't dare sleep, and I looked forward with dread to the coming blackness of night.

The silence was broken only by an occasional muttering from Cowley across the room, unintelligible, as he mumbled to himself of horrors I tried not to imagine. Blackness came, and I waited, straining to hear a sound, waiting to hear Cowley move, for the attack I knew must come. His breathing was regular and slow, he seemed to be asleep, but I couldn't trust him. I was imprisoned with a madman, my only hope of survival was in staying awake, watching him every second until the rescuers came. And the rescuers must come. I couldn't have gone through all this for nothing. They would come, they must come.

My terror and need kept me awake all night long and all through the next day. Cowley slept much of the time, and when he was awake he contented himself with low mumbling or with glowering silence.

But I couldn't stay awake forever. As darkness returned again, as the third day ended without salvation, a heavy fog seemed to lower around me, and although I fought it, although I could feel the terror in my vitals, the fog closed in and I slept.

I woke suddenly. It was day again, and I couldn't breathe. Cowley stood over me, his hands around my neck, squeezing, shutting off the air from my lungs, and I felt as though my head were about to burst. My eyes bulged, my mouth opened and closed helplessly. Cowley's face, indistinct above me, gleamed with madness, his eyes bored into me and his mouth hung open in a hideous laugh.

I pulled at his hands, but they held me tight, I couldn't move them, I couldn't get air, air. I flailed away at his face, and my heart pounded in fear as I struggled. My fingers touched his face, perspiring face, slid away, I lunged at his eyes. My finger drove into his eye, and he screamed and released me. He fell back, his hands against his face, and I felt the warm jelly of his eye on my finger.

I stumbled out of the chair, looking madly for escape, but the room was sealed, we were prisoners together. He came at me again, his clutching hands reaching out for me, his face terrible now with the bloody wound where his left eye had been. I ran, and the breath rattled in my throat as I gulped in air. Choking, sobbing, I ran from him, my arms outstretched in the gloom, and I fell against one of the billiard tables. My hands touched a cuestick, I picked it up, turned, swung at Cowley with it. Cowley fell back, howling like an animal, but then came on again. Screaming, I jabbed the cuestick full into his open mouth. The stick snapped in two, part of it still in my hands, part jutting out of his mouth, and he started a shriek that ended in a terrible gurgling wail. He toppled face forward to the floor, driving the piece of stick through the back of his head.

I turned away and collapsed over a table. I was violently ill, my stomach jerking spasmodically, my throat heaving and retching. But it had been so long since I had eaten that I could bring nothing up, but could only lie helplessly, coughing and shaking and terribly, terribly sick.

That was three days ago, and still they haven't come. They must come soon now. The air is growing foul in here, I can hardly breathe any more. And I find that I am talking to myself, and every once in a while I will pick up a billiard ball and look longingly at the window. I am coming to long for death, and I know that that is madness. So they must come soon.

And the worst thing is the hunger. Cowley is gone, now, all gone, and I am hungry again.

THE MASTER OF THE HOUNDS

by Algis Budrys

The white sand road led off the state highway through the
sparse pines. There were no tire tracks in the road, but,
as Malcolm turned the car onto it, he noticed the footprints of dogs, or perhaps of only one dog, running along
the middle of the road toward the combined general store
and gas station at the intersection.

"Well, it's far enough away from everything, all right,"
Virginia said. She was lean and had dusty black hair. Her
face was long, with high cheekbones. They had married ten
years ago, when she had been girlish and very slightly
plump.

"Yes," Malcolm said. Just days ago, when he'd been
turned down for a Guggenheim Fellowship that he'd expected to get, he had quit his job at the agency and made
plans to spend the summer, somewhere as cheap as possible, working out with himself whether he was really
an artist or just had a certain commercial talent. Now
they were here.

He urged the car up the road, following a line of infre-
quent and weathered utility poles that carried a single
strand of power line. The real-estate agent already had
told them there were no telephones. Malcolm had taken
that to be a positive feature, but somehow he did not like
the looks of that one thin wire sagging from pole to pole.
The wheels of the car sank in deeply on either side of the
dog prints, which he followed like a row of bread crumbs
through a forest.

Several hundred yards farther along, they came to a sign
at the top of a hill:

MARINE VIEW SHORES! NEW JERSEY'S NEWEST, FAST-
EST-GROWING RESIDENTIAL COMMUNITY. WELCOME
HOME! FROM $9,990. NO DN PYT FOR VETS.

Below them was a wedge of land—perhaps ten acres altogether that pushed out into Lower New York Bay. The road became a gullied, yellow gravel street, pointing straight toward the water and ending in three concrete posts, one of which had fallen and left a gap wide enough for a car to blunder through. Beyond that was a low drop-off where the bay ran northward to New York City and, in the other direction, toward the open Atlantic.

On either side of the roughed-out street, the bulldozed land was overgrown with scrub oak and sumac. Along the street were rows of roughly rectangular pits—some with half-finished foundation walls in them—piles of excavated clay, and lesser quantities of sand, sparsely weed-grown and washed into ravaged mounds like Dakota Territory. Here and there were houses with half-completed frames, now silvered and warped.

There were only two exceptions to the general vista. At the end of the street, two identically designed, finished houses faced each other. One looked shabby. The lot around it was free of scrub, but weedy and unsodded. Across the street from it stood a house in excellent repair. Painted a charcoal gray and roofed with dark asphalt shingles, it sat in the center of a meticulously green and level lawn, which was in turn surrounded by a wide fence approximately four feet tall and splendid with fresh aluminum paint. False shutters, painted stark white, flanked high, narrow windows along the side Malcolm could see. In front of the house, a line of whitewashed stones the size of men's heads served as curbing. There wasn't a thing about the house and its surroundings that couldn't have been achieved with a straight string, a handsaw, and a three-inch brush. Malcolm saw a chance to cheer things up. "There now, Marthy!" he said to Virginia. "I've led you safe and sound through the howlin' forest to a snug home right in the shadder of brave Fort Defiance."

"It's orderly," Virginia said. "I'll bet it's no joke, keeping up a place like that out here."

As Malcolm was parking the car parallel to where the curb would have been in front of their house, a pair of handsome young Doberman pinschers came out from behind the gray house across the street and stood together on the lawn with their noses just short of the fence, looking out. They did not bark. There was no movement at the front window, and no one came out into the yard. The dogs simply stood there, watching, as Malcolm walked over the clay to his door.

The house was furnished—that is to say, there were chairs in the living room, although there was no couch, and a chromium-and-plastic dinette set in the area off the kitchen. Though one of the bedrooms was completely empty, there was a bureau and a bed in the other. Malcolm walked through the house quickly and went back out to the car to get the luggage and groceries. Nodding toward the dogs, he said to Virginia, "Well! The latest thing in iron deer." He felt he had to say something light, because Virginia was staring across the street.

He knew perfectly well, as most people do and he assumed Virginia did, that Doberman pinschers are nervous, untrustworthy, and vicious. At the same time, he and his wife did have to spend the whole summer here. He could guess how much luck they'd have trying to get their money back from the agent now.

"They look streamlined like that because their ears and tails are trimmed when they're puppies," Virginia said. She picked up a bag of groceries and carried it into the house.

When Malcolm had finished unloading the car, he slammed the trunk lid shut. Although they hadn't moved until then, the Dobermans seemed to regard this as a sign. They turned smoothly, the arc of one inside the arc of the other, and keeping formation, trotted out of sight behind the gray house.

Malcolm helped Virginia put things away in the closets and in the lone bedroom bureau. There was enough to do to keep both of them busy for several hours, and it was dusk when Malcolm happened to look out through the living-room window. After he had glanced that way, he stopped.

Across the street, floodlights had come on at the four corners of the gray house. They poured illumination downward in cones that lighted the entire yard. A crippled man was walking just inside the fence, his legs stiff and his body bent forward from the waist, as he gripped the projecting handles of two crutch-canes that supported his weight at the elbows. As Malcolm watched, the man took a precise square turn at the corner of the fence and began walking along the front of his property. Looking straight ahead, he moved regularly and purposefully, his shadow thrown out through the fence behind the composite shadow of the two dogs walking at his pace immediately ahead of him. None of them was looking in Malcolm's direction. He watched as the man made another turn, followed the fence toward the back of his property, and disappeared behind the house.

Later Virginia served cold cuts in the little dining alcove. Putting the house in order seemed to have had a good effect on her morale.

"Listen, I think we're going to be all right here, don't you?" Malcolm said.

"Look," she said reasonably, "any place you can get straightened out is fine with me."

This wasn't quite the answer he wanted. He had been sure in New York that the summer would do it—that in four months a man would come to *some* decision. He had visualized a house for them by the ocean, in a town with a library and a movie and other diversions. It had been a shock to discover how expensive summer rentals were and how far in advance you had to book them. When the last agent they saw described this place to them and told them how low the rent was, Malcolm had jumped at it immediately. But so had Virginia, even though there wasn't anything to do for distraction. In fact, she had made a point of asking the agent again about the location of the house, and the agent, a fat, gray man with ashes on his shirt, had said earnestly, "Mrs. Lawrence, if you're looking for a place where nobody will bother your husband from working, I can't think of anything better." Virginia had nodded decisively.

It had bothered her, his quitting the agency; he could understand that. Still, he wanted her to be happy, because he expected to be surer of what he wanted to do by the end of the summer. She was looking at him steadily now. He cast about for something to offer her that would interest her and change the mood between them. Then he remembered the scene he had witnessed earlier that evening. He told her about the man and his dogs, and this did raise her eyebrows.

"Do you remember the real-estate agent telling us anything about him?" she asked. "I don't."

Malcolm, searching through his memory, did recall that the agent had mentioned a custodian they could call on if there were any problems. At the time he had let it pass, because he couldn't imagine either agent or custodian really caring. Now he realized how dependent he and Virginia were out here if it came to things like broken plumbing or bad wiring, and the custodian's importance altered accordingly. "I guess he's the caretaker," he said.

"Oh."

"It makes sense—all this property has got to be worth something. If they didn't have someone here, people would just carry stuff away or come and camp or something."

"I suppose they would. I guess the owners let him live here rent-free, and with those dogs he must do a good job."

"He'll get to keep it for a while, too," Malcolm said. "Whoever started to build here was a good ten years ahead of himself. I can't see anybody buying into these places until things have gotten completely jammed up closer to New York."

"So, he's holding the fort," Virginia said, leaning casually over the table to put a dish down before him. She glanced over his shoulder toward the living-room window, widened her eyes, and automatically touched the neckline of her housecoat, and then snorted at herself.

"Look, he can't possibly scc in here," Malcolm said. "The living room, yes, but to look in here he'd have to be standing in the far corner of his yard. And he's back inside his house." He turned his head to look, and it was indeed true, except that one of the dogs was standing at that corner looking toward their house, eyes glittering. Then its head seemed to melt into a new shape, and it was looking down the road. It pivoted, moved a few steps away from the fence, turned, soared, landed in the street, and set off. Then, a moment later, it came back down the street running side by side with its companion, whose jaws were lightly pressed together around the rolled-over neck of a small paper bag. The dogs trotted together companionably and briskly, their flanks rubbing against one another, and when they were a few steps from the fence they leaped over it in unison and continued across the lawn until they were out of Malcolm's range of vision.

"For heaven's sake! He lives all alone with those dogs!" Virginia said.

Malcolm turned quickly back to her. "How do you come to think that?"

"Well, it's pretty plain. You saw what they were doing

out there just now. They're his servants. He can't get around himself, so they run errands for him. If he had a wife, she would do it."

"You learned all that already?"

"Did you notice how happy they were?" Virginia asked. "There was no need for that other dog to go meet its friend. But it wanted to. They can't be anything but happy." Then she looked at Malcolm, and he saw the old, studying reserve coming back into her eyes.

"For Pete's sake! They're only dogs—what do they know about anything?" Malcolm said.

"They know about happiness," Virginia said. "They know what they do in life."

Malcolm lay awake for a long time that night. He started by thinking about how good the summer was going to be, living here and working, and then he thought about the agency and about why he didn't seem to have the kind of shrewd, limited intuition that let a man do advertising work easily. At about four in the morning he wondered if perhaps he wasn't frightened, and had been frightened for a long time. None of this kind of thinking was new to him, and he knew that it would take him until late afternoon the following day to reach the point where he was feeling pretty good about himself.

When Virginia tried to wake him early the next morning he asked her to please leave him alone. At two in the afternoon, she brought him a cup of coffee and shook his shoulder. After a while, he walked out to the kitchen in his pajama pants and found that she had scrambled up some eggs for the two of them.

"What are your plans for the day?" Virginia said when he had finished eating.

He looked up. "Why?"

"Well, while you were sleeping, I put all your art things in the front bedroom. I think it'll make a good studio. With all your gear in there now, you can be pretty well set up by this evening."

At times she was so abrupt that she shocked him. It upset him that she might have been thinking that he wasn't planning to do anything at all today. "Look," he said, "you know I like to get the feel of a new thing."

"I know that. I didn't set anything up in there. I'm no artist. I just moved it all in."

When Malcolm had sat for a while without speaking,

Virginia cleared away their plates and cups and went into the bedroom. She came out wearing a dress, and she had combed her hair and put on lipstick. "Well, you do what you want to," she said. "I'm going to go across the street and introduce myself."

A flash of irritability hit him, but then he said, "If you'll wait a minute, I'll get dressed and go with you. We might as well both meet him."

He got up and went back to the bedroom for a T-shirt and blue jeans and a pair of loafers. He could feel himself beginning to react to pressure. Pressure always made him bind up; it looked to him as if Virginia had already shot the day for him.

They were standing at the fence, on the narrow strip of lawn between it and the row of whitewashed stones, and nothing was happening. Malcolm saw that although there was a gate in the fence, there was no break in the little grass border opposite it. And there was no front walk. The lawn was lush and all one piece, as if the house had been lowered onto it by helicopter. He began to look closely at the ground just inside the fence, and when he saw the regular pockmarks of the man's crutches, he was comforted.

"Do you see any kind of bell or anything?" Virginia asked.

"No."

"You'd think the dogs would bark."

"I'd just as soon they didn't."

"Will you look?" she said, fingering the gate latch. "The paint's hardly scuffed. I'll bet he hasn't been out of his yard all summer." Her touch rattled the gate lightly, and at that the two dogs came out from behind the house. One of them stopped, turned, and went back. The other dog came and stood by the fence, close enough for them to hear its breathing, and watched them with its head cocked alertly.

The front door of the house opened. At the doorway there was a wink of metal crutches, and then the man came out and stood on his front steps. When he had satisfied himself as to who they were, he nodded, smiled, and came toward them. The other dog walked beside him. Malcolm noticed that the dog at the fence did not distract himself by looking back at his master.

The man moved swiftly, crossing the ground with nimble swings of his body. His trouble seemed to be not in the spine, but in the legs themselves, for he was trying to help himself along with them. It could not be called walking, but it could not be called total helplessness either.

Although the man seemed to be in his late fifties, he had not gone to seed any more than his property had. He was wiry and clean-boned, and the skin on his face was tough and tanned. Around his small blue eyes and at the corners of his thin lips were many fine, deep-etched wrinkles. His yellowish-white hair was brushed straight back from his temples in the classic British military manner. And he even had a slight mustache. He was wearing a tweed jacket with leather patches at the elbows, which seemed a little warm for this kind of day, and a light flannel pale-gray shirt with a pale-blue bow tie. He stopped at the fence, rested his elbows on the crutches, and held out a firm hand with short nails the color of old bones.

"How do you do," he said pleasantly, his manner polished and well-bred. "I have been looking forward to meeting my new neighbors. I am Colonel Ritchey." The dogs stood motionless, one to each side of him, their sharp black faces pointing outward.

"How do you do," Virginia said. "We are Malcolm and Virginia Lawrence."

"I'm very happy to meet you," Colonel Ritchey said. "I was prepared to believe Cortelyou would fail to provide anyone this season."

Virginia was smiling. "What beautiful dogs," she said. "I was watching them last night."

"Yes. Their names are Max and Moritz. I'm very proud of them."

As they prattled on, exchanging pleasantries, Malcolm wondered why the Colonel had referred to Cortelyou, the real-estate agent, as a provider. There was something familiar, too, about the colonel.

Virginia said, "You're the famous Colonel Ritchey."

Indeed he was, Malcolm now realized, remembering the big magazine series that had appeared with the release of the movie several years before.

Colonel Ritchey smiled with no trace of embarrassment. "I am the famous Colonel Ritchey, but you'll notice I certainly don't look much like that charming fellow in the motion picture."

"What in hell are you doing *here?*" Malcolm asked.

Ritchey turned his attention to him. "One has to live somewhere, you know."

Virginia said immediately, "I was watching the dogs last night, and they seemed to do very well for you. I imagine it's pleasant having them to rely on."

"Yes, it is, indeed. They're quite good to me, Max and Moritz. But it is much better with people here now. I had begun to be quite disappointed in Cortelyou."

Malcolm began to wonder whether the agent would have had the brass to call Ritchey a custodian if the colonel had been within earshot.

"Come in, please," the colonel was saying. The gate latch resisted him momentarily, but he rapped it sharply with the heel of one palm and then lifted it. "Don't be concerned about Max and Moritz—they never do anything they're not told."

"Oh, I'm not the least bit worried about them," Virginia said.

"Ah, to some extent you should have been," the colonel said. "Dobermans are not to be casually trusted, you know. It takes many months before one can be at all confident in dealing with them."

"But you trained them yourself, didn't you?" Virginia said.

"Yes, I did," Colonel Ritchey said, with a pleased smile. "From imported pups." The voice in which he now spoke to the dogs was forceful, but as calm as his manner had been to Virginia. "Kennel," he said, and Max and Moritz stopped looking at Malcolm and Virginia and smoothly turned away.

The colonel's living room, which was as neat as a sample, contained beautifully cared for, somewhat old-fashioned furniture. The couch, with its needle-point upholstery and carved framing, was the sort of thing Malcolm would have expected in a lady's living room. Angling out from one wall was a Morris chair, placed so that a man might relax and gaze across the street or, with a turn of his head, rest his eyes on the distant lights of New York. Oil paintings in heavy gilded frames depicted landscapes, great eye-stretching vistas of rolling, open country. The furniture in the room seemed sparse to Malcolm until it occurred to him that the colonel needed extra clearance to get arou d in and had no particular need to keep additional chairs for visitors.

"Please do sit down," the colonel said. "I shall fetch some tea to refresh us."

When he had left the room, Virginia said, "Of all people! Neighborly, too."

Malcolm nodded. "Charming," he said.

The colonel entered holding a silver tray perfectly steady, its edges grasped between his thumbs and forefingers, his other fingers curled around each of the projecting black-rubber handgrips of his crutches. He brought tea on the tray and, of all things, homemade cookies. "I must apologize for the tea service," he said, "but it seems to be the only one I have."

When the colonel offered the tray, Malcolm saw that the utensils were made of the common sort of sheet metal used to manufacture food cans. Looking down now into his cup, he saw it had been enameled over its original tin-plate, and he realized that the whole thing had been made literally from a tin can. The teapot—handle, spout, vented lid, and all—was the same. "Be damned—you made this for yourself at the prison camp, didn't you?"

"As a matter of fact, I did, yes. I was really quite proud of my handiwork at the time, and it still serves. Somehow, living as I do, I've never brought myself to replace it. It's amazing, the fuddy-duddy skills one needs in a camp and how important they become to one. I find myself repainting these poor objects periodically and still taking as much smug pleasure in it as I did when that attitude was quite necessary. One is allowed to do these things in my position, you know. But I do hope my *ersatz* Spode isn't uncomfortably hot in your fingers."

Virginia smiled. "Well, of course, it's trying to be." Malcolm was amazed. He hadn't thought Virginia still remembered how to act so coquettish. She hadn't grown apart from the girl who'd always attracted a lot of attention at other people's gallery openings; she had simply put that part of herself away somewhere else.

Colonel Ritchey's blue eyes were twinkling in response. He turned to Malcolm. "I must say, it will be delightful to share this summer with someone as charming as Mrs. Lawrence."

"Yes," Malcolm said, preoccupied now with the cup, which was distressing his fingers with both heat and sharp edges. "At least, I've always been well satisfied with her," he added.

"I've been noticing the inscription here," Virginia said quickly, indicating the meticulous freehand engraving on the tea tray. She read out loud, " 'To Colonel David N. Ritchey, R.M.E., from his fellow officers at *Oflag* XXXI*b*, on the occasion of their liberation, May 14, 1945. Had he not been there to lead them, many would not have been present to share of this heartfelt token.' " Virginia's eyes shone, as she looked up at the colonel. "They must all have been very fond of you."

"Not all," the colonel said, with a slight smile. "I was senior officer over a very mixed bag. Mostly younger officers gathered from every conceivable branch. No followers at all—just budding leaders, all personally responsible for having surrendered once already, some apathetic, others desperate. Some useful, some not. It was my job to weld them into a disciplined, responsive body, to choose whom we must keep safe and who was best suited to keeping the Jerries on the jump. And we were in, of course, from the time of Dunkirk to the last days of the war, with the strategic situation in the camp constantly changing in various ways. All most of them understood was tactics—when they understood at all."

The colonel grimaced briefly, then smiled again. "The tray was presented by the survivors, of course. They'd had a tame Jerry pinch it out of the commandant's sideboard a few days earlier, in plenty of time to get the inscription on. But even the inscription hints that not all survived."

"It wasn't really like the movie, was it?" Virginia said.

"No, and yet—" Ritchey shrugged, as if remembering a time when he had accommodated someone on a matter of small importance. "That was a question of dramatic values, you must realize, and the need to tell an interesting and exciting story in terms recognizable to a civilian audience. Many of the incidents in the motion picture are literally true—they simply didn't happen in the context shown. The Christmas tunnel was quite real, obviously. I did promise the men I'd get at least one of them home for Christmas if they'd pitch in and dig it. But it wasn't a serious promise, and they knew it wasn't. Unlike the motion picture actor, I was not being fervent; I was being ironic.

"It was late in the war. An intelligent man's natural desire would be to avoid risk and wait for liberation. A

great many of them felt exactly that way. In fact, many
of them had turned civilian in their own minds and were
talking about their careers outside, their families—all that
sort of thing. So by couching in sarcasm trite words about
Christmas tunnels, I was reminding them what and where
they still were. The tactic worked quite well. Through de-
vices of that sort, I was able to keep them from going to
seed and coming out no use to anyone." The colonel's expression grew absent. "Some of them called me 'The
Shrew,' " he murmured. "*That* was in the movie, too, but
they were all shown smiling when they said it."

"But it was your duty to hold them all together any
way you could," Virginia said encouragingly.

Ritchey's face twisted into a spasm of tension so fierce
that there might have been strychnine in his tea. But it was
gone at once. "Oh, yes, yes, I held them together. By lying
and cajoling and tricking them. But the expenditure of
energy was enormous. And demeaning. It ought not to
have made any difference that we were cut off from higher
authority. If we had all still been home, there was not
a man among the prisoners who would have dared not
jump to my simplest command. But in the camp they
could shilly-shally and evade; they could settle down into
little private ambitions. People will do that. People will
not hold true to common purposes unless they are shown
discipline." The colonel's uncompromising glance went
from Virginia to Malcolm. "It's no good telling people what
they ought to do. The only surety is in being in a position
to tell people what they *must* do."

"Get some armed guards to back you up. That the idea,
Colonel? Get permission from the Germans to set up your
own machine-gun towers inside the camp?" Malcolm liked
working things out to the point of absurdity.

The colonel appraised him imperturbably. "I was never
quite that much my own man in Germany. But there is a
little story I must tell you. It's not altogether off the point."
He settled back, at ease once again.

"You may have been curious about Max and Moritz.
The Germans, as you know, have always been fond of
training dogs to perform all sorts of entertaining and useful things. During the war the Jerries were very much
given to using Dobermans for auxiliary guard duty at the
various prisoner-of-war camps. In action, Mr. Lawrence,
or simply in view, a trained dog is far more terrifying than

any soldier with a machine pistol. It takes an animal to stop a man without hesitation, no matter if the man is cursing or praying.

"Guard dogs at each camp were under the charge of a man called the *Hundführer*—the master of the hounds, if you will—whose function, after establishing himself with the dogs as their master and director, was to follow a few simple rules and to take the dogs to wherever they were needed. The dogs had been taught certain patrol routines. It was necessary only for the *Hundführer* to give simple commands such as 'Search' or 'Arrest,' and the dogs would know what to do. Once we had seen them do it, they were very much on our minds, I assure you.

"A Doberman, you see, has no conscience, being a dog. And a trained Doberman has no discretion. From the time he is a puppy, he is bent to whatever purpose has been preordained for him. And the lessons are painful—and autocratic. Once an order has been given, it must be enforced at all costs, for the dog must learn that all orders are to be obeyed unquestioningly. That being true, the dog must also learn immediately and irrevocably that only the orders from one particular individual are valid. Once a Doberman has been trained, there is no way to retrain it. When the American soldiers were seen coming, the Germans in the machine-gun towers threw down their weapons and tried to flee, but the dogs had to be shot. I watched from the hospital window, and I shall never forget how they continued to leap at the kennel fencing until the last one was dead. Their *Hundführer* had run away. . . ."

Malcolm found that his attention was wandering, but Virginia asked, as if on cue, "How did you get into the hospital—was that the Christmas tunnel accident?"

"Yes," the colonel said to Virginia, gentleman to lady. "The sole purpose of the tunnel was, as I said, to give the men a focus of attention. The war was near enough its end. It would have been foolhardy to risk actual escape attempts. But we did the thing up brown, of course. We had a concealed shaft, a tunnel lined with bed slats, a trolley for getting to and from the tunnel entrance, fat lamps made from shoe-blacking tins filled with margarine— all the normal appurtenances. The Germans at that stage were quite experienced in ferreting out this sort of operation, and the only reasonable assurance of continued progress was to work deeply and swiftly. Tunneling is always a calculated risk—the accounts of that sort of operation are biased in favor of the successes, of course.

"At any rate, by the end of November, some of the men were audibly thinking it was my turn to pitch in a bit, so one night I went down and began working. The shoring was as good as it ever was, and the conditions weren't any worse than normal. The air was breathable, and as long as one worked—ah—unclothed, and brushed down immediately on leaving the tunnel, the sand was not particularly damaging to one's skin. Clothing creates chafes in those circumstances. Sand burns coming to light at medical inspections were one of the surest signs that such an operation was under way.

"However that may be, I had been down there for about an hour and a half, and was about to start inching my way back up the tunnel, feetfirst on the trolley like some Freudian symbol, when there was a fall of the tunnel roof that buried my entire chest. It did not cover my face, which was fortunate, and I clearly remember my first thought was that now none of the men would be able to feel the senior officer hadn't shared their physical tribulations. I discovered, at once, that the business of clearing the sand that had fallen was going to be extremely awkward. First, I had to scoop some extra clearance from the roof over my face. Handfuls of sand began falling directly on me, and all I could do about that was to thrash my head back and forth. I was becoming distinctly exasperated at that when there was another slight fall behind the original collapse. This time, the fat lamp attached to the shoring loosened from its fastenings and spilled across my thighs. The hot fat was quite painful. What made it rather worse was that the string wick was not extinguished by the fall, and accordingly, the entire lower part of my body between navel and knees, having been saturated with volatile fat. . . ." The colonel grimaced in embarrassment.

"Well, I was immediately in a very bad way, for there was nothing I could do about the fire until I had dug my way past the sand on my chest. In due course, I did indeed free myself and was able to push my way backward up the tunnel after extinguishing the flames. The men at the shaft head had seen no reason to become alarmed—tunnels always smell rather high and sooty, as you can imagine. But they did send a man down when I got near the entrance shaft and made myself heard.

"Of course, there was nothing to do but tell the Jerries, since we had no facilities whatever for concealing my condition or treating it. They put me in the camp hospital, and there I stayed until the end of the war with plenty of time to lie about and think my thoughts. I was even able to continue exercising some control over my men. I shouldn't be a bit surprised if that hadn't been in the commandant's mind all along. I think he had come to depend on my presence to moderate the behavior of the men.

"That is really almost the end of the story. We were liberated by the American Army, and the men were sent home. I stayed in military hospitals until I was well enough to travel home, and there I dwelt in hotels and played the retired, invalided officer. After that journalist's book was published and the dramatic rights were sold, I was called to Hollywood to be the technical adviser for the movie. I was rather grateful to accept the employment, frankly— an officer's pension is not particularly munificent—and what with selectively lending my name and services to various organizations while my name was still before the public, I was able to accumulate a sufficient nest egg.

"Of course, I cannot go back to England, where the Inland Revenue would relieve me of most of it, but, having established a relationship with Mr. Cortelyou and acquired and trained Max and Moritz, I am content. A man must make his way as best he can and do whatever is required for survival." The colonel cocked his head brightly and regarded Virginia and Malcolm. "Wouldn't you say?"

"Y—es," Virginia said slowly. Malcolm couldn't decide what the look on her face meant. He had never seen it before. Her eyes were shining, but wary. Her smile showed excitement and sympathy, but tension too. She seemed caught between two feelings.

"Quite!" the colonel said, smacking his hands together. "It is most important to me that you fully understand the situation." He pushed himself up to his feet and, with the same move, brought the crutches out smoothly and positioned them to balance him before he could fall. He stood leaning slightly forward, beaming. "Well, now, having heard my story, I imagine the objectives of this conversation are fully attained, and there is no need to detain you here further. I'll see you to the front gate."

"That won't be necessary," Malcolm said.

"I insist," the colonel said in what would have been a perfectly pleasant manner if he had added the animated twinkle to his eyes. Virginia was staring at him, blinking slowly.

"Please forgive us," she said. "We certainly hadn't meant to stay long enough to be rude. Thank you for the tea and cookies. They were very good."

"Not at all, my dear," the colonel said. "It's really quite pleasant to think of looking across the way, now and then, and catching glimpses of someone so attractive at her domestic preoccupations. I cleaned up thoroughly after the last tenants, of course, but there are always little personal touches one wants to apply. And you will start some plantings at the front of the house, won't you? Such little activities are quite precious to me—someone as charming as you, in her summer things, going about her little fussings and tendings, resting in the sun after weeding—that sort of thing. Yes, I expect a most pleasant summer. I assume there was never any question you wouldn't stay all summer. Cortelyou would hardly bother with anyone who could not afford to pay him that much. But little more, eh?" The urbane, shrewd look returned to the colonel's face. "Pinched resources and few ties, eh? Or what would you be doing here, if there were somewhere else to turn to?"

"Well, good afternoon, Colonel," Virginia said with noticeable composure. "Let's go, Malcolm."

"Interesting conversation, Colonel," Malcolm said.

"Interesting and necessary, Mr. Lawrence," the colonel said, following them out onto the lawn. Virginia watched him closely as she moved toward the gate, and Malcolm noticed a little downward twitch at the corners of her mouth.

"Feeling a bit of a strain, Mrs. Lawrence?" the colonel asked solicitously. "Please believe that I shall be as considerate of your sensibilities as intelligent care of my own comfort will permit. It is not at all in my code to offer offense to a lady, and in any case—" the colonel smiled deprecatingly "—since the mishap of the Christmas tunnel, one might say the spirit is willing but . . ." The colonel frowned down absently at his canes. "No, Mrs. Lawrence," he went on, shaking his head paternally, "is a flower the less for being breathed of? And is the cultivated flower, tended and nourished, not more fortunate than the wild rose that blushes unseen? Do not regret your present social situation too much, Mrs. Lawrence—some might find it enviable. Few things are more changeable than points of view. In the coming weeks your viewpoint might well change."

"Just what the hell are you saying to my wife?" Malcolm asked.

Virginia said quickly, "We can talk about it later."

The colonel smiled at Virginia. "Before you do that, I have something else to show Mr. Lawrence." He raised his voice slightly: "Max! Moritz! Here!"—and the dogs were there. "Ah, Mr. Lawrence, I would like to show you first how these animals respond, how discriminating they can be." He turned to one of the dogs. "Moritz," he said sharply, nodding toward Malcolm. "Kill."

Malcolm couldn't believe what he had heard. Then he felt a blow on his chest. The dog was on him, its hind legs making short, fast, digging sounds in the lawn as it pressed its body against him. It was inside the arc of his arms, and the most he could have done was to clasp it closer to him. He made a tentative move to pull his arms back and then push forward against its rib cage, but the minor shift in weight made him stumble, and he realized if he completed the gesture he would fall. All this happened in a very short time, and then the dog touched open lips with him. Having done that, it dropped down and went back to stand beside Colonel Ritchey and Max.

"You see, Mr. Lawrence?" the colonel asked conversationally. "A dog does not respond to literal meaning. It is conditioned. It is trained to perform a certain action when it hears a certain sound. The cues one teaches a dog with pain and patience are not necessarily cues an educated organism can understand. Pavlov rang a bell and a dog salivated. Is a bell food? If he had rung a different bell, or said, 'Food, doggie,' there would have been no response. So, when I speak in a normal tone, rather than at command pitch, 'kill' does not mean 'kiss,' even to Moritz. It means nothing to him—unless I raise my voice. And I could just as easily have conditioned him to perform that sequence in association with some other command—such as, oh, say, 'gingersnaps'—but then you might not have taken the point of my little, instructive jest. There is no way anyone but myself can operate these creatures. Only when I command do they respond. And now you respond, eh, Mr. Lawrence? I dare say. . . . Well, good day. As I said, you have things to do."

They left through the gate, which the colonel drew shut behind them. "Max," he said, "watch," and the dog froze in position. "Moritz, come." The colonel turned, and he and the other dog crossed the lawn and went into his house.

Malcolm and Virginia walked at a normal pace back to the rented house, Malcolm matching his step to Virginia's. He wondered if she were being so deliberate because she wasn't sure what the dog would do if she ran. It had been a long time since Virginia hadn't been sure of something.

In the house, Virginia made certain the door was shut tight, and then she went to sit in the chair that faced away from the window. "Would you make me some coffee, please?" she said.

"All right, sure. Take a few minutes. Catch your breath a little."

"A few minutes is what I need," she said. "Yes, a few minutes, and everything will be fine." When Malcolm returned with the coffee, she continued, "He's got some kind of string on Cortelyou, and I bet those people at the store down at the corner aren't too happy about those dogs walking in and out of there all the time. He's got us. We're locked up."

"Now, wait," Malcolm said, "there's the whole state of New Jersey out there, and he can't—"

"Yes, he can. If he thinks he can get away with it, and he's got good reasons for thinking he can. Take it on faith. There's no bluff in *him*."

"Well, look," he said, "just what can he do to us?"

"Any damn thing he pleases."

"That can't be right." Malcolm frowned. "He's got us pretty well scared right now, but we ought to be able to work out some way of—"

Virginia said tightly, "The dog's still there, right?" Malcolm nodded. "Okay," she said. "What did it feel like when he hit you? It looked awful. It looked like he was going to drive you clear onto your back. Did it feel that way? What did you *think?*"

"Well, he's a pretty strong animal," Malcolm said. "But,

to tell you the truth, I didn't have time to believe it. You know, a man just saying 'kill' like that is a pretty hard thing to believe. Especially just after tea and cookies."

"He's very shrewd," Virginia said. "I can see why he had the camp guards running around in circles. He deserved to have a book written about him."

"All right, and then they should have thrown him into a padded cell."

"Tried to throw," Virginia amended.

"Oh, come on. This is his territory, and he dealt the cards before we even knew we were playing. But all he is is a crazy old cripple. If he wants to buffalo some people in a store and twist a two-bit real-estate salesman around his finger, fine—if he can get away with it. But he doesn't own us. We're not in his army."

"We're inside his prison camp," Virginia said.

"Now, look," Malcolm said. "When we walk in Cortelyou's door and tell him we know all about the colonel, there's not going to be any trouble about getting the rent back. We'll find someplace else, or we'll go back to the city. But whatever we do to get out of this, it's going to work out a lot smoother if the two of us think about it. It's not like you to be sitting there and spending a lot of time on how we can't win."

"Well, Malcolm. Being a prisoner certainly brings out your initiative. Here you are, making noises just like a senior officer. Proposing escape committees and everything."

Malcolm shook his head. Now of all times, when they needed each other so much, she wouldn't let up. The thing to do was to move too fast for her.

"All right," he said, "let's get in the car." There was just the littlest bit of sweat on his upper lip.

"*What?*" He had her sitting up straight in the chair, at least. "Do you imagine that that dog will let us get anywhere near the car?"

"You want to stay here? All right. Just keep the door locked. I'm going to try it, and once I'm out I'm going to come back here with a nice healthy state cop carrying a nice healthy riot gun. And we're either going to do something about the colonel and those two dogs, or we're at least going to move you and our stuff out of here."

He picked up the car keys, stepped through the front door very quickly, and began to walk straight for the car.

The dog barked sharply, once. The front door of Ritchey's house opened immediately, and Ritchey called out, "Max! Hold!" The dog on the lawn was over the fence and had its teeth thrust carefully around Malcolm's wrist before he could take another eight steps, even though he had broken into a run. Both the dog and Malcolm stood very still. The dog was breathing shallowly and quietly, its eyes shining. Ritchey and Moritz walked as far as the front fence. "Now, Mr. Lawrence," Ritchey said, "in a moment I am going to call to Max, and he is to bring you with him. Do not attempt to hold back, or you will lacerate your wrist. Max! Bring here!"

Malcolm walked steadily toward the colonel. By some smooth trick of his neck, Max was able to trot alongside him without shifting his grip. "Very good, Max," Ritchey said soothingly when they had reached the fence. "Loose now," and the dog let go of Malcolm's wrist. Malcolm and Ritchey looked into each other's eyes across the fence, in the darkening evening. "Now, Mr. Lawrence," Ritchey said, "I want you to give me your car keys." Malcolm held out the keys, and Ritchey put them into his pocket. "Thank you." He seemed to reflect on what he was going to say next, as a teacher might reflect on his reply to a child who has asked why the sky is blue. "Mr. Lawrence, I want you to understand the situation. As it happens, I also want a three-pound can of Crisco. If you will please give me all the money in your pocket, this will simplify matters."

"I don't have any money on me," Malcolm said. "Do you want me to go in the house and get some?"

"No, Mr. Lawrence, I'm not a thief. I'm simply restricting your radius of action in one of the several ways I'm going to do so. Please turn out your pockets."

Malcolm turned out his pockets.

"All right, Mr. Lawrence, if you will hand me your wallet and your address book and the thirty-seven cents, they will all be returned to you whenever you have a legitimate use for them." Ritchey put the items away in the pockets of his jacket. "Now, a three-pound can of Crisco is ninety-eight cents. Here is a dollar bill. Max will walk with you to the corner grocery store, and you will buy the Crisco for me and bring it back. It is too much for a dog to carry in a bag, and it is three days until my next monthly delivery of staples. At the store you will please tell them that it will not be necessary for them to come here with monthly deliveries any longer—that you will be in to do my shopping for me from now on. I expect you to take a minimum amount of time to accomplish all this and to come back with my purchase, Mr. Lawrence. Max!" The colonel nodded toward Malcolm. "Guard. Store." The dog trembled and whined. "Don't stand still, Mr. Lawrence. Those commands are incompatible until you start toward the store. If you fail to move, he will grow increasingly tense. Please go now. Moritz and I will keep Mrs. Lawrence good company until you return."

The store consisted of one small room in the front of a drab house. On unpainted pine shelves were brands of goods that Malcolm had never heard of. "Oh! You're with one of those nice dogs," the tired, plump woman behind the counter said, leaning down to pat Max, who had approached her for that purpose. It seemed to Malcolm that the dog was quite mechanical about it and was pretending to itself that nothing caressed it at all. He looked around the place, but he couldn't see anything or anyone that offered any prospect of alliance with him.

"Colonel Ritchey wants a three-pound can of Crisco," he said, bringing the name out to check the reaction.

"Oh, you're helping him?"

"You could say that."

"Isn't he brave?" the woman said in low and confidential tones, as if concerned that the dog could overhear. "You know, there are some people who would think you should feel sorry for a man like that, but I say it would be a sin to do so. Why, he gets along just fine, and he's got more pride and spunk than any whole man I've ever seen. Makes a person proud to know him. You know, I think it's just wonderful the way these dogs come and fetch little things for him. But I'm glad he's got somebody to look out for him now. 'Cept for us, I don't think he sees anybody from one year to the next—'cept summers, of course."

She studied Malcolm closely. "You're summer people too, aren't you? Well, glad to have you, if you're doin' some good for the colonel. Those people last year were a shame. Just moved out one night in September, and neither the colonel nor me or my husband seen hide nor hair of them since. Owed the colonel a month's rent, he said when we was out there."

"Is he the landlord?" Malcolm asked.

"Oh, sure, yes. He owns a lot of land around here. Bought it from the original company after it went bust."

"Does he own this store, too?"

"Well, we lease it from him now. Used to own it, but we sold it to the company and leased it from them. Oh, we was all gonna be rich. My husband took the money from the land and bought a lot across the street and was gonna set up a real big gas station there—figured to be real shrewd—but you just can't get people to live out here. I mean, it isn't as if this was *ocean*-front property. But the colonel now, he's got a head on his shoulders. Value's got to go up someday, and he's just gonna hold on until it does."

The dog was getting restless, and Malcolm was worried about Virginia. He paid for the can of Crisco, and he and Max went back up the sand road in the dark. There really, honestly, didn't seem to be much else to do.

At his front door, he stopped, sensing that he should knock. When Virginia let him in, he saw that she had changed to shorts and a halter. "Hello," she said, and then stood aside quietly for him and Max. The colonel, sitting pertly forward on one of the chairs, looked up. "Ah, Mr. Lawrence, you're a trifle tardy, but the company has been delightful, and the moments seemed to fly."

Malcolm looked at Virginia. In the past couple of years, a little fat had accumulated above her knees, but she still had long, good legs. Colonel Ritchey smiled at Malcolm. "It's a rather close evening. I simply suggested to Mrs. Lawrence that I certainly wouldn't be offended if she left me for a moment and changed into something more comfortable."

It seemed to Malcolm that she could have handled that. But apparently she hadn't.

"Here's your Crisco," Malcolm said. "The change is in the bag."

"Thank you very much," the colonel said. "Did you tell them about the grocery deliveries?"

Malcolm shook his head. "I don't remember. I don't think so. I was busy getting an earful about how you owned them, lock, stock, and barrel."

"Well, no harm. You can tell them tomorrow."

"Is there going to be some set time for me to run your

errands every day, Colonel? Or are you just going to whenever something comes up?"

"Ah, yes. You're concerned about interruptions in your mood. Mrs. Lawrence told me you were some sort of artist. I'd wondered at your not shaving this morning." The colonel paused and then went on crisply. "I'm sure we'll shake down into whatever routine suits best. It always takes a few days for individuals to hit their stride as a group. After that, it's quite easy—regular functions, established duties, that sort of thing. A time to rise and wash, a time to work, a time to sleep. Everything and everyone in his proper niche. Don't worry, Mr. Lawrence, you'll be surprised how comfortable it becomes. Most people find it a revelation." The colonel's gaze grew distant for a moment. "Some do not. Some are as if born on another planet, innocent of human nature. Dealing with that sort, there comes a point when one must cease to try; at the camp, I found that the energy for over-all success depended on my admitting the existence of the individual failure. No, some do not respond. But we needn't dwell on what time will tell us."

Ritchey's eyes twinkled. "I have dealt previously with creative people. Most of them need to work with their hands; do stupid, dull, boring work that leaves their minds free to soar in spirals and yet forces them to stay away from their craft until the tension is nearly unbearable." The colonel waved in the direction of the unbuilt houses. "There's plenty to do. If you don't know how to use a hammer and saw as yet, I know how to teach that. And when from time to time I see you've reached the proper pitch of creative frustration, then you shall have what time off I judge will best serve you artistically. I think you'll be surprised how pleasingly you'll take to your studio. From what I gather from your wife, this may well be a very good experience for you."

Malcolm looked at Virginia. "Yes. Well, that's been bugging her for a long time. I'm glad she's found a sympathetic ear."

"Don't quarrel with your wife, Mr. Lawrence. That sort of thing wastes energy and creates serious morale problems." The colonel got to his feet and went to the door. "One thing no one could ever learn to tolerate in a fellow *Kriegie* was pettiness. That sort of thing was always

ne, Max. Come, Moritz. Good night." He

over to the door and put the chain on.

w, look—"

d up one finger. "Hold it. Nobody likes a
me *Kriegie*. We're not going to fight. We're going
talk, and we're going to think." He found himself looking at her halter and took his glance away. Virginia
blushed.

"I just want you to know it was exactly the way he described it," she said. "He said he wouldn't think it impo-
lite if I left him alone in the living room while I went to
change. And I wasn't telling him our troubles. We were
talking about what you did for a living, and it didn't take
much for him to figure out—"

"I don't want you explaining," Malcolm said. "I want
you to help me tackle this thing and get it solved."

"How are you going to solve it? This is a man who always uses everything he's got! He never quits! How is
somebody like *you* going to solve that?"

All these years, it occurred to Malcolm, at a time like
this, now, she finally had to say the thing you couldn't
make go away.

When Malcolm did not say anything at all for a while
but only walked around frowning and thinking, Virginia
said she was going to sleep. In a sense, he was relieved; a
whole plan of action was forming in his mind, and he did
not want her there to badger him.

After she had closed the bedroom door, he went into
the studio. In a corner was a carton of his painting stuff,
which he now approached, detached but thinking. From
this room he could see the floodlights on around the colonel's house. The colonel had made his circuit of the yard,
and one of the dogs stood at attention, looking across the
way. The setting hadn't altered at all from the night before. Setting, no, Malcolm thought, bouncing a jar of
brown tempera in his hand; mood, *si*. His arm felt good all
the way down from his shoulder, into the forearm, wrist,
and fingers.

When Ritchey had been in his house a full five minutes,
Malcolm said to himself aloud, "Do first, analyze later."
Whipping open the front door, he took two steps forward
on the bare earth to gather momentum and pitched the jar

of paint in a shallow arc calculated to end against the aluminum fence.

It was going to fall short, Malcolm thought, and it did, smashing with a loud impact against one of the white-washed stones and throwing out a fan of gluey, brown spray over the adjacent stones, the fence, and the dog, which jumped back but, lacking orders to charge, stood its ground, whimpering. Malcolm stepped back into his open doorway and leaned in it. When the front door of Ritchey's house opened he put his thumbs to his ears and waggled his fingers, *"Gute Nacht, Herr Kommandant,"* he called, then stepped back inside and slammed and locked the door, throwing the spring-bolt latch. The dog was already on its way. It loped across the yard and scraped its front paws against the other side of the door. Its breath sounded like giggling.

Malcolm moved over to the window. The dog sprang away from the door with a scratching of toenails and leaped upward, glancing off the glass. It turned, trotted away for a better angle, and tried again. Malcolm watched it; this was the part he'd bet on.

The dog didn't make it. Its jaws flattened against pane, and the whole sheet quivered, but there was too much going against success. The window was pretty high above the yard, and the dog couldn't get a proper combination of momentum and angle of impact. If he did manage to break it, he'd never have enough momentum left to clear the break; he'd fall on the sharp edges of glass in the frame while other chunks fell and cut his neck, and then the colonel would be down to one dog. One dog wouldn't be enough; the system would break down somewhere.

The dog dropped down, leaving nothing on the glass but a wet brown smear.

It seemed to Malcolm equally impossible for the colonel to break the window himself. He couldn't stride forward to throw a small stone hard enough to shatter the pane, and he couldn't balance well enough to heft a heavy one from nearby. The lock and chain would prevent him from entering through the front door. No, it wasn't efficient for the colonel any way you looked at it. He would rather take a few days to think of something shrewd and economical. In fact, he was calling the dog back now. When the dog reached its master, he shifted one crutch and did his best to kneel while rubbing the dog's head. There was something rather like affection in the scene. Then the colonel straightened up and called again. The other dog came out of the house and took up its station at the corner of the yard. The colonel and the dirty dog went back into the colonel's house.

Malcolm smiled, then turned out the lights, double-checked the locks, and went back through the hall to the bedroom. Virginia was sitting up in bed, staring in the direction from which the noise had come.

"What did you do?" she asked.

"Oh, changed the situation a little," Malcolm said, grinning. "Asserted my independence. Shook up the colonel. Smirched his neatness a little bit. Spoiled his night's sleep for him, I hope. Standard *Kriegie* tactics. I hope he likes them."

Virginia was incredulous. "Do you know what he could do to you with those dogs if you step outside this house?"

"I'm not going to step outside. Neither are you. We're just going to wait a few days."

"What do you mean?" Virginia said, looking at him as if he were the maniac.

"Day after tomorrow, maybe the day after that," Malcolm explained, "he's due for a grocery delivery I didn't turn off. Somebody's going to be here with a car then, lugging all kinds of things. I don't care how beholden those storekeepers are to him; when we come out the door, he's not going to have those dogs tear us to pieces right on the front lawn in broad daylight and with a witness. We're going to get into the grocery car, and sooner or later we're going to drive out in it, because *that* car and driver have to turn up in the outside world again."

Virginia sighed. "Look," she said with obvious control, "all he has to do is send a note with the dogs. He can stop the delivery that way."

Malcolm nodded. "Uh-huh. And so the groceries don't come. Then what? He starts trying to freight flour and eggs in here by dog back? By remote control? What's he going to do? All right, so it doesn't work out so neatly in two or three days. But we've got a fresh supply of food, and he's almost out. Unless he's planning to live on Crisco, he's in a bad way. And even so, he's only got three pounds of that." Malcolm got out of his clothes and lay down on the bed. "Tomorrow's another day, but I'll be damned if I'm going to worry any more about it tonight. I've got a good head start on frustrating the legless wonder, and tomorrow I'm going to have a nice clear mind, and I'm going to see what other holes I can pick in his defense. I learned a lot of snide little tricks from watching jolly movies about clever prisoners and dumb guards." He reached up and turned out the bed light. "Good night, love," he said. Virginia rolled away from him in the dark. "Oh, my God," she said in a voice with a brittle edge around it.

It was a sad thing for Malcolm to lie there thinking that she had that kind of limitation in her, that she didn't really understand what had to be done. On the other hand, he thought sleepily, feeling more relaxed than he had in years, he had his own limitations. And she had put up with them for years. He fell asleep wondering pleasantly what tomorrow would bring.

He woke to a sound of rumbling and crunching under the earth, as if there were teeth at the foundations of the house. Still sleeping in large portions of his brain, he cried out silently to himself with a madman's lucidity, "Ah, of course, he's been tunneling!" And his mind gave him all the details—the careful transfer of supporting timber from falling houses, the disposal of the excavated clay in the piles beside the other foundations. Perhaps there were tunnels leading toward those other foundations, too, for when the colonel had more people. . . .

Now one corner of the room showed a jagged line of yellow, and Malcolm's hands sprang to the light switch. Virginia jumped from sleep. In the corner was a trap door, its uneven joints concealed by boards of different lengths. The trap door crashed back, releasing a stench of body odor and soot.

A dog popped up through the opening and scrambled into the bedroom. Its face and body were streaked, and it shook itself to get the sand from its coat. Behind it, the colonel dragged himself up, naked, and braced himself on his arms, half out of the tunnel mouth. His hair was matted down with perspiration over his narrow-boned skull. He was mottled yellow-red with dirt, and half in the shadows. Virginia buried her face in her hands, one eye glinting out between spread fingers, and cried to Malcolm, "Oh my God, what have you done to us?"

"Don't worry, my dear," the colonel said crisply to her. Then he screamed at Malcolm, "I will not be abused!"

Trembling with strain as he hung on one corded arm, he said to the dog at command pitch, pointing at Malcolm, "Kiss!"

THE CANDIDATE

by Henry Slesar

"A man's worth can be judged by the calibre of his enemies." Burton Grunzer, encountering the phrase in a
pocket-sized biography he had purchased at a newsstand,
put the book in his lap and stared reflectively from the
murky window of the commuter train. Darkness silvered
the glass and gave him nothing to look at but his own
image, but it seemed appropriate to his line of thought.
How many people were enemies of that face, of the eyes
narrowed by a myopic squint denied by vanity that cor-
rection of spectacles, of the nose he secretly called patri-
cian, of the mouth that was soft in relaxation and hard
when animated by speech or smiles or frowns? How many
enemies? Grunzer mused. A few he could name, others he
could guess. But it was their calibre that was important.
Men like Whitman Hayes, for instance, there was a 24-
carat opponent for you. Grunzer smiled, darting a sidelong glance at the seat-sharer beside him, not wanting to
be caught indulging in a secret thought. Grunzer was
thirty-four; Hayes was twice as old, his white hairs synony-
mous with experience, an enemy to be proud of. Hayes
knew the food business, all right, knew it from every
angle: he'd been a wagon jobber for six years, a broker
for ten, a food company executive for twenty before the
old man had brought him into the organization to sit on
his right hand. Pinning Hayes to the mat wasn't easy, and
that made Grunzer's small but increasing triumphs all the
sweeter. He congratulated himself. He had twisted Hayes's
advantages into drawbacks, had made his long years seem
tantamount to senility and outlived usefulness; in meetings,
he had concentrated his questions on the new supermarket
and suburbia phenomena to demonstrate to the old man
that times had changed, that the past was dead, that new
merchandising tactics were needed, and that only a younger
man could supply them. . . .

Suddenly, he was depressed. His enjoyment of remembered victories seemed tasteless. Yes, he'd won a minor battle or two in the company conference room; he'd made Hayes' ruddy face go crimson, and seen the old man's parchment skin wrinkle in a sly grin. But what had been accomplished? Hayes seemed more self-assured than ever, and the old man more dependent upon his advice. . . .

When he arrived home, later than usual, his wife Jean didn't ask questions. After eight years of a marriage in which, childless, she knew her husband almost too well, she wisely offered nothing more than a quiet greeting, a hot meal, and the day's mail. Grunzer flipped through the bills and circulars, and found an unmarked letter. He slipped it into his hip pocket, reserving it for private perusal, and finished the meal in silence.

After dinner, Jean suggested a movie and he agreed; he had a passion for violent action movies. But first, he locked himself in the bathroom and opened the letter. Its heading was cryptic: *Society for United Action.* The return address was a post office box. It read:

> Dear Mr. Grunzer:
>   Your name has been suggested to us by a mutual acquaintance. Our organization has an unusual mission which cannot be described in this letter, but which you may find of exceeding interest. We would be gratified by a private discussion at your earliest convenience. If I do not hear from you to the contrary in the next few days, I will take the liberty of calling you at your office.

It was signed, *Carl Tucker, Secretary.* A thin line at the bottom of the page read: *A Non-Profit Organization.*

His first reaction was a defensive one; he suspected an oblique attack on his pocketbook. His second was curiosity: he went to the bedroom and located the telephone directory, but found no organization listed by the letterhead name. *Okay, Mr. Tucker,* he thought wryly, *I'll bite.*

When no call came in the next three days, his curiosity was increased. But when Friday arrived, he forgot the letter's promise in the crush of office affairs. The old man called a meeting with the bakery products division. Grunzer sat opposite Whitman Hayes at the conference table, poised to pounce on fallacies in his statements. He almost had him once, but Eckhardt, the bakery products manager, spoke up in defense of Hayes's views. Eckhardt had only been with the company a year, but he had evidently chosen sides already. Grunzer glared at him, and reserved a place for Eckhardt in the hate chamber of his mind.

At three o'clock, Carl Tucker called.

"Mr. Grunzer?" The voice was friendly, even cheery. "I haven't heard from you, so I assume you don't mind me calling today. Is there a chance we can get together sometime?"

"Well, if you could give me some idea, Mr. Tucker—"

The chuckle was resonant. "We're not a charity organization, Mr. Grunzer, in case you got that notion. Nor do we sell anything. We're more or less a voluntary service group: our membership is over a thousand at present."

"To tell you the truth," Grunzer frowned, "I never heard of you."

"No, you haven't, and that's one of the assets. I think you'll understand when I tell you about us. I can be over at your office in fifteen minutes, unless you want to make it another day."

Grunzer glanced at his calendar. "Okay, Mr. Tucker. Best time for me is right now."

"Fine! I'll be right over."

Tucker was prompt. When he walked into the office, Grunzer's eyes went dismayed at the officious briefcase in the man's right hand. But he felt better when Tucker, a florid man in his early sixties with small, pleasant features, began talking.

"Nice of you to take the time, Mr. Grunzer. And believe me, I'm not here to sell you insurance or razor blades. Couldn't if I tried; I'm a semi-retired broker. However, the subject I want to discuss is rather—intimate, so I'll have to ask you to bear with me on a certain point. May I close the door?"

"Sure," Grunzer said, mystified.

Tucker closed it, hitched his chair closer, and said:

"The point is this. What I have to say must remain in the strictest confidence. If you betray that confidence, if you publicize our society in any way, the consequences could be most unpleasant. Is that agreeable?"

Grunzer, frowning, nodded.

"Fine!" The visitor snapped open the briefcase and produced a stapled manuscript. "Now, the society has prepared this little spiel about our basic philosophy, but I'm not going to bore you with it. I'm going to go straight to the heart of our argument. You may not agree with our first principle at all, and I'd like to know that now."

"How do you mean, first principle?"

"Well . . ." Tucker flushed slightly. "Put in the crudest form, Mr. Grunzer, the Society for United Action believes that—*some* people are just not fit to live." He looked up quickly, as if anxious to gauge the immediate reaction. "There, I've said it," he laughed, somewhat in relief. "Some of our members don't believe in my direct approach; they feel the argument has to be broached more discreetly. But frankly, I've gotten excellent results in this rather crude manner. How do you feel about what I've said, Mr. Grunzer?"

"I don't know. Guess I never thought about it much."

"Were you in the war, Mr. Grunzer?"

"Yes. Navy." Grunzer rubbed his jaw. "I suppose I didn't think the Japs were fit to live, back then. I guess maybe there are other cases. I mean, you take capital punishment, I believe in that. Murderers, rape-artists, perverts, hell, I certainly don't think *they're* fit to live."

"Ah," Tucker said. "So you really accept our first principle. It's a question of category, isn't it?"

"I guess you could say that."

"Good. So now I'll try another blunt question. Have you—personally—ever wished someone dead? Oh, I don't mean those casual, fleeting wishes everybody has. I mean a real, deep-down, uncomplicated wish for the death of someone *you* thought was unfit to live. Have you?"

"Sure." Grunzer said frankly. "I guess I have."

"There are times, in your opinion, when the removal of someone from this earth would be beneficial?"

Grunzer smiled. "Hey, what is this? You from Murder Incorporated or something?"

Tucker grinned back. "Hardly, Mr. Grunzer, hardly. There is absolutely no criminal aspect to our aims or our methods. I'll admit we're a 'secret' society, but we're no Black Hand. You'd be amazed at the quality of our membership; it even includes members of the legal profession. But suppose I tell you how the society came into being.

"It began with two men; I can't reveal their names just now. The year was 1949, and one of these men was a lawyer attached to the district attorney's office. The other man was a state psychiatrist. Both of them were involved in a rather sensational trial, concerning a man accused of a hideous crime against two small boys. In their opinion, the man was unquestionably guilty, but an unusually persuasive defense counsel, and a highly suggestible jury, gave him his freedom. When the shocking verdict was announced, these two, who were personal friends as well as colleagues, were thunderstruck and furious. They felt a great wrong had been committed, and they were helpless to right it . . .

"But I should explain something about this psychiatrist. For some years, he had made studies in a field which might be called anthropological psychiatry. One of these researches related to the Voodoo practice of certain groups, the Haitian in particular. You've probably heard a great deal about Voodoo, or Obeah as they call it in Jamaica, but I won't dwell on the subject lest you think we hold tribal rites and stick pins in dolls . . . But the chief feature of his study was the uncanny *success* of certain strange practices. Naturally, as a scientist, he rejected the supernatural explanation and sought the rational one. And of course, there was only one answer. When the Vodun priest decreed the punishment or death of a malefactor, it was the malefactor's own convictions concerning the efficacy of the death-wish, his own faith in the Voodoo power, that eventually made the wish come true. Sometimes, the process was organic—his body reacted psychosomatically to the Voodoo curse, and he would sicken and die. Sometimes, he would die by 'accident'—an accident prompted by the secret belief that once cursed, he *must* die. Eerie, isn't it?"

"No doubt," Grunzer said, dry-lipped.

"Anyway, our friend, the psychiatrist, began wondering aloud if *any* of us have advanced so far along the civilized path that we couldn't be subject to this same sort of 'suggested' punishment. He proposed that they experiment on this choice subject, just to see.

"How they did it was simple," he said. "They went to see this man, and they announced their intentions. They told him they were going to *wish him dead*. They explained how and why the wish would become reality, and while he laughed at their proposal, they could see the look of superstitious fear cross his face. They promised him that regularly, every day, they would be wishing for his death, until he could no longer stop the mystic juggernaut that would make the wish come true."

Grunzer shivered suddenly, and clenched his fist. "That's pretty silly," he said softly.

"The man died of a heart attack two months later."

"Of course. I knew you'd say that. But there's such a thing as coincidence."

"Naturally. And our friends, while intrigued, weren't satisfied. *So they tried it again.*"

"Again?"

"Yes, again. I won't recount who the victim was, but I will tell you that this time they enlisted the aid of four associates. This little band of pioneers was the nucleus of the society I represent today."

Grunzer shook his head. "And you mean to tell me there's a *thousand* now?"

"Yes, a thousand and more, all over the country. A society whose one function is to *wish people dead.* At first, membership was purely voluntary, but now we have a system. Each new member of the Society for United Action joins on the basis of submitting one potential victim. Naturally, the society investigates to determine whether the victim is deserving of his fate. If the case is a good one, the *entire* membership then sets about to *wish him dead.* Once the task has been accomplished, naturally, the new member must take part in all future concerted action. That and a small yearly fee, is the price of membership."

Carl Tucker grinned.

"And in case you think I'm not serious, Mr. Grunzer—" He dipped into the briefcase again, this time producing a blue-bound volume of telephone directory thickness. "Here are the facts. To date, two hundred and twenty-nine victims were named by our selection committee. Of those, *one hundred and four* are no longer alive. Coincidence, Mr. Grunzer?

"As for the remaining one hundred and twenty-five— perhaps that indicates that our method is not infallible. We're the first to admit that. But new techniques are being developed all the time. I assure you, Mr. Grunzer, *we will get them all.*"

He flipped through the blue-bound book.

"Our members are listed in this book, Mr. Grunzer. I'm

going to give you the option to call one, ten, or a hundred of them. Call them and see if I'm not telling the truth."

He flipped the manuscript toward Grunzer's desk. It landed on the blotter with a thud. Grunzer picked it up.

"Well?" Tucker said. "Want to call them?"

"No." He licked his lips. "I'm willing to take your word for it, Mr. Tucker. It's incredible, but I can see how it works. *Just knowing* that a thousand people are wishing you dead is enough to shake hell out of you." His eyes narrowed. "But there's one question. You talked about a 'small' fee—"

"It's fifty dollars, Mr. Grunzer."

"Fifty, huh? Fifty times a thousand, that's pretty good money, isn't it?"

"I assure you, the organization is not motivated by profit. Not the kind you mean. The dues merely cover expenses, committee work, research, and the like. Surely you can understand that?"

"I guess so," he grunted.

"Then you find it interesting?"

Grunzer swiveled his chair about to face the window. *God!* he thought.

God! if it *really* worked!

But how could it? If wishes became deeds, he would have slaughtered dozens in his lifetime. Yet, that was different. His wishes were always secret things, hidden where no man could know them. But this method was different, more practical, more terrifying. Yes, he could see how it might work. He could visualize a thousand minds burning with the single wish of death, see the victim sneering in disbelief at first, and then slowly, gradually, surely succumbing to the tightening, constricting chain of fear that it *might* work, that so many deadly thoughts could indeed emit a mystical, malevolent ray that destroyed life.

Suddenly, ghost-like, he saw the ruddy face of Whitman Hayes before him.

He wheeled about and said:

"But the victim has to *know* all this, of course? He has to know the society exists, and has succeeded, and is wishing for *his* death? That's essential, isn't it?"

"Absolutely essential," Tucker said, replacing the manuscripts in his briefcase. "You've touched on the vital point, Mr. Grunzer. The victim must be informed, and that, precisely, is what I have done." He looked at his watch.

"Your death wish began at noon today. The society has begun to work. I'm very sorry."

At the doorway, he turned and lifted both hat and briefcase in one departing salute.

"Goodbye, Mr. Grunzer," he said.

IT

by Theodore Sturgeon

It walked in the woods.

It was never born. It existed. Under the pine needles the fires burn, deep and smokeless in the mold. In heat and in darkness and decay there is growth. There is life and there is growth. It grew, but it was not alive. It walked unbreathing through the woods, and thought and saw and was hideous and strong, and it was not born and it did not live. It grew and moved about without living.

It crawled out of the darkness and hot damp mold into the cool of a morning. It was huge. It was lumped and crusted with its own hateful substances, and pieces of it dropped off as it went its way, dropped off and lay writhing, and stilled, and sank putrescent into the forest loam.

It had no mercy, no laughter, no beauty. It had strength and great intelligence. And—perhaps it could not be destroyed. It crawled out of its mound in the wood and lay pulsing in the sunlight for a long moment. Patches of it shone wetly in the golden glow, parts of it were nubbled and flaked. And whose dead bones had given it the form of a man?

It scrabbled painfully with its half-formed hands, beating the ground and the bole of a tree. It rolled and lifted itself up on its crumbling elbows, and it tore up a great handful of herbs and shredded them against its chest, and it paused and gazed at the gray-green juices with intelligent calm. It wavered to its feet, and seized a young sapling and destroyed it, folding the slender trunk back on itself again and again, watching attentively the useless, fibered splinters. And it snatched up a fear-frozen field-creature, crushing it slowly, letting blood and pulpy flesh and fur ooze from between its fingers, run down and rot on the forearms.

It began searching.

Kimbo drifted through the tall grasses like a puff of dust, his bushy tail curled tightly over his back and his long jaws agape. He ran with an easy lope, loving his freedom and the power of his flanks and furry shoulders. His tongue lolled listlessly over his lips. His lips were black and serrated, and each tiny pointed liplet swayed with his doggy gallop. Kimbo was all dog, all healthy animal.

He leaped high over a boulder and landed with a startled yelp as a long-eared cony shot from its hiding place under the rock. Kimbo hurtled after it, grunting with each great thrust of his legs. The rabbit bounced just ahead of him, keeping its distance, its ears flattened on its curving back and its little legs nibbling away at distance hungrily. It stopped, and Kimbo pounced, and the rabbit shot away at a tangent and popped into a hollow log. Kimbo yelped again and rushed snuffling at the log, and knowing his failure, curvetted but once around the stump and ran on into the forest. The thing that watched from the wood raised its crusted arms and waited for Kimbo.

Kimbo sensed it there, standing dead-still by the path. To him it was a bulk which smelled of carrion not fit to roll in, and he snuffled distastefully and ran to pass it.

The thing let him come abreast and dropped a heavy twisted fist on him. Kimbo saw it coming and curled up tight as he ran, and the hand clipped stunningly on his rump, sending him rolling and yipping down the slope. Kimbo straddled to his feet, shook his head, shook his body with a deep growl, came back to the silent thing with green murder in his eyes. He walked stiffly, straight-legged, his tail as low as his lowered head and a ruff of fury round his neck. The thing raised its arm again, waited.

Kimbo slowed, then flipped himself through the air at the monster's throat. His jaws closed on it; his teeth clicked together through a mass of filth, and he fell choking and snarling at its feet. The thing leaned down and struck twice, and after the dog's back was broken, it sat beside him and began to tear him apart.

"Be back in an hour or so," said Alton Drew, picking up his rifle from the corner behind the wood box. His brother laughed.

"Old Kimbo 'bout runs your life, Alton," he said.

"Ah, I know the ol' devil," said Alton. "When I whistle for him for half an hour and he don't show up, he's in a jam or he's treed something wuth shootin' at. The ol' son of a gun calls me by not answerin'."

Cory Drew shoved a full glass of milk over to his nine-year-old daughter and smiled. "You think as much o' that houn' dog o' yours as I do of Babe here."

Babe slid off her chair and ran to her uncle. "Gonna catch me the bad fella, Uncle Alton?" she shrilled. The "bad fella" was Cory's invention—the one who lurked in corners ready to pounce on little girls who chased the chickens and played around mowing machines and hurled green apples with powerful young arms at the sides of the hogs, to hear the synchronized thud and grunt; little girls who swore with an Austrian accent like an ex-hired man they had had; who dug caves in haystacks till they tipped over, and kept pet crawfish in tomorrow's milk cans, and rode work horses to a lather in the night pasture.

"Get back here and keep away from Uncle Alton's gun!" said Cory. "If you see the bad fella, Alton, chase him back here. He has a date with Babe here for that stunt of hers last night." The preceding evening, Babe had kind-heartedly poured pepper on the cows' salt block.

"Don't worry, kiddo," grinned her uncle, "I'll bring you the bad fella's hide if he don't get me first."

Alton Drew walked up the path toward the wood, thinking about Babe. She was a phenomenon—a pampered farm child. Ah well—she had to be. They'd both loved Clissa Drew, and she'd married Cory, and they had to love Clissa's child. Funny thing, love. Alton was a man's man, and thought things out that way; and his reaction to love was a strong and frightened one. He knew what love was because he felt it still for his brother's wife and would feel it as long as he lived for Babe. It led him through his life, and yet he embarrassed himself by thinking of it. Loving a dog was an easy thing, because you and the old devil could love one another completely without talking about it. The smell of gun smoke and wet fur in the rain were perfume enough for Alton Drew, a grunt of satisfaction and the scream of something hunted and hit were poetry enough. They weren't like love for a human, that choked his throat so he could not say words he could not have thought of anyway. So Alton loved his dog Kimbo and his Winchester for all to see, and let his love for his brother's women, Clissa and Babe, eat at him quietly and unmentioned.

His quick eyes saw the fresh indentations in the soft earth behind the boulder, which showed where Kimbo had turned and leaped with a single surge, chasing the rabbit. Ignoring the tracks, he looked for the nearest place where a rabbit might hide, and strolled over to the stump. Kimbo had been there, he saw, and had been there too late. "You're an ol' fool," muttered Alton. "Y' can't catch a cony by chasin' it. You want to cross him up some way." He gave a peculiar trilling whistle, sure that Kimbo was digging frantically under some nearby stump for a rabbit that was three counties away by now. No answer. A little puzzled, Alton went back to the path. "He never done this before," he said softly.

He cocked his .32-40 and cradled it. At the county fair someone had once said of Alton Drew that he could shoot at a handful of corn and peas thrown in the air and hit only the corn. Once he split a bullet on the blade of a knife and put two candles out. He had no need to fear anything that could be shot at. That's what he believed.

The thing in the woods looked curiously down at what it had done to Kimbo, and tried to moan the way Kimbo had before he died. It stood a minute storing away facts in its foul, unemotional mind. Blood was warm. The sunlight was warm. Things that moved and bore fur had a muscle to force the thick liquid through tiny tubes in their bodies. The liquid coagulated after a time. The liquid on rooted green things was thinner and the loss of a limb did not mean loss of life. It was very interesting, but the thing, the mold with a mind, was not pleased. Neither was it displeased. Its accidental urge was a thirst for knowledge, and it was only—interested.

It was growing late, and the sun reddened and rested awhile on the hilly horizon, teaching the clouds to be inverted flames. The thing threw up its head suddenly, noticing the dusk. Night was ever a strange thing, even for those of us who have known it in life. It would have been frightening for the monster had it been capable of fright, but it could only be curious; it could only reason from what it had observed.

What was happening? It was getting harder to see. Why? It threw its shapeless head from side to side. It was true—things were dim, and growing dimmer. Things were changing shape, taking on a new and darker color. What did the creatures it had crushed and torn apart see? How did they see? The larger one, the one that had attacked, had used two organs in its head. That must have been it, because after the thing had torn off two of the dog's legs it had struck at the hairy muzzle; and the dog, seeing the blow coming, had dropped folds of skin over the organs—closed its eyes. Ergo, the dog saw with its eyes. But then after the dog was dead, and its body still, repeated blows had had no effect on the eyes. They remained open and staring. The logical conclusion was, then, that a being that had ceased to live and breathe and move about lost the use of its eyes. It must be that to lose sight was, conversely, to die. Dead things did not walk about. They lay down and did not move. Therefore the thing in the wood concluded that it must be dead, and so it lay down by the path, not far away from Kimbo's scattered body, lay down and believed itself dead.

Alton Drew came up through the dusk to the wood. He was frankly worried. He whistled again, and then called, and there was still no response, and he said again, "The ol' flea-bus never done this before," and shook his heavy head. It was past milking time, and Cory would need him. "Kimbo!" he roared. The cry echoed through the shadows, and Alton flipped on the safety catch of his rifle and put the butt on the ground beside the path. Leaning on it, he took off his cap and scratched the back of his head, wondering. The rifle butt sank into what he thought was soft earth; he staggered and stepped into the chest of the thing that lay beside the path. His foot went up to the ankle in its yielding rottenness, and he swore and jumped back.

"*Whew!* Somp'n sure dead as hell there! Ugh!" He swabbed at his boot with a handful of leaves while the monster lay in the growing blackness with the edges of the deep footprint in its chest sliding into it, filling it up. It lay there regarding him dimly out of its muddy eyes, thinking it was dead because of the darkness, watching the articulation of Alton Drew's joints, wondering at this new uncautious creature.

Alton cleaned the butt of his gun with more leaves and went on up the path, whistling anxiously for Kimbo.

Clissa Drew stood in the door of the milk shed, very

lovely in red-checked gingham and a blue apron. Her hair was clean yellow, parted in the middle and stretched tautly back to a heavy braided knot. "Cory! Alton!" she called a little sharply.

"Well?" Cory responded gruffly from the barn, where he was stripping off the Ayrshire. The dwindling streams of milk plopped pleasantly into the froth of a full pail.

"I've called and called," said Clissa. "Supper's cold, and Babe won't eat until you come. Why—where's Alton?"

Cory grunted, heaved the stool out of the way, threw over the stanchion lock and slapped the Ayrshire on the rump. The cow backed and filled like a towboat, clattered down the line and out into the barn-yard. "Ain't back yet."

"Not back?" Clissa came in and stood beside him as he sat by the next cow, put his forehead against the warm flank. "But, Cory, he said he'd—"

"Yeh, yeh, I know. He said he'd be back fer the milkin'. I heard him. Well, he ain't."

"And you have to—Oh, Cory, I'll help you finish up. Alton would be back if he could. Maybe he's—"

"Maybe he's treed a bluejay," snapped her husband. "Him an' that damn dog." He gestured hugely with one hand while the other went on milking. "I got twenty-six head o' cows to milk. I got pigs to feed an' chickens to put to bed. I got to toss hay for the mare and turn the team out. I got harness to mend and a wire down in the night pasture. I got wood to split an' carry." He milked for a moment in silence, chewing on his lip. Clissa stood twisting her hands together, trying to think of something to stem the tide. It wasn't the first time Alton's hunting had interfered with the chores. "So I got to go ahead with it. I can't interfere with Alton's spoorin'. Every damn time that hound o' his smells out a squirrel I go without my supper. I'm gettin' sick an'—"

"Oh, I'll help you!" said Clissa. She was thinking of the spring, when Kimbo had held four hundred pounds of raging black bear at bay until Alton could put a bullet in its brain, the time Babe had found a bear cub and started to carry it home, and had fallen into a freshet, cutting her head. You can't hate a dog that has saved your child for you, she thought.

"You'll do nothin' of the kind!" Cory growled. "Get back to the house. You'll find work enough there. I'll be along when I can. Dammit, Clissa, don't cry! I didn't mean to—Oh, shucks!" He got up and put his arms around her. "I'm wrought up," he said. "Go on now. I'd no call to speak that way to you. I'm sorry. Go back to Babe. I'll put a stop to this for good tonight. I've had enough. There's work here for four farmers an' all we've got is me an' that . . . that huntsman.

"Go on now, Clissa."

"All right," she said into his shoulder. "But, Cory, hear him out first when he comes back. He might be unable to come back. He might be unable to come back this time. Maybe he . . . he—"

"Ain't nothin' kin hurt my brother that a bullet will hit. He can take care of himself. He's got no excuse good enough this time. Go on, now. Make the kid eat."

Clissa went back to the house, her young face furrowed. If Cory quarreled with Alton now and drove him away, what with the drought and the creamery about to close and all, they just couldn't manage. Hiring a man was out of the question. Cory'd have to work himself to death, and he just wouldn't be able to make it. No one man could. She sighed and went into the house. It was seven o'clock, and the milking not done yet. Oh, why did Alton have to—

Babe was in bed at nine when Clissa heard Cory in the shed, slinging the wire cutters into a corner. "Alton back yet?" they both said at once as Cory stepped into the kitchen; and as she shook her head he clumped over to the stove, and lifting a lid, spat into the coals. "Come to bed," he said.

She laid down her stitching and looked at his broad back. He was twenty-eight, and he walked and acted like a man ten years older, and looked like a man five years younger. "I'll be up in a while," Clissa said.

Cory glanced at the corner behind the wood box where Alton's rifle usually stood, then made an unspellable, disgusted sound and sat down to take off his heavy muddy shoes.

"It's after nine," Clissa volunteered timidly. Cory said nothing, reaching for house slippers.

"Cory, you're not going to—"

"Not going to what?"

"Oh, nothing. I just thought that maybe Alton—"

"Alton," Cory flared. "The dog goes hunting field mice. Alton goes hunting the dog. Now you want me to go hunting Alton. That's what you want?"

"I just—He was never this late before."

"I won't do it! Go out lookin' for him at nine o'clock in the night? I'll be damned! He has no call to use us so, Clissa."

Clissa said nothing. She went to the stove, peered into the wash boiler set aside at the back of the range. When she turned around, Cory had his shoes and coat on again.

"I knew you'd go," she said. Her voice smiled though she did not.

"I'll be back durned soon," said Cory. "I don't reckon he's strayed far. It is late. I ain't feared for him, but—" He broke his 12-gauge shotgun, looked through the barrels, slipped two shells in the breech and a box of them into his pocket. "Don't wait up," he said over his shoulder as he went out.

"I won't," Clissa replied to the closed door, and went back to her stitching by the lamp.

The path up the slope to the wood was very dark when Cory went up it, peering and calling. The air was chill and quiet, and a fetid odor of mold hung in it. Cory blew the taste of it out through impatient nostrils, drew it in again with the next breath, and swore. "Nonsense," he muttered. "Houn' dawg Huntin', at ten in th' night, too. Alton!" he bellowed. "Alton Drew!" Echoes answered him, and he entered the wood. The huddled thing he passed in the dark heard him and felt the vibrations of his footsteps and did not move because it thought it was dead.

Cory strode on, looking around and ahead and not down since his feet knew the path.

"Alton!"

"That you, Cory?"

Cory Drew froze. That corner of the wood was thickly set and as dark as a burial vault. The voice he heard was choked, quiet, penetrating.

"Alton?"

"I found Kimbo, Cory."

"Where the hell have you been?" shouted Cory furiously. He disliked this pitch-darkness; he was afraid at the tense hopelessness of Alton's voice, and he mistrusted his ability to stay angry at his brother.

"I called him, Cory. I whistled at him, an' the ol' devil didn't answer."

"I can say the same for you, you . . . you louse. Why

weren't you to milkin'? Where are you? You caught in a trap?"

"The houn' never missed answerin' me before, you know," said the tight, monotonous voice from the darkness.

"Alton! What the devil's the matter with you? What do I care if your mutt didn't answer? Where—"

"I guess because he ain't never died before," said Alton, refusing to be interrupted.

"You *what?*" Cory clicked his lips together twice and then said, "Alton, you turned crazy? What's that you say?"

"Kimbo's dead."

"Kim . . . oh! Oh!" Cory was seeing that picture again in his mind—Babe sprawled unconscious in the freshet, and Kimbo raging and snapping against a monster bear, holding her back until Alton could get there. "What happened, Alton?" he asked more quietly.

"I aim to find out. Someone tore him up."

"*Tore him up?*"

"There ain't a bit of him left tacked together, Cory. Every damn joint in his body tore apart. Guts out of him."

"Good God! Bear, you reckon?"

"No bear, nor nothin' on four legs. He's all here. None of him's been et. Whoever done it just killed him an'—tore him up."

"Good God!" Cory said again. "Who could've—" There was a long silence, then. "Come 'long home," he said almost gently. "There's no call for you to set up by him all night."

"I'll set. I aim to be here at sunup, an' I'm going to start trackin', an' I'm goin' to keep trackin' till I find the one done this job on Kimbo."

"You're drunk or crazy, Alton."

"I ain't drunk. You can think what you like about the rest of it. I'm stickin' here."

"We got a farm back yonder. Remember? I ain't going to milk twenty-six head o' cows again in the mornin' like I did jest now, Alton."

"Somebody's got to. I can't be there. I guess you'll just have to, Cory."

"You dirty scum!" Cory screamed. "You'll come back with me now or I'll know why!"

Alton's voice was still tight, half-sleepy. "Don't you come no nearer, bud."

Cory kept moving toward Alton's voice.

"I said"—the voice was very quiet now—"*stop where you are*." Cory kept coming. A sharp click told of the release of the .32–40's safety. Cory stopped.

"You got your gun on me, Alton?" Cory whispered.

"Thass right, bud. You ain't a-trompin' up these tracks for me. I need 'em at sunup."

A full minute passed, and the only sound in the blackness was that of Cory's pained breathing. Finally:

"I got my gun, too, Alton. Come home."

"You can't see to shoot me."

"We're even on that."

"We ain't. I know just where you stand, Cory. I been here four hours."

"My gun scatters."

"My gun kills."

Without another word Cory Drew turned on his heel and stamped back to the farm.

Black and liquidescent it lay in the blackness, not alive, not understanding death, believing itself dead. Things that were alive saw and moved about. Things that were not alive could do neither. It rested its muddy gaze on the line of trees at the crest of the rise, and deep within it thoughts trickled wetly. It lay huddled, dividing its new-found facts, dissecting them as it had dissected live things when there was light; comparing, concluding, pigeonholing.

The trees at the top of the slope could just be seen, as their trunks were a fraction of a shade lighter than the dark sky behind them. At length they, too, disappeared, and for a moment sky and trees were a monotone. The thing knew it was dead now, and like many a being before it, it wondered how long it must stay like this. And then the sky beyond the trees grew a little lighter. That was a manifestly impossible occurrence, thought the thing, but it could see it and it must be so. Did dead things live again? That was curious. What about dismembered dead things? It would wait and see.

The sun came hand over hand up a beam of light. A bird somewhere made a high yawning peep, and as an owl killed a shrew, a skunk pounced on another, so that the night-shift deaths and those of the day could go on without cessation. Two flowers nodded archly to each other, comparing their pretty clothes. A dragonfly nymph decided it was tired of looking serious and cracked its back open, to crawl out and dry gauzily. The first golden ray sheared down between the trees, through the grasses, passed over the mass in the shadowed bushes. "I am alive again," thought the thing that could not possibly live. "I am alive, for I see clearly." It stood up on its thick legs, up into the golden glow. In a little while the wet flakes that had grown during the night dried in the sun, and when it took its first steps, they cracked off and a small shower of them fell away. It walked up the slope to find Kimbo, to see if he, too, were alive again.

Babe let the sun come into her room by opening her eyes. Uncle Alton was gone—that was the first thing that ran through her head. Dad had come home last night and had shouted at mother for an hour. Alton was plumb crazy. He'd turned a gun on his own brother. If Alton ever came ten feet into Cory's land, Cory would fill him so full of holes, he'd look like a tumbleweed. Alton was lazy, shiftless, selfish, and one or two other things of questionable taste but undoubted vividness. Babe knew her father. Uncle Alton would never be safe in this county.

She bounced out of bed in the enviable way of the very young, and ran to the window. Cory was trudging down to the night pasture with two bridles over his arm, to get the team. There were kitchen noises from downstairs.

Babe ducked her head in the washbowl and shook off the water like a terrier before she toweled. Trailing clean shirt and dungarees, she went to the head of the stairs, slid into the shirt, and began her morning ritual with the trousers. One step down was a step through the right leg. One more, and she was into the left. Then, bouncing step by step on both feet, buttoning one button per step, she reached the bottom fully dressed and ran into the kitchen.

"Didn't Uncle Alton come back a-tall, Mum?"

"Morning, Babe. No, dear." Clissa was too quiet, smiling too much, Babe thought shrewdly. Wasn't happy.

"Where's he go, Mum?"

"We don't know, Babe. Sit down and eat your breakfast."

"What's a misbegotten, Mum?" the Babe asked suddenly. Her mother nearly dropped the dish she was drying. "Babe! You must never say that again!"

"Oh. Well, why is Uncle Alton, then?"

"Why is he what?"

Babe's mouth muscled around an outsize spoonful of oatmeal. "A misbe—"

"Babe!"

"All right, Mum," said Babe with her mouth full. "Well, why?"

"I told Cory not to shout last night," Clissa said half to herself.

"Well, whatever it means, he isn't," said Babe with finality. "Did he go hunting again?"

"He went to look for Kimbo, darling."

"Kimbo? Oh Mummy, is Kimbo gone, too? Didn't he come back either?"

"No dear. Oh, please, Babe, stop asking questions!"

"All right. Where do you think they went?"

"Into the north woods. Be quiet."

Babe gulped away at her breakfast. An idea struck her; and as she thought of it she ate slower and slower, and cast more and more glances at her mother from under the lashes of her tilted eyes. It would be awful if daddy did anything to Uncle Alton. Someone ought to warn him.

Babe was halfway to the woods when Alton's .32-40 sent echoes giggling up and down the valley.

Cory was in the south thirty, riding a cultivator and cussing at the team of grays when he heard the gun. "Hoa," he called to the horses, and sat a moment to listen to the sound. "One-two-three. Four," he counted. "Saw someone, blasted away at him. Had a chance to take aim and give him another, careful. My God!" He threw up the cultivator points and steered the team into the shade of three oaks. He hobbled the gelding with swift tosses of a spare strap, and headed for the woods. "Alton a killer," he murmured, and doubled back to the house for his gun. Clissa was standing just outside the door.

"Get shells!" he snapped and flung into the house. Clissa followed him. He was strapping his hunting knife on before she could get a box off the shelf. "Cory—"

"Hear that gun, did you? Alton's off his nut. He don't waste lead. He shot at someone just then, and he wasn't fixin' to shoot pa'tridges when I saw him last. He was out to get a man. Gimmee my gun."

"Cory, Babe—"

"You keep her here. Oh, God, this is a helluva mess. I

can't stand much more." Cory ran out the door.

Clissa caught his arm: "Cory I'm trying to tell you. Babe isn't here. I've called, and she isn't here."

Cory's heavy, young-old face tautened. "Babe—Where did you last see her?"

"Breakfast." Clissa was crying now.

"She say where she was going?"

"No. She asked a lot of questions about Alton and where he'd gone."

"Did you say?"

Clissa's eyes widened, and she nodded, biting the back of her hand.

"You shouldn't ha' done that, Clissa," he gritted, and ran toward the woods, Clissa looking after him, and in that moment she could have killed herself.

Cory ran with his head up, straining with his legs and lungs and eyes at the long path. He puffed up the slope to the woods, agonized for breath after the forty-five minutes' heavy going. He couldn't even notice the damp smell of mold in the air.

He caught a movement in a thicket to his right, and dropped. Struggling to keep his breath, he crept forward until he could see clearly. There was something in there, all right. Something black, keeping still. Cory relaxed his legs and torso completely to make it easier for his heart to pump some strength back into them, and slowly raised the 12-gauge until it bore on the thing hidden in the thicket.

"Come out!" Cory said when he could speak.

Nothing happened.

"Come out or by God I'll shoot!" rasped Cory.

There was a long moment of silence, and his finger tightened on the trigger.

"You asked for it," he said, and as he fired, the thing leaped sideways into the open, screaming.

It was a thin little man dressed in sepulchral black, and bearing the rosiest baby-face Cory had ever seen. The face was twisted with fright and pain. The man scrambled to his feet and hopped up and down saying over and over, "Oh, my hand. Don't shoot again! Oh, my hand. Don't shoot again!" He stopped after a bit, when Cory had climbed to his feet, and he regarded the farmer out of sad china-blue eyes. "You shot me," he said reproachfully, holding up a little bloody hand. "Oh, my goodness."

Cory said, "Now, who the hell are you?"

The man immediately became hysterical, mouthing such a flood of broken sentences that Cory stepped back a pace pace and half-raised his gun in self-defense. It seemed to consist mostly of "I lost my papers," and "I didn't do it," and "It was horrible. Horrible. Horrible," and "The dead man," and "Oh, don't shoot again."

Cory tried twice to ask him a question, and then he stepped over and knocked the man down. He lay on the ground writhing and moaning and blubbering and putting his bloody hand to his mouth where Cory had hit him.

"Now what's going on around here?"

The man rolled over and sat up. "I didn't do it!" he sobbed. "I didn't. I was walking along and I heard the gun and I heard some swearing and an awful scream and I went over there and peeped and I saw the dead man and I ran away and you came and I hid and you shot me and—"

"*Shut up!*" The man did, as if a switch had been thrown. "Now," said Cory, pointing along the path, "you say there's a dead man up there?"

The man nodded and began crying in earnest. Cory helped him up. "Follow this path back to my farmhouse," he said. "Tell my wife to fix up your hand. *Don't* tell her anything else. And wait there until I come. Hear?"

"Yes. Thank you. Oh, thank you. *Snff.*"

"Go on now." Cory gave him a gentle shove in the right direction and went alone, in cold fear, up the path to the spot where he had found Alton the night before.

He found him here now, too, and Kimbo. Kimbo and Alton had spent several years together in the deepest friendship; they had hunted and fought and slept together and the lives they owed each other were finished now. They were dead together.

It was terrible that they died the same way. Cory Drew was a strong man, but he gasped and fainted dead away when he saw what the thing of the mold had done to his brother and his brother's dog.

The little man in black hurried down the path, whimpering and holding his injured hand as if he rather wished he could limp with it. After a while the whimper faded away, and the hurried stride changed to a walk as the gibbering terror of the last hour receded. He drew two deep breaths, said: "My goodness!" and felt almost normal. He bound a linen handkerchief around his wrist, but the hand kept bleeding. He tried the elbow, and that made it hurt. So he stuffed the handkerchief back in his pocket and simply waved the hand stupidly in the air until the blood clotted. He did not see the great moist horror that clumped along behind him, although his nostrils crinkled with its foulness.

The monster had three holes close together on its chest, and one hole in the middle of its slimy forehead. It had three close-set pits in its back and one on the back of its head. These marks were where Alton Drew's bullets had struck and passed through. Half of the monster's shapeless face was sloughed away, and there was a deep indentation on its shoulder. This was what Alton Drew's gun butt had done after he clubbed it and struck at the thing that would not lie down after he put his four bullets through it. When these things happened the monster was not hurt or angry. It only wondered why Alton Drew acted that way. Now it followed the little man without hurrying at all, matching his stride step by step and dropping little particles of muck behind it.

The little man went on out of the wood and stood with his back against a big tree at the forest's edge, and he thought. Enough had happened to him here. What good would it do to stay and face a horrible murder inquest, just to continue this silly, vague search? There was supposed to be the ruin of an old, old hunting lodge deep in this wood somewhere, and perhaps it would hold the evidence he wanted. But it was a vague report—vague enough to be forgotten without regret. It would be the height of foolishness to stay for all the hick-town red tape that would follow that ghastly affair back in the wood. Ergo, it would be ridiculous to follow that farmer's advice, to go to his house and wait for him. He would go back to town.

The monster was leaning against the other side of the big tree.

The little man snuffled disgustedly at a sudden overpowering odor of rot. He reached for his handkerchief, fumbled and dropped it. As he bent to pick it up, the monster's arm *whuffed* heavily in the air where his head had been—a blow that would certainly have removed that baby-face protuberance. The man stood up and would have put the handkerchief to his nose had it not been so bloody. The creature behind the tree lifted its arm again just as the little man tossed the handkerchief away and stepped out into the field, heading across country to the distant highway that would take him back to town. The monster pounced on the handkerchief, picked it up, studied it, tore it across several times and inspected the tattered edges. Then it gazed vacantly at the disappearing figure of the little man, and finding him no longer interesting turned back into the woods.

Babe broke into a trot at the sound of the shots. It was important to warn Uncle Alton about what her father had said, but it was more interesting to find out what he had bagged. Oh, he'd bagged it, all right. Uncle Alton never fired without killing. This was about the first time she had ever heard him blast away like that. Must be a bear, she thought excitedly, tripping over a root, sprawling, rolling to her feet again, without noticing the tumble. She'd love to have another bearskin in her room. Where would she put it? Maybe they could line it and she could have it for a blanket. Uncle Alton could sit on it and read to her in the evening—Oh, no. No. Not with this trouble between him and dad. Oh, if she could only do something! She tried to run faster, worried and anticipating, but she was out of breath and went more slowly instead.

At the top of the rise by the edge of the woods she stopped and looked back. Far down in the valley lay the south thirty. She scanned it carefully, looking for her father. The new furrows and the old were sharply defined, and her keen eyes saw immediately that Cory had left the line with the cultivator and had angled the team over to the shade trees without finishing his row. That wasn't like him. She could see the team now, and Cory's pale-blue denim was nowhere in sight. She giggled lightly to herself as she thought of the way she would fool her father. And the little sound of laughter drowned out, for her, the sound of Alton's hoarse dying scream.

She reached and crossed the path and slid through the brush beside it. The shots came from up around here somewhere. She stopped and listened several times, and then suddenly heard something coming toward her, fast. She ducked under cover, terrified, and a little baby-faced man in black, his blue eyes wide with horror, crashed blindly past her, the leather case he carried catching on the branches. It spun a moment and then fell right in front of her. The man never missed it.

Babe lay there for a long moment and then picked up the case and faded into the woods. Things were happening too fast for her. She wanted Uncle Alton, but she dared not call. She stopped again and strained her ears. Back toward the edge of the wood she heard her father's voice, and another's—probably the man who had dropped the briefcase. She dared not go over there. Filled with enjoyable terror, she thought hard, then snapped her fingers in triumph. She and Alton had played Injun many times up here; they had a whole repertoire of secret signals. She had practiced birdcalls until she knew them better than the birds themselves. What would it be? Ah—bluejay. She threw back her head and by some youthful alchemy produced a nerve-shattering screech that would have done justice to any jay that ever flew. She repeated it, and then twice more.

The response was immediate—the call of a bluejay, four times, spaced two and two. Babe nodded to herself happily. That was the signal that they were to meet immediately at The Place. The Place was a hide-out that he had discovered and shared with her, and not another soul knew of it; an angle of rock beside a stream not far away. It wasn't exactly a cave, but almost. Enough so to be entrancing. Babe trotted happily away toward the brook. She had just known that Uncle Alton would remember the call of the bluejay, and what it meant.

In the tree that arched over Alton's scattered body perched a large jay bird, preening itself and shining in the sun. Quite unconscious of the presence of death, hardly noticing the Babe's realistic cry, it screamed again four times, two and two.

It took Cory more than a moment to recover himself from what he had seen. He turned away from it and leaned weakly against a pine, panting. Alton. That was Alton lying there, in—parts.

"God! God, God, God—"

Gradually his strength returned, and he forced himself to turn again. Stepping carefully, he bent and picked up the .32-40. Its barrel was bright and clean, but the butt and stock were smeared with some kind of stinking rottenness. Where had he seen the stuff before? Somewhere—

no matter. He cleaned it off absently, throwing the be-
fouled bandanna away afterward. Through his mind ran
Alton's words—was that only last night?—"*I'm goin' to
start trackin'. An' I'm goin' to keep trackin' till I find the
one done this job on Kimbo.*"

Cory searched shrinkingly until he found Alton's box
of shells. The box was wet and sticky. That made it—better, somehow. A bullet wet with Alton's blood was the
right thing to use. He went away a short distance, circled
around till he found heavy footprints, then came back.

"I'm a-trackin' for you, bud," he whispered thickly,
and began. Through the brush he followed its wavering
spoor, amazed at the amount of filthy mold about, gradually associating it with the thing that had killed his brother.
There was nothing in the world for him any more but hate
and doggedness. Cursing himself for not getting Alton
home last night, he followed the tracks to the edge of the
woods. They led him to a big tree there, and there he saw
something else—the footprints of the little city man.
Nearby lay some tattered scraps of linen, and—what was
that?

Another set of prints—small ones. Small, stub-toed ones.
"Babe!"

No answer. The wind sighed. Somewhere a bluejay
called.

Babe stopped and turned when she heard her father's
voice, faint with distance, piercing.

"Listen at him holler," she crooned delightedly. "Gee,
he sounds mad." She sent a jay bird's call disrespectfully
back to him and hurried to The Place.

It consisted of a mammoth boulder beside the brook.
Some upheaval in the glacial age had cleft it, cutting out
a huge V-shaped chunk. The widest part of the cleft was
at the water's edge, and the narrowest was hidden by
bushes. It made a little ceilingless room, rough and uneven and full of pot-holes and cavelets inside, and yet
with quite a level floor. The open end was at the water's
edge.

Babe parted the bushes and peered down the cleft.

"Uncle Alton!" she called softly. There was no answer.
Oh, well, he'd be along. She scrambled in and slid down
to the floor.

She loved it here. It was shaded and cool, and the chattering stream filled it with shifting golden lights and laugh-

ing gurgles. She called again, on principle, and then perched on an outcropping to wait. It was only then she realized that she still carried the little man's brief case.

She turned it over a couple of times and then opened it. It was divided in the middle by a leather wall. On one side were a few papers in a large yellow envelope, and on the other some sandwiches, a candy bar, and an apple. With a youngster's complacent acceptance of manna from heaven, Babe fell to. She saved one sandwich for Alton, mainly because she didn't like its highly spiced bologna. The rest made quite a feast.

She was a little worried when Alton hadn't arrived, even after she had consumed the apple core. She got up and tried to skim some flat pebbles across the roiling brook, and she stood on her hands, and she tried to think of a story to tell herself, and she tried just waiting. Finally, in desperation, she turned again to the brief case, took out the papers, curled up by the rocky wall and began to read them. It was something to do, anyway.

There was an old newspaper clipping that told about strange wills that people had left. An old lady had once left a lot of money to whoever would make the trip from the Earth to the Moon and back. Another had financed a home for cats whose masters and mistresses had died. A man left thousands of dollars to the first person who could solve a certain mathematical problem and prove his solution. But one item was blue-penciled. It was:

> One of the strangest of wills still in force is that of Thaddeus M. Kirk, who died in 1920. It appears that he built an elaborate mausoleum with burial vaults for all the remains of his family. He collected and removed caskets from all over the country to fill the designated niches. Kirk was the last of his line; there were no relatives when he died. His will stated that the mausoleum was to be kept in repair permanently, and that a certain sum was to be set aside as a reward for whoever could produce the body of his grandfather, Roger Kirk, whose niche is still empty. Anyone finding this body is eligible to receive a substantial fortune.

Babe yawned vaguely over this, but kept on reading because there was nothing else to do. Next was a thick sheet of business correspondence, bearing the letterhead of a firm of lawyers. The body of it ran:

> In regard to your query regarding the will of Thaddeus Kirk, we are authorized to state that his grandfather was a man about five feet, five inches, whose left arm had been broken and who had a triangular silver plate set into his skull. There is no information as to the whereabouts of his death. He disappeared and was declared legally dead after the lapse of fourteen years.
>
> The amount of the reward as stated in the will, plus accrued interest, now amounts to a fraction over sixty-two thousand dollars. This will be paid to anyone who produces the remains, providing that said remains answer descriptions kept in our private files.

There was more, but Babe was bored. She went on to the little black notebook. There was nothing in it but penciled and highly abbreviated records of visits to libraries; quotations from books with titles like "History of Angelina and Tyler Counties" and "Kirk Family History." Babe threw that aside, too. Where could Uncle Alton be?

She began to sing tunelessly, "Tumalumalum tum, ta ta ta," pretending to dance a minuet with flowing skirts like a girl she had seen in the movies. A rustle of the bushes at the entrance to The Place stopped her. She peeped upward, saw them being thrust aside. Quickly she ran to a tiny cul-de-sac in the rock wall, just big enough for her to hide in. She giggled at the thought of how surprised Uncle Alton would be when she jumped out at him.

She heard the newcomer come shuffling down the steep slope of the crevice and land heavily on the floor. There was something about the sound—What was it? It occurred to her that though it was a hard job for a big man like Uncle Alton to get through the little opening in the bushes, she could hear no heavy breathing. She heard no breathing at all!

Babe peeped out into the main cave and squealed in utmost horror. Standing there was, not Uncle Alton, but a massive caricature of a man: a huge thing like an irregular mud doll, clumsily made. It quivered and parts of it glistened and parts of it were dried and crumbly. Half of the lower left part of its face was gone, giving it a lopsided look. It had no perceptible mouth or nose, and its eyes were crooked, one higher than the other, both a dingy brown with no whites at all. It stood quite still looking at her, its only movement a steady unalive quivering.

It wondered about the queer little noise Babe had made.

Babe crept far back against a little pocket of stone, her brain running round and round in tiny circles of agony. She opened her mouth to cry out, and could not. Her eyes bulged and her face flamed with the strangling effort, and the two golden ropes of her braided hair twitched and twitched as she hunted hopelessly for a way out. If only she were out in the open—or in the wedge-shaped half-cave where the thing was—or home in bed!

The thing clumped toward her, expressionless, moving with a slow inevitability that was the sheer crux of horror. Babe lay wide-eyed and frozen, mounting pressure of terror stilling her lungs, making her heart shake the whole world. The monster came to the mouth of the little pocket, tried to walk to her and was stopped by the sides. It was such a narrow little fissure, and it was all Babe could do to get in. The thing from the wood stood straining against the rock at its shoulders, pressing harder and harder to get to Babe. She sat up slowly, so near to the thing that its odor was almost thick enough to see, and a wild hope burst through her voiceless fear. It couldn't get in! It couldn't get in because it was too big!

The substance of its feet spread slowly under the tremendous strain and at its shoulder appeared a slight crack. It widened as the monster unfeelingly crushed itself against the rock, and suddenly a large piece of the shoulder came away and the being twisted slushily three feet farther in. It lay quietly with its muddy eyes fixed on her, and then brought one thick arm up over its head and reached.

Babe scrambled in the inch farther she had believed impossible, and the filthy clubbed hand stroked down her back, leaving a trail of muck on the blue denim of the shirt she wore. The monster surged suddenly and, lying full length now, gained that last precious inch. A black hand seized one of her braids, and for Babe the lights went out.

When she came to, she was dangling by her hair from that same crusted paw. The thing held her high, so that her face and its featureless head were not more than a foot apart. It gazed at her with a mild curiosity in its eyes, and it swung her slowly back and forth. The agony of her pulled hair did what fear could not do—gave her a voice. She screamed. She opened her mouth and puffed up her powerful young lungs, and she sounded off. She held her throat in the position of the first scream, and her chest labored and pumped more air through the frozen throat. Shrill and monotonous and infinitely piercing, her screams.

The thing did not mind. It held her as she was, and watched. When it had learned all it could from this phenomenon, it dropped her jarringly, and looked around the half-cave, ignoring the stunned and huddled Babe. It reached over and picked up the leather brief case and tore it twice across as if it were tissue. It saw the sandwich Babe had left, picked it up, crushed it, dropped it.

Babe opened her eyes, saw she was free, and just as the thing turned back to her she dove between its legs and out into the shallow pool in front of the rock, paddled across and hit the other bank screaming. A vicious little light of fury burned in her; she picked up a grapefruit-sized stone and hurled it with all her frenzied might. It flew low and fast, and struck squashily on the monster's ankle. The thing was just taking a step toward the water; the stone caught it off balance, and its unpracticed equilibrium could not save it. It tottered for a long, silent moment at the edge and then splashed into the stream. Without a second look Babe ran shrieking away.

Cory Drew was following the little gobs of mold that somehow indicated the path of the murderer, and he was nearby when he first heard her scream. He broke into a run, dropping his shotgun and holding the .32-40 ready to fire. He ran with such deadly panic in his heart that he ran right past the huge cleft rock and was a hundred yards past it before she burst out through the pool and ran up the bank. He had to run hard and fast to catch her, because anything behind her was that faceless horror in the cave, and she was living for the one idea of getting away from there. He caught her in his arms and swung her to him, and she screamed on and on and on.

Babe didn't see Cory at all, even when he held her and quieted her.

The monster lay in the water. It neither liked nor disliked this new element. It rested on the bottom, its massive head a foot beneath the surface, and it curiously considered the facts that it had garnered. There was the little humming noise of Babe's voice that sent the monster questing into the cave. There was the black material of the brief case that resisted so much more than green things when he tore it. There was the little two-legged one who sang and brought him near, and who screamed when he came. There was this new cold moving thing he had fallen into. It was washing his body away. That had never happened before. That was interesting. The monster decided to stay and observe this new thing. It felt no urge to save itself; it could only be curious.

The brook came laughing down out of its spring, ran down from its source beckoning to the sunbeams and embracing freshets and helpful brooklets. It shouted and played with streaming little roots, and nudged the minnows and pollywogs about in its tiny backwaters. It was a happy brook. When it came to the pool by the cloven rock it found the monster there, and plucked at it. It soaked the foul substances and smoothed and melted the molds, and the waters below the thing eddied darkly with its diluted matter. It was a thorough brook. It washed all it touched, persistently. Where it found filth, it removed filth; and if there were layer on layer of foulness, then layer by foul layer it was removed. It was a good brook. It did not mind the poison of the monster, but took it up and thinned it and spread it in little rings round water rocks downstream, and let it drift to the rootlets of water plants, that they might grow greener and lovelier. And the monster melted.

"I am smaller," the thing thought. "That is interesting. I could not move now. And now this part of me which thinks is going, too. It will stop in just a moment, and drift away with the rest of the body. It will stop thinking and I will stop being, and that, too, is a very interesting thing."

So the monster melted and dirtied the water, and the water was clean again, washing and washing the skeleton that the monster had left. It was not very big, and there was a badly-healed knot on the left arm. The sunlight flickered on the triangular silver plate set into the pale skull, and the skeleton was very clean now. The brook laughed about it for an age.

They found the skeleton, six grimlipped men who came to find a killer. No one had believed Babe, when she told her story days later. It had to be days later because Babe had screamed for seven hours without stopping, and had lain like a dead child for a day. No one believed her at all, because her story was all about the bad fella, and they knew that the bad fella was simply a thing that her father had made up to frighten her with. But it was through her that the skeleton was found, and so the men at the bank sent a check to the Drews for more money than they had ever dreamed about. It was old Roger Kirk, sure enough, that skeleton, though it was found five miles from where he had died and sank into the forest floor where the hot molds builded around his skeleton and emerged—a monster.

So the Drews had a new barn and fine new livestock and they hired four men. But they didn't have Alton. And they didn't have Kimbo. And Babe screams at night and has grown very thin.